Definition of a Bad Girl

Definition of a Bad Girl

MìChaune

www.urbanbooks.net

Urban Books, LLC
300 Farmingdale Road, NY-Route 109
Farmingdale, NY 11735

ISBN 13: 978-1-62286-571-0
ISBN 10: 1-62286-571-5

First Trade Paperback Printing September 2017
Printed in the United States of America

10 9 8 7 6 5 4 3 2 1

Distributed by Kensington Publishing Corp.
Submit orders to:
Customer Service
400 Hahn Road
Westminster, MD 21157-4627
Phone: 1-800-733-3000
Fax: 1-800-659-2436

Chapter One

Leshaun pulled at the crisp white bed sheet as Zay tongued her pussy from the back. Face down, ass up, she moaned into the soft pillow and twirled herself against his face. His slurps met her ears as her body shivered from his tongue and prodding fingers.

"Mmm, shit feels sooo good!" she shouted. "Don't stop! Ooohh, shiiit!"

Zay spread her phat pussy lips and flicked his tongue up and down. Smack, he slapped her ass and jabbed his tongue in and out. A breath later he parted her fleshy ass and teased her asshole.

"Ooohh, fuck! Ooohh, fuck! Hmmm! Right there, baby! Yesss, eat my ass!" Leshaun bit the pillow.

Zay feasted on Leshaun with a feverish passion. He slurped hard on her pussy lips while thumbing the pink nub that made Leshaun's eyes roll. She wiggled her ass side to side and begged him to make her bust a second nut on his lips.

"I need some dick!" she gasped. "Please fuck me! Please, I want it sooo bad." She squirmed as his tongue shoveled in and out of her pink cherry.

Zay pulled his mouth from her sweet wetness and sat back on his heels. He licked his slippery mouth and stared at Leshaun's willing position with his heart pounding. Sweat covered every inch of their nude flesh. Zay looked down at his raging erection and then at Leshaun's phat pussy.

"Please," she whined out of breath. "Just slide it in and out a few times."

Zay stayed quiet as Leshaun crawled to the edge of the bed. Her soft ass held him in a trance. She picked up a condom off the bedside table with her teeth. On the prowl, she crawled back toward him, her heavy breasts swinging with her seductive moves. He didn't move an inch as she dropped the condom between his legs. She crawled closer and circled her fingers around his long penis. She discovered it was wet and slippery at the tip.

"Wait—" he tried to protest, but his words were axed by the gentle strokes of her hand. He laid his head back, closed his eyes, and immersed himself in the pleasure of a woman. He moaned when her thumb circled the mushroom head of his dick, smearing his precum all over it. His stomach flipped when she toyed with his balls. Up and down she jacked him off.

Leshaun had no shame about wrapping her lips around a dick. In truth, she enjoyed the feeling of a dick poking in and out of her mouth and the power that came with it. At the moment, she had no such urge to suck Zay's dick. Instead, Leshaun looked into Zay's eyes as she continued her slow hand job in full view of her hidden iPhone.

Zay reached for Leshaun's shoulders as she opened the condom wrapper with her teeth. He stared at what she did, throbbing as he anticipated what she was going to do next. All of his self-control began to flicker as she rolled the condom over his veined pipe.

Leshaun shoved her hair over her shoulder and pushed Zay on his back. "Hmmm! This is gonna be fun, baby!" She smiled down at him as she straddled his waist. "You want to feel my pussy?" She reached back and pulled his erection toward her pounding slit. "I'll make it feel real good."

Zay's hunger for some pussy won out. His body responded to the woman above as she pounded up and down the stretch of his penis. Her bare ass bounced and smacked against his thighs as her nails dug into his shoulders.

She fucked him silly; up and down she raced him in and out of her squishy hole. She took the dick, fucking herself hard and fast. Her titties wobbled, and she sped up, slamming herself at a stressed beat on his penis. Caught up in the haze of lust, neither heard the door unlock with a motorized click. Leshaun kept riding Zay, the sounds of her rebounding ass intermingled with their guttural moans.

What the hell is that on the stove? Leshaun jerked her head up so fast, one of her rollers fell against her eye. On her left side was Zay, lying on his back still asleep; and on his other side was one of her whores. No sheet was on the bed to conceal their naked bodies. As she removed the spongy pink curler from her face, it dawned on her: not only did she forget to wear her favorite scarf, but it wasn't three o'clock in the afternoon, her usual waking time.

Leshaun had warned Lysa and Janae, the two whores she let stay with her on occasion, plenty of times about cooking shit on the gotdamn stove and leaving it without telling someone. *See, this is why I am never going to get these bitches to go from hookers to housewives, shit like this.* Leshaun was beyond frustrated, and the smoke was messing with her ability to think straight.

"Uughh!" Leshaun moaned as she struggled to collect herself. She slowly hopped up out of the bed. She owned a nice little hotel where she handled her business. The hotel had been in the Gamble family since her great-grandfather had it in the 1920s. He was one of the very few blacks to own some property and Leshaun had no intention of letting Price Street Hotel, aka the Gamble property, fall on her watch.

As Jeremih was singing about "you and I," the scorching smell of whatever the hell it was burning on the stove got stronger. While Leshaun loved the infectious beat, it was stomping a migraine into her head, causing her left temple to throb. The breaths she took were like forced labor pains and Leshaun struggled to keep count of the pace in which she was breathing.

Something in her spirit wasn't right, and other than the bright neon green digital time stamp reflecting eleven thirty-two in the morning and the fine, sexy muthafucker singing and trying to croon her panties off from the radio, Leshaun couldn't put her finger on it.

"I know it's not eleven thirty!" Leshaun could barely hear herself complain.

The search for her white robe led her to the door adjacent to the bathroom, and Leshaun quickly grabbed it and threw it over her plump body. She caught a glimpse of herself in the mirror. She was still black, still hadn't had a bath, still five foot seven and 200 pounds, still part of the big bitches club.

"Bitch Better Have My Money" by Rihanna boomed from the iPhone Leshaun had to look for. As she bent down to look beside the bed, she covered her nose and mouth; then she remembered the phone was placed on the bookshelf she had mounted to the wall next to the window, which gave her a clear view of Tunnel Road. On the shelf were the hottest street li'l classics from Nikki Turner, Brick & Storm, and De'Nesha Diamond. Unfortunately, the saying was true: if you wanted to hide something, put it in a book. Or in this case, leave enough space between *Stone Cold Liar* by Noire and *Prison Snatch* by Cairo. Everything Leshaun wanted to hide, including the phone that had filmed her sexcapade the night before, was safe there.

When it came to Leshaun's hoes or her time, she didn't have many rules. Let her tell it, these broads were grown, and she didn't have the time to be no damn babysitter; that's why she always only let the girls who didn't have kids work out of her rooms. Never compare her to an insecure man who felt the need to stand over a girl's neck and tell her how to suck dick or which man she needed to wear or not wear a condom with. Hell, the answer to the last statement was all of them. The expectation was these hoes were old enough to know better. And calling Leshaun before it was time for her to wake up was one of her few, but big no-no's.

Leshaun got up from the floor and sat on the bed, slipped her feet into pink flip-flops, and reached over to grab the phone, knocking over some of the books on both ends of the shelf. When she finally got the iPhone in her hand, Kofi flashed across the screen. Even though he was one of Leshaun's few male hoes and he gave good dick, Leshaun wore two condoms with that muthafucker 'cause she never knew where that dick went. As Rihanna continued to sing about a shady muthafucka who owed her, the phone seemed to ring for the millionth time. Leshaun finally pressed the TALK button. She just knew that whatever was wrong, it didn't involve him.

"Hello," Leshaun spoke with clarity. It seemed as if hours had passed before she got a response. She didn't think that this phone call would change her life forever.

"Leshaun!" Kofi yelled. As he continued to yell and scream, Leshaun struggled to keep up with him as Kofi seemed to speak 1,000 words a minute. She wasn't used to this. When Kofi spoke, he was eloquent, bringing to life some of the education college had afforded him. As the words crashed into Leshaun's ear, she wondered how was she going to find out what was wrong when she couldn't understand him.

"Kofi, calm down." Leshaun was slightly confused, sad, and aggravated that she couldn't figure out what was wrong with this boy. She prayed to God he didn't fuck the wrong man's wife again and got stranded out in the middle of Bumfuck, Tennessee. Last time that happened, she ended up with a $50,000 hospital bill that she just got done paying a few weeks ago. *His ass better not be in jail again, either.* She couldn't afford the trouble. Bailing his sleazy ass out was getting old, and Leshaun had half a mind to leave his ass there.

"Leshaun. Leshaun!"

Leshaun understood that much out of everything that he had said. "Kofi, what's wrong?" Leshaun knew before she had asked the question she wasn't going to like the answer. But it was important. In the pit of her stomach, Leshaun could feel a knot forming, and she almost wanted to roll over. Her stomach twisted and turned like water being wrung from a bath cloth. Sweat left her body like water being flung to the basin. The fear was something had happened to one of the girls.

"Leshaun, you can't smell that your hotel is on fire?"

She finally understood him. The smell hit her nose again. "Hell yeah, I can smell it," Leshaun confirmed as she moved about the room. She looked back on her bed and noticed her toys were sprawled all over, buck-naked, and if they had awakened they could've had a round twelve. "Tiana, Zay, get y'all asses up!"

The night before had turned wild as Tiana and Leshaun took turns wearing Zay out and teaching him the ropes. Zay had the right body and the right equipment, but Leshaun needed him to get his skill level up so that he could throw dick in a way that made women give him the same amount of money and pleasure that they got from Kofi. That pink roller found its way in front of Leshaun's face. Agitated, she unsnapped it and tossed it to the side.

"Tiana, Zay, get up!" Leshaun hated repeating herself. She knew her voice was loud enough to wake the dead and that it carried. After finding her white and brown oversized purse, Leshaun grabbed it and tried to stuff as much money and as many personal possessions inside as possible.

The phone rang again, and Leshaun shook her head. Answering the phone would've only caused her to get pissed off even more, so she tossed it into the purse along with a few pairs of panties, a few bras, all the rolled-up bills, and two flimsy summer dresses. When she got to her closet, the best she could do was slip into a pair of loose-fitting jeans and an old 'Pac T-shirt.

"I'm gonna get them girls for burning my hotel down."

Tiana and Zay finally got their asses up, and they struggled to get dressed. Leshaun could them hear fussing about the smoke, which started to creep into their room. Zay opened the window, and the fire trucks and ambulance could be heard making their way to her establishment. While her tastes required a stay on the top floor of any hotel she paid for, when it came to the master suite of the hotel she lived in, all Leshaun wanted was the best room in the building. At that moment, she thanked God all the rooms were on one floor.

They made their exit through the window and walked on the freshly cut grass and headed to the sidewalk, where some spectators were already looking as a large fire engulfed the other end of Leshaun's nearly one-hundred-year-old property. Fortunately, only one of her hoes was working in the room, but Leshaun needed to figure out where they were going to work tonight because money still needed to be made and Leshaun had every intention of getting the hotel fixed fast.

Chapter Two

"The Price Street Hotel is up in flames! We toasted that bitch!" Lysa bragged as she and Janae walked on the dirt side of Meadow Road, walking alongside the Swannanoa River.

Janae shook her head at Lysa's immaturity. This dumb bitch confirmed for any eavesdropper, or someone unaware of their crime, that they were the culprits.

The breeze was light and the air was thin. The watermelon Four Loko Lysa downed with her chicken biscuit from Bojangles had a stronghold on her mind.

Janae wished she had worn a jacket, underestimating the cool weather at seven thirty in the morning. Janae wasn't feeling walking out in the morning without a prospective customer in sight, especially to meet no new pimp.

Nicki Minaj spit the first verse of "Roman's Revenge," and Janae shook her head. It was the tenth time the phone rang, and Janae dug it from her pants. Leshaun's number displayed on the screen. "I wish I could throw this muthafucka in the river!" Janae vented as she tried to power down the phone. She thought she'd accomplished the task before, but with Nicki lyrics taunting her, she knew she'd failed.

"I'd toss that muthafucka." Lysa reached for the phone, and Janae put it back in her pocket. "We're getting new phones anyway."

"Well, until then—" Janae barely got the words out before "Beez in the Trap" started blaring.

"I'm getting sick of Nicki and shit!" Lysa yelled. "I wish you'd figure out how to work that phone."

"I'm almost tempted to see what she said, but I don't want her to know I seen the message," Janae admitted as she and Lysa kept walking.

"Girl, you have some knockoff Android phone," Janae pointed out. "She can only see that shit if you got an iPhone like she do."

"Anyway, where's Lloyd?" Janae questioned. "And why we meeting at a river and not in a motel or a restaurant or something?"

"Because the river has no walls," Lysa pointed out as she extended her hand to all the open space. Lysa twirled and danced in the space and slured the words to Sia's "Chandelier," rocking her hips as if she were on the rungs of one hanging from a cloud in the sky. No question about it, Lysa was drunk. Nicki Minaj cut in again. "Black folks go kayaking too, not just white people. And Lloyd comes here so often that people don't pay him no attention. Shit, he gets customers this way. He's where the rich dick is at, and this is where I wanna be."

Janae wanted new customers too. Part of the reason she started tricking was because it was easy money. Lysa had been all on Lloyd's dick since she met him at Bele Chere a few years back. Hustlers and tourists came from all over the world to celebrate Asheville, North Carolina's music and arts festival. While the event didn't bring as much revenue for many of Asheville's businesses, local pimps used the festival as an opportunity to network with artists and wealthy visitors to build new clientele. The women strutted in their best eclectic summer wear that ranged from neon throwbacks of the sixties' hippie movement to the colorful designs and hairstyles of the eighties. Lloyd came to see if Asheville was a destination worthy enough to be placed on his radar. With the growth of the local pubs and Asheville being designated as the

Craft Beer Capital, the city tapped into a new tourist revenue stream, and Lloyd found another home.

As they walked along the river, nothing spectacular stood out other than various bland metal buildings that were vandalized. The one they were looking for looked like a makeshift trailer. Once they found it, Janae was amazed and felt like she had stepped into a high-end department store. She couldn't believe her eyes when she saw the large number of name brand clothes, shoes, and perfumes lined against the walls. On her right, Janae saw various sizes of baby clothes, and antique dining and living room sets.

Nicki Minaj was in the trap again. Before Janae could address the phone, a young white girl in a big purple bandana, a loose-fitting, hand-knit jacket, and a long, flowing jean skirt approached them. "Lloyd said y'all would be on your way."

Who the fuck is this plain Jane and what can she do? Janae thought as she followed Lysa and the fake gypsy woman inside the building. She took out the phone and tried to power it down again.

"Damn, Leigh Ann, I could have gotten a better welcome than that." Lysa copped an attitude.

"No," Leigh Ann turned and answered her with a big smile. "I only put on my Southern charm when the racetrack boys and dirty politicians come around. You regular bitches get treated as such until you prove yourselves otherwise."

"Regular bitches?" Janae mouthed to herself. Before she could think, they found themselves among a group of girls and a few guys having conversations about what they were doing and what they wanted to do for the weekend. Right away, Janae did not like that there were only four black girls in the room. And both of them bitches had arms and legs as thin as rails, and weave that pulled at their scalp and fell halfway down their backs.

The darker-skinned one wore dark red makeup and had small Granny Smith apple–sized breasts. The lighter one was a shade of unfinished furnish on a sand-colored desk. Janae didn't want to stare to hard, but she had a hard time finding the girl's breasts. As she profiled their side views, neither one had an ass.

The other ten white girls seemed to be in their early to midtwenties. Hair came in every color of the rainbow. Five of them looked like they suffered from anorexia and looked more like white boys starting puberty. The other five girls were no thicker than a swimsuit model. One had a fuller face and was very top heavy. The other four looked like they belonged on the volleyball team.

Janae could tell the wafer-thin white boy who was the height of a basketball player was gay by the way he rolled his eyes and turned his head away as she and Lysa continued into the room. The Hispanic man maybe had an inch or two on her five foot four frame. He had blond streaks in his spiked hair and wore a dog leash around his neck. The faded pink KEEP ASHEVILLE WEIRD T-shirt he wore was at least two sizes too small, revealing his navel ring. And his black spandex hugged every inch of his hippopotamus-shaped ass; it was a wonder his skinnier legs held his frame up. He smiled, and Janae smiled back.

After a few minutes, Lloyd walked in the room. Everyone got quiet and moved quickly to form a line in order of height before him. Janae checked out their routine, chose not to follow it, and took a place next to the line a few feet from the tallest person. Lloyd approached Leigh Ann and shook his head disapprovingly.

"What's up with your hair? And why do you have on that hideous outfit?" Lloyd should have been the last one to talk, with a buttoned-up checkered shirt, crisp black jeans, and scuffed black work boots, looking more like a misplaced black cowboy than somebody's pimp. Leigh Ann was about to fend for herself, but Lloyd cut her off.

"No damn excuses." Lloyd backed away from them as if he were the drill sergeant getting ready to shape a bunch of army recruits into shape.

Janae noticed that most of the girls looked straight ahead, scared to look their leader in his eyes. "You have to look good at all times. The first thing customers look at when you approach them is your appearance: who are you with and can they pass you off as their armpiece for the night. Ladies and gentlemen, I tell you all, all the time your looks talk before you do, so make sure you're looking tight. Now down to business. The last time we went met up with the baseball team at the Indigo Hotel we only came out with fourteen thousand dollars for our services. What the hell is going on, Britany?"

Janae looked on as Lloyd approached the girl who was equal to him in height. "You had the star player on your arm. You should have had fourteen thousand dollars yourself. What the hell happened?" Lloyd berated her.

"These minor-league players are broke as hell. His wife makes more money than he does and they wanted to do more than eat my pussy and fuck me strange. I'm not into pissing and shitting on folks. I do have morals." Britany looked away from Lloyd.

Janae expected Lloyd to knock the shit out of her. She was surprised when he didn't. Lloyd stepped away and shook his head, unsatisfied with the answer he had been given. He made his way to the next girl. "Cheyenne, what is your excuse?"

Cheyenne shrugged her shoulders and mumbled, "I don't know."

Lloyd shook his head. He spotted Janae and Lysa at the end of the line. Truthfully, Janae was nervous because even though she was confident that she had the ability to hold her own, Janae knew she was still in the lion's den and that anything could happen. Soon, Lloyd and Janae were face to face.

"I'm glad you could make it." A small smile escaped his lips. "Are you ready to get paid?"

"Hell yeah. What I got to do?" Janae looked him in the eye and showed no fear, just like Leshaun had taught her.

"Just follow directions. I think you and Lysa will be joining me for a special project later tonight. Leigh Ann, get them an Uber and take them to my favorite spot in Montford."

Uber? Janae questioned. *What the hell?* Strike one was meeting in a warehouse made to resemble a high-end department store, and strike two was that this mutha-fucker had the nerve to send them around in an Uber. Janae was waiting on strike three to be lit so she could bounce and try to figure things out on her own.

"A'ight, bitches, you come this way," Leigh Ann instructed.

Strike three!

"Call me that again." Janae reached up to her left ear to remove the small hoop she was wearing and did the same for the other side. "And you won't have to worry about how come you can't bring this nigga his money, because I'm going to make him watch me bury your ass six feet under where you're standing."

Leigh Ann turned her head to the side, and her eyes got big. She couldn't believe Janae had to the gall to talk to her like that.

"Now, ladies." Lloyd stepped between them. "Let's play nice. I need Leigh Ann to be the white trash bitch she's pretending to be to get my money from them rich hillbillies in Waynesville later today. I need you two to get ready for a meet and greet I want y'all to be part of."

Janae stared Lloyd in the face while Lysa tugged her shoulder. "Come on. He gonna take care of us, I promise."

"Roman's Revenge" cut into her thoughts. Janae looked at Lysa and couldn't believe she let this girl talk her into this shit.

***

Lysa had been pacing the small hotel room on Tunnel Road ever since the Uber dropped them off an hour ago. Janae knew her way around Asheville enough to know that they were at least five miles from where they needed to be. Montford was an old community in North Asheville that supported the Grove Park Inn and had some of the city's historical houses and neighborhoods. She started to correct the Uber driver but chose to go with the program just in case Lloyd had something better planned.

"Yo, Lloyd, what's up? Thanks for the new phones and all but I thought we were going to do this." Lysa didn't give him a chance to greet her or whatever. Lysa got straight to the point of why she was calling, and she expected him to have an acceptable answer.

"We still are." Lloyd's baritone could be heard smoothly over the speaker. "Some of the girls got caught slipping. I want y'all to get ready for this private house party I'm setting up for later today."

"You gonna bail the other girls out?" Janae needed to know where Lloyd's head was at. She worked on the new Android phone Lloyd got them from MetroPCS so she could reset her settings and add important numbers to it.

"Hell no!" Lloyd's answer was blunt. "Their misstep could have been prevented, so they had to deal with the consequences. Lloyd is not going to bail them out. But I do have some good news for you. The money they could've made will be yours if you and your sister work that party right."

Sister? Janae wondered what the hell they had gotten themselves into and if the drama was even worth it. Lloyd wasn't moving like the pimps she was used to. For starters, Lloyd let a trick explain why she couldn't make money. Leshaun's mantra was get the dough by hook or by crook. Janae knew that if she and Lysa hadbeen there, Lloyd's money would've been right. If they couldn't afford to pay, a minor-league baseball player wouldn't have seen her face. And morals. Morals. There was no such thing. If the the valet had the money, he could get what service he could afford. And if Leshaun needed to arrange for a gay escort to come up there and do the work, then all Janae had to do was watch, pretend to like it, and get the money. Simple shit any ho should be able to do.

And from the looks of things, Lloyd wasn't just into selling pussy. So there was no excuse. Leshaun would've got that money. Janae hated admitting that leaving her for Lloyd might've been a mistake. She had no intention of her and Lysa being the only hoes pulling in money; and if she had to become a madam, she, Lysa, and Lloyd would be starting from scratch because she'd reject every last ho in Lloyd's stable.

"Pull out that red one-piece with the spaghetti straps," Lysa ordered as she hung up the phone.

"I don't have the shoes to go with that." Janae looked at the bag that was on her bed. She regretted not packing all her stuff, but they only had a few hours to send their bags ahead of them before they set the kitchen on fire. For three weeks, Janae and Lysa plotted their escape. They left Leshaun because Lloyd made it seem like he could get them more money and a steady high-end clientele. Leshaun did a good job at bringing in the D-list celebrities, the reality television stars, and the extremely wealthy people who had fame.

Janae saw Lloyd on Instagram popping bottles with his boys and making it rain on strippers in Vegas. Lloyd hung out with and featured celebrities on his Snapchats. And on Lloyd's Tumblr and ConnectPal accounts, the freak parties looked clean and high maintenance.

Where the hell were the rich rappers and how was she getting on their dicks?

"Don't worry about that. We'll get some at the warehouse before we go to the house party," Lysa suggested.

Janae could picture being able to find something on short notice at the warehouse. It did look like a mini Macy's with some Ashley Furniture thrown in on the side. Janae showered and quickly got dressed and put on the tennis shoes she was rocking earlier.

"I think you can get away with that look." Lysa looked her over. She didn't look too bad herself with a low-cut pink blouse and a pink threaded jean skirt. "This is a house party, and we expect to fuck, not sit around and look pretty."

It had been a minute since Janae had been to a sex party. Leshaun always thought those events were beneath her.

"Our Uber's here," Lysa interrupted her thoughts. Janae quickly looked herself over, and she and Lysa raced out the door.

"Damn, who you come to see?" Janae heard one of Lloyd's friends ask as they entered the quaint house in West Asheville. They weren't too far from the infamous Haywood Road, and some of the nightlife was already cramming the streets.

"Chill," Lloyd answered the question from a distance, "they're here for me."

Janae could see Lloyd smiling at them. This dude was full of tricks. "Is that right?" Janae asked, slyly looking around to see if there were some other chicks waiting on Lloyd's friend to finish talking.

"You're here aren't you?"

Leigh Ann rolled her eyes as she looked over Lloyd's shoulder. Gone was her hippie gear. Her short brunette hair featured micro curls, and her white dress made her more sophisticated than she appeared earlier. "Lloyd, where is Ron Ron?"

Lloyd got agitated. "Do I look like Ron Ron's keeper to you?"

"Did I ask you that?" Leigh Ann got smart.

"No. He went to the store. He'll be right back," Lloyd answered as they followed him throughout the house. Lloyd got closer to Janae and asked, "What took you so long to get back at me?"

"'I got my mind on my money and my money on me.'" Janae quoted one of her favorite New Edition lines. She wanted guys to hit her off and not just between her pants. Lloyd letting these females talk back to him was getting on her nerves. Admittedly, Leshaun was a little informal with them. Leshaun was more like everyone's big sister, but she made it known she was the oldest. Leigh Ann acted like Lloyd was her man, and she was wearing his ring.

"Well, get that money." A devious grin formed on Lloyd's face. Janae knew he was getting ready to get at her on something sly. "How can I be down?"

Janae could see the lust in his eyes, and that did nothing but piss her off. Janae needed to set ol' boy straight because she didn't know what he thought but this wasn't that type of party. He must've had her confused with them other hoes he'd been dealing with. "What do you mean how can you be down? Nigga, do I look like the type who would ho and give a nigga my money? You got me twisted. I don't work like that." If his hoes talked to him like that, shouldn't nothing have been wrong with her speaking her mind.

"Damn, I was just messing with you. Slow your roll. I ain't here to break you. I'm here to be your friend." Lloyd put some distance between them. He must've thought Janae was going to swing on him. Janae should've knocked him into next week coming at her like that.

Lloyd thought he was going to get easy access to Janae's pants, but he was sadly mistaken. Janae watched as he crossed his arms and leaned against the wall and smiled. Janae was about to give him a piece of her mind.

She got distracted when "For Free" by DJ Khaled and Drake bumped from the car Ron Ron was driving as he parked the car.

"What's up?" he addressed a few of the patrons as he came in. Janae was surprised that he scrunched his face upon seeing Leigh Ann. "Why didn't you call first? You can't just pop up and think it's cool."

Drake faded into the background. The thumping bass line in Bryson Tiller's "Exchange" encouraged everyone to relax and huddle into small groups. No one danced or two-stepped. The bartender could be seen serving drinks from a mobile cart, but nothing serious was going on.

"Oh, is that right?" Leigh Ann didn't hide the anger in her voice. Janae knew his head was spinning with some of the same thoughts she had. "I don't have a problem with leaving."

"That's not the point. You ain't trying to be with a nigga like me then you're just wasting time."

"What are you tripping on? You never had a problem with me coming through before." Leigh Ann rolled her eyes before looking at him. "Look, Lloyd, I'm leaving. I will see you at the house!"

Through the open door, Janae watched as Leigh Ann walked down the street by herself. Lloyd grabbed Janae's hand and led her past the dining room and into the kitchen. Lloyd opened a door that led to some stairs heading into a basement. Janae hadn't been in a basement in a long time. As they descended the stairs, she could see a young lady peeping in through a window outside surrounded by potted flowers and rocks. As her face pressed against the window, Janae could see the girl may not have been out of high school. She started to call Lloyd on the situation but decided to wait until later. When they got to a room, Lloyd opened a door and guided her to the edge of a bed.

Strike four!

"Who is that at the window?" Janae was still freaked out about the young lady staring at her. The room smelled of recently burned vanilla incense. The white walls were bare, which made the king-sized bed appear to take up the entire room. The dresser with the mirror on top added to the claustrophobia. Neither side of the bed had much room to walk. Whoever's room it was left little detail to who they were or what they were into.

"She my sister." Lloyd didn't bother to look at Janae as he had the audacity to lie to her face. Janae didn't believe that girl was his sister any more than she still believed in Santa Claus.

"How old is your sister?" Janae pressed because Lloyd and Lysa failed to mention any siblings. As she recollected the scene in the living room, there were no pictures of family of any sort. No statues or flowers to liven the place up. The home looked clean and as if basic yard work was attended to on the outside, but nothing stood out to make the house pop.

"Twenty-five," Lloyd responded.

"This chick doesn't look to be twenty-five," Janae answered as Lloyd took off the watch he was wearing and put it on the dresser. "She looks like she's about sixteen or seventeen."

"You asking me all these questions." Lloyd shook his head and looked at her from the mirror.

Janae hated when dudes got on the defensive. It meant they were lying. "We can make this *Snapped,* so who's the bitch in the window?"

The bluntness of her words made Lloyd smile. This was a game to him, and Janae didn't feel like playing. She had half a mind to go back to Leshaun and apologize, but she and Lysa had already gone too far. Her only way of contact with Leshaun had been traded in at a cell phone recycling machine at Walmart for four dollars, which she used to buy dollar menu items at the McDonald's inside.

They'd heard vague news reports about Price Street Hotel being on fire, but she didn't put too much stock into it.

Lloyd exhaled hard and glared at her through the mirror. "That's one of my hoes. She doesn't have a place to live, so she came to stay with us."

"So this is your place?" Janae did an once-over of the bare room again. "This is a disappointment. No famous people. The music wack and you probably sexing that jealous bitch who thinks I want your dick."

"I fuck all my hoes," Lloyd answered without a break as he took his shirt off, revealing a modest frame that a few push-ups and sit-ups could whip into shape. "I'm about to fuck you."

Janae was *this* close to ending it all. When she left Leshaun, she was supposed to upgrade, not witness her situation getting worse. What the hell! Janae knew that "sister" thing was a bunch of crap and Lysa was just gullible to believe anything he would spit. In the back of her mind, Janae wished she'd checked things out on her own, and she'd meant to. She knew Lloyd pimped from Philly to Atlanta to Houston. Lloyd owned strip clubs in each of these cities that had tight body dancers with pretty faces, so she was confused to why all the hoes she met in Asheville were dog faced and basic. Asheville was a hot spot destination, let some of the major tourist and family publications tell it, so Asheville should have bad bitches too. Had Janae met Leigh Ann, she would have rode it out with Leshaun a little while longer. Lloyd tried to play her for a simple girl. She knew he was used to the girls who oohed and aahed at his every move. He walked away from the dresser and unbuckled his Gucci belt. Janae studied the buckle and determined the belt to be real.

Lloyd sat next to her and leaned in for a kiss. Janae put her hand up and backed away. Lloyd's hands tried to swim across her legs, but Janae shoved him away. "I'm not one of your hoes," she told him forcefully as she put some space between the two of them.

"What I got to do to change that?" Lloyd reached into his pants and pulled out his hardening erection. Janae admitted to herself that Lloyd was one of the biggest. It curved to the left, and the skin was smooth. She'd heard the rumors and seen a few pictures of him wearing gray sweatpants with his package bulking at the midsection. But she'd never seen him do some work with it.

She started to wrap her hand around it but then restrained herself. "I hope you can fuck."

Lloyd stood up and pulled his pants down, lifting one leg at a time to remove them and his mesh underwear in one move. Janae noticed he had shaved the hair that would've given him a happy trail from his navel to his package. The way his dick throbbed seemed to be in sync with his heartbeat. Thump thump. Thump thump.

Lloyd got on his knees before Janae and reached for her panties under her dress. He pulled the pair down slowly and tossed them over her shoulder. He parted her legs and kissed her inner thigh while cupping her ass. As he nipped and sucked his way to her prize, Janae hoped he wasn't marking her with his lips. A moan escaped her mouth as Lloyd proceeded to bring his face closer to her freshly shaved lips and he parted them with his tongue. It felt surprisingly cool, and Janae was impressed by the length as it tickled her walls. The slurping and his skills had her hissing and cooing in a matter of minutes. Janae stole a glance and, unlike most guys who put that tongue down first if they were lacking something, Lloyd had nothing to hide or be ashamed of. In fact, Janae tried to figure out how he hid the perfectly shaped muscle with a slight left curve and marshmallow-sized head in his drawers.

"Umm," Janae moaned as she found Lloyd undressed and her legs behind her head. Without hesitation, Lloyd filled her up and started throwing that pimp game down.

Chapter Three

"What is a young, sweet lady like yourself doing out on the city streets of Asheville at two thirty in the morning?" Kofi asked the young lady standing near the entrance of the tunnel. 9ine stood next to him and ignored him while focused on his Samsung.

The young lady rolled her eyes. Kofi knew his pickup line was weak, but he also knew she was young. He wasn't trying to spit his best line at her. He saw her fumble with a prepaid Boost Mobile phone.

"Yo, I know that red rag-wearing bitch ain't trying to ignore you," 9ine butted in the conversation. Loitering at the bus station was a favorite past time. It was across from a small mom-and-pop hotel and near the Papa's and Beer Mexican restaurant he loved to frequent. "What she better do is buy some Ambi and Mabeline to hide all those cat scratches. Trying to act like she stuck-up and shit. Better be glad that a nigga like me even spoke to the broke-down bitch like you."

Between 9ine calling the girl out of her name and the busy signal, Kofi was more than annoyed. He watched as the girl tried the phone number again.

"Hello." Kofi could hear the girl start a conversation. He looked to see if the screen was black to verify if the girl was on the phone for real or just talking to herself.

"9ine, chill out, man. You don't have to be an asshole toward her," Kofi admonished him as he finished eating the last of his soft taco.

"She ain't doing shit," 9ine popped back. "I'm trying to offer the bitch some safety. If she can't handle a nigga like me fucking with her, she might as well let the rusty-ass white dude near the tunnel rape her ass and throw her off Town Mountain Road."

Kofi looked up and caught a glimpse of the amazing view. He knew for a fact that many made the trip up the road but didn't come down alive. 9ine was right, but the approach Kofi wanted to use on her was to be subtle. She showed all the signs of being the perfect chick for Leshaun's stable. She looked young and had a little attitude, and all Kofi needed to know was if she was coachable.

"I am sorry for calling you but can I stay at your house for three days?" Kofi overheard the girl ask. This was going to be easy for him. The girl confirmed that should've made the arrangements before she jumped on the bus and headed to the big city. Kofi surmised that the girl abruptly got out of an abusive situation and she hadn't thought that far ahead.

Whatever her friend said on the other line didn't sound promising. Kofi and 9ine watched as the girl shook her head like she'd been dealt a devastating blow.

"What should I do? I don't have any place to go." The girl looked behind her. 9ine and Kofi still had her in their sights. Each of them viewed her like a meal they were getting ready to devour. "You know of any other place I can go?"

Kofi and 9ine watched as the girl pressed END on the phone and put it in her small pink bag. She walked back to the station and looked to see who was behind her. The girl was scared as she started booking it down Tunnel Road through the tunnel.

"Hey, baby, wait for me."

Kofi and 9ine couldn't see where the voice was coming from, but they both booked it to the tunnel. They knew a lot of mentally deranged folks hung out and walked aimlessly. Cars sped through on either side and honked their horns loudly, mainly just to make noise. Kofi saw the young man in shabby clothes grab her. "Bitch, what do you have, cancer?"

"Nigga, fall back." 9ine caught up with the young man first and separated the two.

"Fuck you, Prince Charming." The stale man spit alcohol and phlegm in 9ine's direction. "I don't want no bald-headed, cancer-looking bitch."

"Then why you got your hands on her then?" 9ine punched the man before waiting for an answer.

While 9ine manhandled the potential rapist, Kofi walked next to her. "Listen, I know my boy was a complete asshole but, as you can see, we had no intentions but to look out for you. We know you by yourself and you have nowhere to turn. Roll with us for the night, meet our Ma, and if you want the help she can offer you, we'll make sure you'll always have a safe passage home. Even if you don't want to fuck with us no more."

Kofi studied the girl. She was easily five inches shorter than him. She had a full body with large breasts, a little pooch, and a thick waist. The young woman before him saw hard times but, he knew if she cleaned herself up, she had potential to fuck with them for a little while.

"She a'ight?" 9ine could be heard yelling from the tunnel.

"Yeah." Kofi put his arm around her. She didn't resist. "She gonna be fine."

"I'm 9ine." 9ine extended his hand. "My name is spelled with a number in it."

"That's cool." The young woman extended her hand and smiled. The full set of teeth sealed the deal for Kofi.

She was worth the time and energy needed to clean her up.

"I'm Kofi, and we got a small, beat-up Toyota Corolla," Kofi offered as he walked to the green car that was parked near a streetlight. He reached in his pocket and pulled out the keys. "We gonna take a ride and get you cleaned up. Then, in the morning, we'll go shopping."

"I'm Chasity," the woman introduced herself. "I can get my own clothes, but I do appreciate the room for the night. Am I gonna have to give you some pussy?"

"Only if you need some dick," 9ine licked his lips and responded sarcastically.

"What my boy is saying is that we not gonna make you do what you don't want to do." Kofi smacked 9ine on the back of the head. "Straight up, we both hustlers and we both make enough money selling dick and other goods and services that we don't need to take no pussy from you."

"You guys get paid to swing wood?" Chasity was amazed. She'd never heard no bullshit like that before in life. "So Ma is—"

"She's my mother and his pimp," 9ine answered.

"Sounds like someone I can fuck with while I'm here." Chasity was impressed. Kofi smiled, knowing that Chasity was letting her guard down around them.

Kofi unlocked the door once they got to the car and he offered her the front seat. "Look, before we go any further, how old are you?"

"I'm nineteen." Chasity took her bag off and opened it. She dug in and pulled out a North Carolina ID that said her name and that she was from Cary. Kofi did the math in his head and realized the young girl was gonna turn twenty in a few weeks.

Kofi pulled off from the parking lot and watched as Chasity leaned against the window and enjoyed the view of the Asheville skyline in the background. They made it down the street to another small motel not too far from the I-240 ramp. As they pulled into the motel, Kofi got up and adjusted his sweatpants. Chasity pulled her scarf down so that no one could see her hair. 9ine looked around to make sure there wasn't anyone around who could cause any drama. They walked past an older lady holding a grocery bag with one hand.

9ine pulled out the room key and turned the key in the lock to open the door. They saw Zay walking around buck-naked with a towel hanging from his neck. The shower was running, and clothes were laid neatly over one of the king-sized beds.

"Hey!" Zay called out as if Chasity were one of their clients. "Where you from?"

"Go put some clothes on!" 9ine ordered.

"She's staying here for the night, and then we'll meet up with Leshaun in the morning," Kofi added.

Zay headed into the shower and shook his head.

"Y'all are wild," Chasity observed. "I have half a mind to get in the shower with him."

"Join him at your own risk." Kofi seemed indifferent as he picked up the remote and turned on the television. Chasity took a seat on the bed, declining the offer. Kofi gave Chasity the remote, and she quickly found BET. They watched a *Girlfriends* rerun, and by time the last commercials were done, Zay and Tiana had come out of the shower. They each quickly dressed. Zay rocked some late-nineties gear with his pants leg rolled up like LL Cool J used to wear, and Tiana's shoulder-length hair was tight and complemented her equally long earrings. She looked like one of those around the way girls LL Cool J rapped about. "We about to go meet up with this couple staying at the Baymont on Hendersonville Road," Zay informed him. "They want a nineties party, and we're giving them one."

"Yeah, we gotta be there in fifteen minutes," Tiana added as she ran her fingers through her hair in the mirror.

Kofi looked at the time on his phone. "You need the nineties car to go with it?"

"Yeah. That will make it easier," Tiana confirmed.

Kofi dug in his pocket and pulled out the keys and tossed them to Zay. In a minute, Zay and Tiana were out the door.

"All of y'all work out of this little-ass room?" Chasity looked around.

"Naw, this is a temporary situation," 9ine replied.

"You really from Cary?" Kofi asked.

"I grew up in Philly, but I'm in Cary now," Chasity answered. "I was going to Central, but I flunked out, and now I'm here."

Kofi made his way to the refrigerator under the television. He pulled out some of the bean burritos he purchased earlier in the day and put them in the microwave. He could hear Chasity's stomach growling.

"It sounds like you haven't eaten in days," Kofi commented as took out a bag of cinnamon twists and handed it to her.

"Thank you." Chasity accepted the generosity and put one in her mouth.

"Normally I'd cook but, like we said, this room is a temporary situation," Kofi offered as he looked Chasity over. The burritos finished, and he tossed 9ine one and gave her two. Kofi studied the Bukkweat Bill–type haircut could not be concealed under the scarf Chasity was wearing. Her face was still fresh from bruises from her mother's brutal attack. The sympathy in his eyes let her know that he wanted to help.

"The room is full. Where will she sleep?" 9ine asked.

"Let's see." Kofi sat at the table with his own cinnamon twist. "She can have my bed for the night. I doubt Tiana and Zay are coming back so you can sleep in the other bed and I'll just chill right here."

"I'm not gonna put you out," Chasity offered. "I can sleep on top of the covers, and you can sleep under them."

"It should be the other way around," Kofi corrected her.

"Why don't both of y'all sleep under the covers?" 9ine suggested. "That way, y'all won't feel awkward and y'all can get that shit over with."

Kofi shook his head. He didn't have any intention of messing around with Chasity unless she started something.

9ine got up to go to the bathroom, and Kofi watched as Chasity took off the scarf she was wearing and put her bag on his bed. "So who putting their hands on you?" he asked as she sat on bed.

"My mom, she just likes to hit a little bit too much, and I don't hit her back," Chasity admitted softly. She never wanted to admit to anyone the type of abuse she was putting up with from her mother on a day-to-day basis. "I was trying to help her, but I can only do so much."

Kofi shook his head. "I don't know how you do it."

She finally sat on the bed with him and fiddled through her things. "I just do."

Chasity opened up to Kofi and told him how she felt about her mother and how she always hit her. Chasity told him how she got her "haircut" and how her mother spit on her, in addition to the things her mother threw at her or hit her with. Chasity almost brought herself to tears. Kofi gave her a hug and promised everything was going to be okay and, for the first time in her life, Chasity believed that.

Chapter Four

"Bitch, wake up!" Janae later shoved Lysa after Lloyd made his exit. She sprayed flowery-scented air freshener. She was still in the room Lloyd brought her in earlier.

"Damn, girl, I ain't 'sleep!" Lysa rolled over and sat up. "You making all that fucking noise like you never had any dick before." She frowned.

"That's because it was good!" Janae smiled as she sat down and rubbed her sore breasts. Lloyd wasted no time folding her every which way but sideways and testing out all her holes. "Guess what I made Lloyd do?" She grinned.

Lysa shrugged and pulled at the hem of the black boy shorts that circled her chocolate thick hips. "Probably something stupid or nasty."

"I made him lick my ass!" Janae bragged as she turned over and shook her ass in the air.

"Eww." Lysa covered her mouth.

"Fuck you ewwing for?" Janae rolled her neck, offended that her girl thought she was nasty. "That nigga loved it! And I liked it too."

"That's TMI for me, girl." Lysa shook her head. "I don't think nothing is sexy about licking or fucking an ass. Nope, that ain't for me. It's exit only."

"You don't know what you're missing." Janae laughed. "For real! It felt good!"

Lysa glanced at her watch and saw it was ten minutes to midnight. "What's up with this lick?"

Janae sighed. "I need a damn cigarette!"

"I'm out too." Lysa didn't bother to reach for her purse.

"Damn! I don't feel like walking to the store," Janae complained. "Uh, you feel like going to the corner store for me?"

"Yeah. But I want to hear more about this new lick you got lined up." Lysa studied Janae. Any idea to get money was good as long as she didn't get hurt.

Janae sat on the bed and slid her legs up under her. "Okay, all bullshit aside, this lick won't be like nothing we ever done. We won't be dealing with no true-to-life street dudes, and that will play in our favor."

"How?" Lysa asked.

"A street nigga don't give a fuck. These pimps, they have an image to maintain. They're in the public eye and can't be on no dumb shit."

Lysa nodded. "All right, that makes sense. But what I don't get is this: how do we get their bread in our hands?"

"Blackmail!" Janae rubbed her hands together. "We'll hit them muthafuckers with a choice. The only choice. Run us our money."

"This shit sounds too damn complicated." Lysa crossed her arms.

"Nothing about robbing anyone is supposed to be easy," Janae explained. "This ain't no gun-and-mask lick. We gotta be up on our shit to pull this off. All you gotta do is trust me on this. We ain't about to waste our time on no nickel-and-dime lick. If we do this shit right, we can get up outta these projects!"

Lysa scratched behind her ear. "How much bread can we get?"

"Depends on who we get. Like I told you, Lloyd, he's hiding his paper! From what I overheard last night, he got more than one revenue stream, some legit, some illegal. I'm willing to bet he's sitting on a hundred fucking racks!"

"So?" Lysa shrugged with a confused look.

"Bitch, do you know we can get the fuck out of Asheville with that kind of loot? And that's just half of the lick."

"How?" Lysa asked with a load of doubt.

Janae sighed and rolled her eyes. "Once I find where the rest of his shit is at, we'll blackmail his ass and take his ride and whatever jewels he's rocking. He looks like an old Rolex-ass dude anyway."

"I get the robbing part," Lysa concurred, "but the shit about a blackmail move, explain."

Janae smiled. "This is where you come in. Name one pussy-loving dude who can resist you."

Lysa shifted on the couch. For all it was worth, she held the title of being one of the baddest bitches in Buncombe County. Her ghetto thick frame and chocolate skin tone had all the rowdy hustlers ready to fuck. She was hood, but far from being a ho. Even in a pair of plain shorts and a T-shirt, her every voluptuous curve had to be admired. In truth, Lysa was a certified dime piece, and she was still poor and stressed the fuck out.

"Okay. You might have a point. But what's my role?" Lysa wanted to know.

"Remember what I said about these pimps having an image to uphold. Well, they'll come up off that bread when we hang a rape scandal over their heads."

"Rape!" Lysa stared at Janae like she'd lost her fucking mind.

"Yes, rape. It won't be true, but they will pay us to stay quiet regardless. They ain't about to let something like a rape charge go public. They got too much to lose."

"And I guess I'll be the bait," Lysa replied straight-faced.

"Yes. And don't act like you ain't never show some ass for a lick."

"That's not what I'm worried about. What concerns me is if this shit will work. If the bread is like you say it is, I'm down for mine, and you know that."

"It's worth it, girl."

"Better be." Lysa stood with the tight boyshorts riding all up in her ass.

"Your butt getting bigger." Janae snickered.

"Fuck you," Lysa sang as she grabbed Janae's keys off the table. "Uh, gimme some money for the cigarettes."

Janae pointed across the living room at the kitchen table. "Take what you need. Lloyd left me a few dollars."

"Bitch, lemme find out yo' ass is prostituting!" Lysa joked.

"Eat my pussy! You know what time it is."

Lysa took what she needed for the cigarettes and ten dollars for herself. She couldn't get from her mind the fact that Janae rocked Lloyd loose. She exited Janae's crib and strutted through a group of thugs posted out on the curb.

"Yo, Lysa!" one of the thugs called.

She didn't pause a step. Tonight she wasn't in the mood to flirt since the heartache over her lover was too fresh. Seconds later she strutted down Tunnel Road with confidence, and she winked at the occasional driver when they rode by. The stress over her mound of issues weighed hard on Lysa. She feared the possibility of things turning for the worse before she had a chance to make it to next month. Halfway to the store, she realized that her current situation would be all the way fucked up if Janae weren't on her side. Janae never sweated the fact that Lysa preferred women but fucked niggas for a quick buck. Tonight proved to Lysa that the bond and friendship she had with Janae was unbreakable. But, in life, it's the unexpected that trips us up; and for Lysa, the unexpected would come next month.

Chapter Five

"Mama," 9ine called Leshaun as she struggled to get through her pancake meal at IHOP. She looked at the one whore in her life who could call her that. Leshaun remembered pushing him out on her Barbie bedspread when she was thirteen and couldn't keep the pregnancy a secret. 9ine had full lips, mocha skin, and a ill bald fade just like three of the cousins who started raping her when she was nine. She couldn't remember which of her mother's sister's children was her son's father. Her parents never believed she was raped and they accused her of being too fast for her own good. Like it was her fault for having B-cups and hair on her pussy at nine, She didn't ask for them.

Leshaun picked up a piece of turkey bacon and bit into it as she fought off the memory. She finally looked at her son and then looked away. While she loved her son dearly, she hated the fact that 9ine knew he was also her cousin, and how they both misused and took advantage of *that* relationship.

"I can't believe I let them dusty-ass bitches burn my hotel to the ground," Leshaun vented as she chewed her piece of bacon fast.

"Ma, don't be like that," 9ine offered as he took a sip of his cranberry juice. "Papa will be proud of us once he sees how fast we got the money together and get Price Street Hotel back together, watch."

"Yeah," Tiana cosigned. "You've always been a hustler, and you'll get beyond this."

"Yeah, Ma, 9ine, and Tiana are right," Zay agreed.

Leshaun cut her eyes at Zay. He smiled and licked his lips. 9ine caught the tension between the two and promptly smacked his best friend in the back of the head. Zay shoved him back. "I don't know what I'm going to do with the three of y'all." Leshaun shook her head.

"First things first. That new Chasity girl y'all brought in, we gotta teach her some new things and make sure she's ready for her schoolgirl gig," Tiana brought up as she brought her strawberry lemonade to her lips.

"How is she doing?" Leshaun had some reservations about Chasity and her mental state. When they introduced her to Leshaun, she could see right away that the girl had potential, but the wardrobe and the attitude needed work.

"Well, I made sure that ID she had was legit," Tiana mentioned as she cut her pancakes with a knife and a fork. "Once I got that done, you know I made sure she was ready. I pulled in a favor from one of my friends who works at the clinic, and she came back clean. Then I watched as she put in some work with 9ine and Zay. She can definitely handle two dicks in one sitting."

Zay looked away, catching the attention of an older lady a few tables away near the window. Leshaun knew he was trying to hide the fact that he enjoyed his time with Chasity. She wasn't jealous; it just meant she'd make up some of the money lost by not having Lysa and Janae.

"You gonna stop letting your head fall, call Kofi, and put the three of us to work," 9ine encouraged her, bringing the conversation back to the business and off his sex life. He knew Tiana was gonna tell his mom how Chasity performed in bed, but he didn't want to be present when the news was presented. Aside from that, he hated seeing his mom angry, upset, or down and he made it his business to lay hands on anyone who brought pain to her doorstep. "We gon' find out who did this and, I promise you, the minute I know will be the minute they take their last breath."

"You so smart." The sarcasm in Zay's voice was hard to ignore. "We making threats in the motherfuckin' IHOP where these scared-ass white people probably are recording us on their smartphones and shit."

"Naw, I'm speaking facts," 9ine defended himself. "You gonna stop coming at me like I'm slow and shit. Best friend or not, you can get your head rocked too."

Leshaun reached out to the two men she loved most. She knew neither one of them would get rowdy in her presence. As she looked at Zay, a part of her felt guilty for sleeping with him. She raised 9ine's friend since he was five years old. She barely could afford to take care of 9ine and his sister, Ten, but when Zay's mom got too strung out on meth and heroin, her heart wouldn't let her allow the department of social services to take the boy and put him in foster care. 9ine and Zay were only three days apart, and while Leshaun didn't care for Zay's mom, she had appreciated that she was one of the few parents who would let their child play with 9ine.

"Okay, Zay, you said we got to be smart right now and you calling it right because the last thing I need is to end up in jail. And, 9ine, you also right: we gon' get whoever had the balls to put a flame to Price Street Hotel, accident or not." Her hunger struck her, and she finally picked up a fork and scooped some of the pancakes on it and brought it to her lips. She enjoyed the taste and swallowed. "I'm just trying to figure out what I'm going to do with all of you. It ain't just the two of y'all; I got eleven other whores to feed and take care of too."

"Well, you know me, Zay, and Kofi got ourselves and can hold our own," 9ine called out. Whether she wanted to admit it or not, 9ine was telling the truth. "You worry about them other bitches and make sure they become resourceful. You been taken care of them for all these years and now it's time they take care of you."

9ine's words rang true to heart as she thought about how she made her younger sister, Gogo, one of her first whores. Their mother hadn't always felt well coming up. Maybe that would explain why getting along with her and living with her could be so difficult at times. Gogo was fifteen and only three years younger than Leshaun. Gogo knew her sister struggled with being on welfare and trying to work a job at Wendy's to support herself and 9ine. Gogo never cosigned on how their parents treated Leshaun once they found out she was pregnant and claiming to be raped by her family members. Gogo knew Leshaun was telling the truth because the same cousins who were touching her sister were touching her too.

Gogo figured out that if she got on her back, opened her legs, and let a few men spend some time dancing and swimming inside of her, releasing their tensions and inner demons, two things would happen: one, the men would pay her hush money to keep their secrets, especially the ones old enough to be her grandfather; and, two, if she kept her body right and stayed on top of her grades at school, she could use both to advance her career.

When Leshaun found out what her sister was doing, and how she was able to give her money for Pampers, apple juice, and brand new baby clothes that came from Belk and JCPenney, she couldn't let Gogo mess with these men unattended. She arranged for her boyfriend and Ten's father, Prince, to stand guard and make sure Gogo was okay. The nigga wasn't doing nothing but smoking weed and stealing knickknacks from the convenience store he was working at.

Thinking about her sister, Leshaun was surprised that Gogo hadn't reached out to her by now. Usually, if one was in trouble, the other was on the way. Even though Gogo lived in Greenville, South Carolina, she made the forty-five-minute trek to Asheville to make sure her sister was all right and had everything she needed.

Maybe Gogo on the way, Leshaun comforted herself as she ate the rest of her food. She looked at her two twenty-year-old gigolos and smiled as they were huddled up, surely looking at something profane on Zay's iPhone. Every year they got a new model, Zay was the first one at the Best Buy to get his hands on it. Zay passed the phone to Tiana, and she passed it back, giggling. When he wasn't looking at something on Facebook, he was filming something lewd and crass to put on his Instagram or Snapchat. That's how she discovered how big Zay's dick was. She crept on the page one time while she was bored and Zay had just briefly uploaded a small clip of some trashy white girl swallowing him and going up and down his length. That intrigued her, and as she looked through his past pics and flicks, she discovered that Zay had the potential to be a full-fledged porn star. Leshaun talked Tiana into hitting him up in his DMs and, the next thing she knew, Zay and Tiana started sending each other nasty pics and posting pics and flicks of them having sex all over the place. Zay's pipe game was all right and, at ten and a half inches, he definitely couldn't hide that with his five foot seven, 210-pound frame. Leshaun thought that if Zay lost a few pounds, ten and a half inches might turn into twelve and she'd really have a killer on her hands.

Leshaun got her mind focused on how she was going to rebuild Price Street Hotel and off of what Zay had going on below the waist. The way 9ine and Zay laughed, some girl was struggling to take all that Zay had to offer, and she was silent when the two of them debated on whether the flick should go on Instagram or the Web site she helped Zay set up where people could pay to view some of his exploits in real time. It linked to the ConnectPal account, which mostly his gay fans paid a monthly subscription to, to watch him jack off, dance, or fuck random chicks, watching his ass move as he laid pipe.

When Leshaun finished her meal, she looked up and could've sworn she saw Prince heading to the back of the restaurant. No, she was sure, because she'd recognize Ten's father anywhere and no one carried off a white button-up shirt, black slacks, and black work shoes the way he did. Leshaun looked at her boys one last time before she got up, left a fifty dollar bill on the table, and headed in Prince's direction.

"Ay, can you ask Prince to come here please?" Leshaun commanded the waitress who was ringing up an order on the computer screen near the kitchen. Leshaun looked at the card and, just that fast, she memorized Sheila Goldfield's name, Discover card number, and the expiration date; and all she had to find out was the security code on the back.

Luck was on Leshaun's side as she saw the waitress being careless with the card as she went to fulfill her request. She repeated the numbers again and again until Prince stood before her. He was still as fine as the day she met him when 9ine was only a year old. He wasn't a day older than twenty-six himself, and he couldn't believe that the fourteen-year-old girl he laid eyes on was built better than some of the women his age. It wasn't until he got inside her that he found out she felt just as good as the women his age, too.

"How's Ten doing?" Prince broke Leshaun's concentration. When Leshaun didn't answer right away, he knew what time it was and stepped to the side so that Leshaun could focus on getting whatever information off the card she needed. "I wish you wouldn't do this shit at my job."

"My bad." Leshaun felt bad for not recognizing Prince standing in front of him. She looked at him again, and he still smelled like that Alpha cologne that he ordered from his aunt who sold Avon. Alpha smelled good on him and defined what kind of man he was. "I saw you, and I just wanted to speak."

"I see your two boys are up to no good." Prince pointed out the pretty and well-built Asian woman who ke-keyed with them, and the waitress brought another order of food to feed them. She thanked God when she saw they mostly had fruit on their plates.

"It's not like that with me." She told Prince the truth. "I saw you, and I didn't think it would be right if we didn't speak. Besides, I had a rough day the other day."

"What happened?" Prince was concerned. No matter what went on between him and Leshaun, he was always concerned about her. "Is Ten okay?" The inquiry confirmed that Prince always looked out for his seed.

"Ten is fine. She's at Western Carolina University tending to her studies. The Price Street Hotel caught on fire yesterday. I lost half the building."

Prince gave Leshaun a hug. That wasn't the reaction she was expecting from him. The careless waitress turned the card over, punched in the three-digit code, and then flipped the card back over. Regardless of their relationship, Prince was more of a help than he was a hindrance. "I'm okay. I'm just pissed because I have to pay rent for the first time in like, years, and I haven't figured out how I'm gonna run my business."

Prince gave her the side eye.

"I mean, running my hotel," Leshaun defended herself. "Don't judge me like that, muthafucker. I had paying customers in those rooms, and dealing with the insurance and the credit card companies has given me a headache.

I don't have a property in sight to purchase immediately, and it could take months before Price Street Hotel is up and running where I need it to be."

"Ma, say no more," Prince replied. "I got to get to work, but as soon as I lay down this nine to five, I'm gonna call you. My ex has a property she ain't using and before you roll your eyes and say no, let me do what I do, and I'll get back with you. I can't fix one area of your business, but I sure can provide you the space to take care of the business you need to handle."

It wasn't what she asked for, but it was a concession she was willing to take for now. Even though she couldn't stand Prince's ex-wife, she knew she didn't want to stay in someone else's hotel, either. Like it or not, she knew she was going to have to have her whores on the road and revamping that part of her business while her property got fixed. Once she figured that out, she could then bring everyone home.

Chapter Six

"Girl! What the fuck are you doing?" Gogo shouted as she and Tiana entered Leshaun's room. Seeing Leshaun out of character across the dimly lit room raised concern.

Leshaun lowered the chrome .22 with a flood of tears streaming down her innocent face. "I'm tired of this life!" she sobbed from the floor.

"Leshaun." Tiana lowered her voice. "Put the gun down, okay? I know you're going through hell right now, but killing yourself ain't the answer."

"Gimme the gun!" Gogo demanded as she and Tiana cautiously approached Leshaun's bed.

"I can't do this!" Leshaun wiped her eyes. "My building is ruined. I haven't been able to get in touch with Lysa and Janae, which confirms for me that they did this shit. I'm living in this damn Grand Bohemian Hotel, and I haven't figured out my next fuckin' move!"

"I know that." Gogo carefully put her arm around Leshaun.

"None of it is worth taking your life." Tiana tried to be the voice of reason. "Especially over them sorry-ass hoes. We kill bitches like them over less."

Leshaun wiped her eyes again with a firm grip on the .22. "But don't you get tired of this life?" She looked up at Gogo. She could barely see the concern on her face for the tears in her eyes. Leshaun shook her head. "It's easier this way." She sobbed.

"No, it's not. Don't say that!" Gogo stated. She couldn't figure out for the life of her what had gotten into Leshaun. Last time Gogo checked in on 9ine, he and Zay were clowning in the IHOP. He was the one who told her his mom was tripping and needed her. The way he said it implied to Gogo that she needed help figuring shit out, not that Gogo needed to try stopping her from committing suicide.

"Nobody is gonna miss me," Leshaun reasoned as she held the gun firmly in her hand.

"Bitch, are you crazy?" Tiana snapped. "I'm gonna miss your ass, but I'm not even going to think like that because you got to be fucked up if you think I'm going to let you take your life like this!"

"What about me?" Gogo shouted as she pointed to herself. "You're my sister, Leshaun. 9ine and Ten are going to miss they crazy-ass mama. Prince still worships the ground you walk on. Kofi and Tiana are loyal as fuck; and Zay, you been raising that nigga for a minute and fucking him for the last two weeks."

Leshaun gave Gogo the side eye. Only Tiana knew she'd crossed that line with Zay. If Gogo knew, she knew it was a matter of time before 9ine and Zay fought and 9ine was standing over her cussing her out.

"I didn't tell her," Tiana defended herself.

"Naw, she didn't tell me but, bitch, that's not the point. You know you're the only one I fucks with. Look at all the bullshit we've been through. And we did it together," Gogo pointed out.

"It's hard," Leshaun sobbed. "I'm trying so hard, but I keep falling flat on my face. I don't have enough money to make this happen overnight. And you know these spiteful-ass muthafuckers in Asheville love to see a bitch fall. I'll be all over Facebook over this shit."

"See?" Tiana walked around turning items over. "Where are the drugs you're on? Because this isn't even like you to be thinking like this. Fuck these people in Asheville, real shit."

"Look at me, Leshaun." Gogo lifted her sister's face and wiped her tears, returning a favor that had been given to her forever ago. "I care about you, and I don't want to lose the only friend I have in this world. What if I was gonna kill myself? What would you do?" Gogo stared at Leshaun as she fought back her own tears.

"I would stop you," Leshaun answered with her lips quivering.

"Oh, we gonna stop your ass. That's for sure." Tiana kept looking for drugs or whatever it was that she thought made Leshaun lose her mind.

"Then let me do the same for you." Gogo held her hand out. "I'll help you through this like I always do. You're stronger than you think you are."

Leshaun stared at the .22 through a haze of tears and wondered if Gogo's words were true. "Something has to change," she cried.

"It will!" Gogo replied. "But we have to fight this shit together."

"Yeah." Tiana gave up her search and took a seat next to Leshaun. "You know you're bigger than this."

Leshaun relaxed her grip on the .22 with a mixture of stressed emotions. "I can't live like this no more." Her breathing was still labored by her failed attempt to take her life.

"I have a plan to get us up out of here," Gogo assured her as she held her hand out for the gun. Her heart beat fast because even though she had the belief she could talk Leshaun out of doing the unthinkable, she knew her sister made snap decisions. One wrong word, one wrong move, and Gogo would be mourning the woman she'd admired and loved since they met.

Leshaun turned the .22 backward and handed it to Gogo.

"C'mere." Gogo slid the .22 behind her and gestured Leshaun and Tiana in for a hug. They sat and cried at the foot of the bed. Gogo didn't even try to imagine how her life would be without Leshaun. In truth, their bond was thicker than blood. Life was simple back then, but the harsh lessons of life came too fast for them to learn.

As a team, as the best of friends, they went against the world after their parents put them out on their own. They stripped together, dated hustlers, tried to sell weed, stole clothes from the mall, and each time they were met with failure. At thirty-three, thirty, and twenty-nine years old, they shared a ton of unneeded stress. Sadly, Leshaun reached her breaking point first.

"Where did you get that gun?" Gogo asked minutes later in the living room.

Leshaun stared at the floor. "I stole it out of Kofi's car last month."

"He's been looking for that gun." Tiana chuckled.

"Girl, you're crazy." Gogo managed to smile.

Leshaun wiped her eyes and turned toward Gogo. "What's this plan you spoke of awhile ago?"

"It's a major lick to get some serious bread!" Gogo was excited.

"Whatever it is, I'm with it." Tiana signed up, down for the team.

Leshaun crossed her arms. "I'm not robbing no more drug dealers. That shit is too fucking dangerous."

"That ain't it." Gogo wanted Leshaun to guess.

"And I'm not stripping." Leshaun hated the pole. Even though she loved being a big girl, she didn't want to put in the work to stay fit and do the trips to get the bands to dance.

"Nope. That ain't it either." Gogo sounded like a little kid.

Bitch. Leshaun was tired of guessing. She cocked her head to the side, nonverbally coaxing Gogo to get to the point.

"We can rob some our rivals' escorts and clients!" Gogo got crunk as she felt like she'd dropped the best news since Leshaun discovered she could balance her legal and illegal revenue streams comfortably.

Leshaun lifted an eyebrow. "Escorts and clients? What the fu—"

"Yes!" Tiana got excited. "It was probably one of your rivals who hit you up, so you get the sons and daughters you got loyal to you to do the same shit."

"Really?" Leshaun thought the plan sounded too good to be true.

"Fuck yeah. Listen, we lie low for a minute. Pretend like everything is over, and then we come back and hit these bitches blind because they will never see us coming. That would be a major lick," Gogo promised. "But, seriously, we can make a big come up with this plan I got."

Leshaun sat back and pushed her fingers through her bone-straight, shoulder-length hair. This wouldn't be the first time for Gogo to have a plan. "I doubt any escort or client who knows us is gonna take a robbery from us seriously," Leshaun spoke her mind.

"I know that. But you got to trust me because I've done my research on this," Gogo insisted.

"Research?" Leshaun frowned. "For this lick you talkin' 'bout?"

"Yeah. We not gonna shit in our backyard. We going to Phoenix, Tuscon, Denver, Colorado Springs, Seattle: low-key West Coast cities."

"Then what?" Leshaun interrupted.

"If you let me finish you'll know how this will pop off." Gogo cleared her throat. "Now, like I was say-ing. I checked out every operation running west of the

Mississippi, and I got a list of all the major ones. Plus, I got a list of the major clients who use the call girls and boy toys regularly. They will be our target. All we gotta do is work what our mama gave us."

Leshaun rolled her eyes. "You ain't making a bit of sense, girl."

"Let her finish." Tiana jumped in.

"That's because I haven't told you everything. For instance, one of the big clients out there is Jackson Young. They just did a spread on him in *USA Today* last week, and he just signed on to do a movie based on Faith's *Church Whore* books. He's loaded, girl! On his Facebook he has a picture of his ride and guess what it is?" Gogo squirmed in her seat with excitement.

Leshaun shrugged, showing little interest.

"A muthfuckin' Maserati sedan and I can't even pronounce the name of it! Shit starts with a Q, and it's fly as fuck! He got that paper, girl, and it's legal."

"True. But how do we get it?" Tiana asked.

"By scheming and working on his weakness." Gogo's answer was straight-forward.

Leshaun sighed and kicked her tennis shoes off. "It sounds wack."

"It ain't wack. FYI, it's the best plan I ever had!" Gogo saw the dollar signs dance in her head.

"How do you plan to even get up with Jackson Young?" Leshaun was skeptical. Everything Gogo presented so far seemed too good to be true. And she was mad at Tiana for being so quick to jump on the opportunity.

Gogo smiled. "Remember that dude I was fucking who worked as a travel agent with AAA?"

Leshaun and Tiana nodded.

"Well, he was the one who told me about the major screening Jackson Young has in Seattle at the Big Picture.

He was the one who booked the reservation. I have his whole itinerary. I know when he's chilling at Starbucks, and which Adam's Mark hotel he's staying in. And he slid me that info."

Leshaun shook her head. "We'd be like the only black folks in the crowd. How the hell can I even think of mingling with that crowd?"

"It will be easy because—"

Click.

"What the fuck!" Gogo jumped off the bed.

Leshaun closed her eyes to keep any new tears at bay.

"Girl!" Gogo looked at the .22 in Leshaun's hand. "This piece of shit don't even got a firing pin!"

Leshaun took a close look at the .22. She shrugged as she flopped down on the floor.

"I'ma spend the night with you."

"Yeah, me too," Tiana added.

Gogo took the gun from Leshaun and made sure she had her mind right before she headed to the bathroom to take a shower. Leshaun waved her out of her face and told her to go and wash her stanking ass. They shared a laugh, but Leshaun did her best to cover her stress.

Left alone on the bed, she broke down in fresh tears. Leshaun hated her life. Hated the streets. Hated the trouble of finding a new property. Hated the backstabbing bitches and the stupid games they played! Life, her life, taught her that a pretty face and a phat ass didn't mean shit when it came to paying the bills. Shit, there were plenty of dimes in the hood. Leshaun turned on her side and blinked her tears away. Gogo had her back, and that was something Leshaun wouldn't doubt.

She thought of Gogo's new lick. Robbing escorts and clients. It still didn't make any sense, but it was a risk she had to take. Truth be told, Leshaun was down for anything. She wasn't honest with herself, Tiana, or Gogo.

Shit! I'd strip on Main Street and rob any dope boy right now! All she wanted and needed was enough money to be set for life.

Leshaun envisioned a future where she could sit back, relax, and enjoy the fruits of her labors. The problem was that she never set a goal for what would make her happy. Price Street Hotel grew in popularity as more visitors toured Asheville and took in the scenery. With the breweries came franchises of popular restaurants in other cities. Many home and tourist magazines ranked Asheville a "Number One Place to Live and See." And Leshaun made good money. She rented the rooms in Price Street Hotel at $160 a night. With thirty rooms, she booked the twenty-four rooms that she'd made available to the public, every night from April fifteenth to the week before Christmas.

The club in Birmingham, Alabama, Dom's Paradice, did well too. It was a revenue stream not many in Asheville knew about. Unlike the hotel, the club was a safe haven because it was close enough to fly to if she wanted to get away for the weekend, but far enough that she didn't have to worry about the club and the hotel crowds comingling. She'd bought the club on a whim a few years ago after the former owner patronized her hotel and she observed the competent staff that ran the operations. Dom's Paradice appealed to her because she could be part of the entertainment scene without having to invest a lot of money in grooming the talent. The management of the hotel worked with local radio stations and promoters to keep the club popping.

Prostitution, larceny, and murder didn't mix well with her legal portfolio. But she remembered the days when she didn't have a hotel. Prince worked two and three jobs at a time so that Leshaun could go to school and do the best for 9ine and Ten that she knew how. Prostitution put food on the table and larceny afforded her luxuries every now and then. The murders weren't frequent but part of the game. And that's what Leshaun liked: she wanted to stay in the game.

After being raped and impregnated by one her cousins, Leshaun saw pimping as a means to an end. Why couldn't she be on both sides of the law? Men did it all the time; she should be able to do it too. Unlike most pimps, Leshaun treated her whores good. She allowed them to pick and choose who they worked with. Mindful that one of the whores was her son, she treated the rest as if they were her children. They were paid well, tested regularly, and they didn't need anything because Leshaun paid for everything out of pocket. She even had them keep legitimate jobs at fast food restaurants, other hotels and, for the two who had education, in their respective professions. Which made the betrayal by Lysa and Janae more troubling. Leshaun never forced the two women to do anything they didn't want to do. Everything a mother was supposed to provide—food, clothing, shelter, love—Leshaun did that. All the things a pimp was supposed to do—protect, keep them maintained, and give loyalty—Leshaun did that, too.

Maybe some things weren't meant to be understood. Leshaun wanted to catch those two, chop them up, and feed them to the hogs and pigs in the pork farms in Michigan. Get her revenge and make them disappear. But she knew moving too fast would not produce the result she wanted.

Leshaun thought about what she was going to attempt to do a few minutes ago and how she missed the blessings in her life, and she cried again.

Chapter Seven

Lysa and Janae kept the textbooks they stole from one of the vacant classrooms close to the chest as the wandered the sidewalk outside of the Victoria building at A-B Tech. Since setting Leshaun's property on fire, the two whores had been keeping a low profile. The best place to hide was around the 20,000 students who went to the community college to start or change careers.

"I'm so glad that bitch ain't over my shoulder." Janae spoke of Leshaun in disgust as she loudly smacked her watermelon-flavored Bubblicious gum.

"See, I knew you'd be happy if we made the move and rocked with Lloyd." Lysa spotted a table and quickly threw her black and pink backpack across the metal grill-styled table, claiming her spot.

"Just because his dick big don't make him good," Janae warned. She took a seat across from Lysa. She wanted to roll her eyes, but her guard was up. In the back of her mind, she expected Leshaun to catch the two of them slipping and make both of them disappear. Guilt began to surface as she thought about how Leshaun and 9ine rescued her from an abusive foster home. But she'd paid her debt to them several times, bringing in money from her older tricks time to time, and aborting 9ine's seed so Leshaun wouldn't become a grandma before thirty. After seven years, Janae just wanted to be free. The plan wasn't for her to be indebted to Leshaun and her "company" forever.

"Girl." Lysa got excited. Janae hated that about her. Lysa always got excited every time she got a trick with a big dick or a well-built body. And she swore Lloyd had both. All Lysa could talk about was how fine and how sexy she thought Lloyd was and how she couldn't wait to spend the day with him. "When we meet with him tonight at the Grove Park Inn, you'll see."

Janae was good on meeting Lloyd again. In her eyes, Lloyd wasn't nothing special. Five foot eleven and 200 pounds, Lloyd often passed for white, thanks to his almond milk–colored skin. He was built like Josh Norman, a former cornerback for the Carolina Panthers. His dark chocolate eyes and full lips gave away his African heritage, but his thin European nose and thin jawbone always threw his ethnicity into question.

"He did deliver on the ten racks he promised us to burn down the Price Street Hotel," Janae conceded, hoping Lysa would shut up. Janae knew Lysa was in love, and she didn't want to hurt her feelings, but she was sick of hearing about Lysa and Lloyd. Janae wasn't jealous because she didn't have a man, but she got sick and tired of hearing the same things about the same person over and over again. Janae knew and accepted her lot in life. She was a whore and an occasional booster, and Janae planned on rocking that train until the wheels fell off.

Lysa's phone rang and Janae shook her head when she caught Lysa in a lie about throwing away the Cricket phone Leshaun had given her last week. *Lloyd again.* She could tell that by the way Lysa giggled and let her hands roam her body freely as if she were at home and not in the middle of a college campus. "Lloyd called, and he wants to see us, but I don't want to go by myself. Please come with me?" Lysa asked as she put her phone next to her bag.

Lysa has lost her damn mind, Janae thought, and she checked her LG smartphone she bought at Walmart. "What am I going to do, be the third wheel?"

"No, Janae," Lysa cooed like a baby and giggled. "I'm going to introduce you to Bryson, his brother. He owns a small used car dealership that only sells Toyotas and Hondas." Lysa moved her fingers fast on her phone. "I got us an Uber, and they'll be here in two minutes."

"Is the driver a woman?" Janae opened her bag and put her phone inside. "You know I'm not getting in a car with no male driver."

"Girl, it's two of us." Lysa stood up and straightened out her loose-fitting dark blue T-shirt. "We can overpower any nigga if we work together."

Lysa's naïveté is going to be the death of me, Janae kept in the forefront of her mind. Janae was sensitive to the fact that Lysa was just nineteen and still learning about life. She thought her smooth skin, light brown eyes, and thick, five foot four frame would get her everything she wanted in life. Janae was twenty-five and knew better. Janae knew the end of life wasn't supposed to be with her face down, ass up, being pounded by some unnamed john. She knew there was more to life than her looks, as they would fade; and, if she was lucky, her black wouldn't crack.

Janae had them all. Big dicks, little dicks, black men, Latin men, Asians, fat, and fit. She admitted to herself that she had Leshaun and Gogo to thank for her street smarts and her burning quest for knowledge for her book sense. Janae still took care of her five foot six, 170-pound frame, but she had plans that did not involve her pussy getting her out of everything. Janae wanted to be a paralegal in three years, but she had yet to register for classes or make an effort to seriously pursue getting accepted into A-B Tech or any other school.

The Uber arrived, and Janae was relieved to see a dark-skinned sister with locks pushing the silver 2014 Hyundai Sonata on the pavement.

"I told you we got a woman," Lysa stated as the Uber driver got out of the car and opened the door for them. Once Janae and Lysa got situated, Janae smiled at the driver.

"I'm Clairese, and I'll be your driver for this ride," the driver introduced herself. "I have an iPhone and an Android charger if you need one. Also, I have satellite radio, or I can pick up the music in your phone with my Bluetooth connection. And if you need water, I have some cold bottles in the trunk."

"I like you," Lysa complimented her. "See, Janae, this is why I always take an Uber."

Janae smiled. She peeped the University of North Carolina Asheville lanyard hanging off the rearview mirror and the student parking decal at the bottom of the driver's side of her windowpane. "What are you studying?" Janae wanted to hear something else other than Lloyd.

"English," Clairese answered. "I'm on the basketball team, and it's one way I can focus on my creative writing."

Janae liked Clairese. In a different world, she could see herself hanging out with someone like Clairese. Janae liked to read in her spare time. She was happy to meet a sister who had brains and a little bit of brawn. One who knew how to make and get money without having to open her legs.

"Girl, Lloyd is fine, so Bryson has to be fine." Lysa brought the attention back to herself and Lloyd again. Janae hadn't been under his leadership for twenty-four hours, and she was already sick of him.

"If he is ugly I'm walking out and leaving your ass right there by yo'self," Janae countered. *Since when did it become Lysa's mission to find a man for me?* Janae tried not to get suspicious. Hell, if Janae wanted one, Janae could get any of these roughnecks on her own. But Janae decided to be a good sport about it because she would've felt guilty if something happened because she refused to go. Janae had taken Lysa under her wing, as Janae looked up to Leshaun.

"Bryson is gonna be fine, I promise," Lysa insisted.

Speak of the devil, the bass for Bryson Tiller's song "Don't" rocked the Sonata as Clairese guided the car down Charlotte Avenue to the turn on Macon Avenue. Janae was glad Clairese didn't take the longer scenic route through Kimberly Avenue. "Whatever. You hear me when I said I'm out of there. Don't play me, Lysa."

"I wouldn't do that." Lysa took out her phone and sent a text message.

Janae heard that line before. "So how many rooms did Lloyd get us?" She had meant to get clarification on that before they got into the Uber.

"He got us three," Lysa confirmed. "We supposed to meet some other girl there, but I don't know her."

Before she could protest, Janae took in the beautiful view of the Grove Park Inn. She'd only been there once before; she was drunk and with a client whom Kofi had gotten rid of. The older granite rock building had a valet waiting at the entrance. As they got out of the Uber, Janae reached in her pocket and pulled out a five dollar bill and handed to Clairese.

"Thank you." Clairese took the money and put it in her pocket.

Janae nodded her head. She knew if she wanted her customers to throw in a little something extra, she had to be a good tipper too. And her karma worked out for that.

"Did you think about what we talked about?" Lysa asked as they stepped into the building.

"No, not really." Janae hadn't thought about it. Janae had hoped to take her mind off the betrayal she dished to Leshaun.

"Well, don't you want to get money?"

"Yeah."

They stopped at the front desk and got their rooms situated. As she looked around, Janae couldn't help but notice that she and Lysa had the only brown faces in the lobby.

Lysa came into the room where Janae was getting ready for this business meeting with Lysa, Lloyd, and Bryson. Janae had to admit, Lloyd had good taste when it came to clothes. The pink satin blouse looked good and matched the threads in her Apple Bottoms jeans. Lysa looked at Janae with a screw face. "Do you think you're going to church?"

Janae looked in the mirror. Her outfit was subtle and didn't scream that she was getting paid to screw the rich and famous. In fact, she fit in with the tourists Asheville was known to attract. "What's wrong with what I got on?"

"Hell no. You're not coming with me with that on. Let me help you with your outfit." Lysa left the room. A few seconds later, she returned with a miniskirt that looked a little too small and a tank top. Janae switched gears and made sure her hair was right. Satisfied, they left the rooms and got on a nearby elevator.

"That's Lloyd in the velour sweat suit." Lysa grabbed Janae's hand and exited the elevator. "You see him?" she continued as they headed into the lobby. Janae saw two men who looked similar. "You see him?"

"Damn, Lysa, I see him," Janae finally told her.

Lloyd acknowledged their presence as he made his way across the lobby, leaving the group of guys he was with as they approached him. When they got close, he reached out to give Lysa a hug. "What's up, girl?" Lloyd asked as he let Lysa go and gave Janae a once-over. "You look good."

"Thank you." Janae hoped it wasn't obvious that she was a hoochie as Lloyd flanked her on the left side. He looked back and nodded to another man who was part of another crew. "Bry," Lloyd called out like he was in the middle of the street and not a three-star hotel. The tall, light-skinned boy turned around, nodded his head, and grinned.

"Damn." Janae admitted he was fine under her breath.

"What's up?" Bryson yelled just as loud as Lloyd. He then turned his attention to his boys and probably said something slick because some of his boys were cracking up.

"Ay, Bryson, come on, man," Lloyd insisted.

Bryson left his group and came over to Lloyd. "What's up, Lysa?" Bryson greeted her as he gave her a small hug. Then he looked at Janae and licked his lips. "You wanted to see a nigga? Where are you from? How old are you?"

"What? Am I on a game show? What's with all these questions and all?"

Bryson stepped closer to Janae and smiled. "I'm just trying to get to know you that's all. I see you and Lysa been on waiting on us for over an hour, so I know how bad you wanted to meet me."

Janae was not about to be played to the left. "Okay. We gon' keep it real. I only came because she didn't want to come alone."

Bryson dismissed what Janae had to say as if he had proof otherwise. "Let's go back to the room. A'ight, fellas,

I got some better friends to entertain. It's time for y'all to be out." Bryson dissed the crew he was hanging with. Some of them responded by calling him a sucker and some other names, but that didn't stop his boys from giving him pounds and man hugs.

Bryson led the way to the elevator. "Go ahead in. Ain't nobody going to bite you. At least not yet," Bryson assured them. He pressed the button leading to the top floor.

Once the elevator stopped, he led them to his suite, which was at the end of the hall. "Why don't y'all have a seat?" Bryson tried to make them feel at home. "I'm about to go put on some Rihanna." The next minute, "Desperado" boomed in the room and set the mood.

Lloyd and Lysa sat at the table, engrossed in their own private conversation. Janae finally took a seat at the edge of his bed after failing to find preferable seating in the room. The last thing Janae wanted was to give him the idea that she was easy, and sitting on his bed would be defeating the purpose of that. Her other options were sitting on random men's laps or on the table and, to get Bryson's attention, she had to come better than that.

Bryson took a seat next to her after a few minutes. "You never did answer my question. I asked, how old are you?"

"Eighteen," Janae lied. "Why? Does age matter to you?"

"Hell yeah, the difference between jail or not. I don't mess with jailbait."

Janae wasn't concerned because she wasn't planning on doing anything stupid with him. "You don't have to worry about that."

"I hope not."

The song switched to "Work" featuring Drake. Rihanna spoke her language because if she did anything with

Bryson, she was going to get paid. Janae noticed that it was five o'clock according to the digital clock on the wall and no action had started. Janae didn't want to waste her time if he wasn't serious about making a move. Bryson was cute, but she didn't come to fuck for free. Janae didn't see a new target who physically brought his game like Bryson, but she was willing to bet that a few of them had cash that went just as long. Time was money, and if he wasn't going to drop that paper, then it was past time for them to go.

"We got to go," Janae let him know as she got up from the bed.

"Man, I feel like I was just getting to know you." Bryson tried to spit game.

Janae looked him over again. She didn't mind that he looked a little like Trey Songz but with the same complexion Lloyd had. "Maybe you'll get to know me another time."

Lloyd and Lysa got up from the couch, and he kissed her lightly on the cheek.

"When will I see you again? Do you have a number?" Bryson asked.

Janae enjoyed watching a man sweat. She smiled flirtatiously. "There you go again with the questions. I'm just saying that's all."

"Well, I will call you. Give me your number?" Bryson grabbed a piece of paper and tore off the end and wrote his number down and gave it to Janae. She smiled and took the paper and put it in her pocket.

It was time for Janae to meet a new trick. Maybe next time, Bryson would do a better job kicking his game.

Chapter Eight

Kofi hated not being around when shit was going down with Leshaun and the crew. A part of him hated that he ignored the inner voice in his spirit that told him to stay his ass in Asheville. But his yearning to see his son drove him to make the trip to Columbus, Ohio. Upon his arrival, he'd hoped to be able to hustle some money and catch a glimpse of his son. It killed him knowing he couldn't hold him, call out his name, or being seen with him.

After looking up his parents' address on Google from his phone, Kofi discovered that his son would've gone to the same elementary school he did when he was younger. With that knowledge, Kofi caught a local craps game and quickly lost fifty dollars. Not being able to afford to lose another dime, Kofi walked to a convenient store near the school and bought ten scratch-off tickets. He made thirty of the dollars back and then checked his social media profiles to see if any women hit him up in his DMs. Luck wasn't in his favor as only older white men in their fifties and sixties wanted the pipe.

Kofi hated that shit. Clearly his profile said he wanted pussy. No dudes, written in big bold letters, was ignored by the men who hit him up. The thought crossed his mind to play along, show some chest and dick pics, meet up with them, and rob a few. If Kofi had planned to stay in town for a long period of time, he could've pulled off a robbery or two, but he didn't know how the local police moved.

Outside of the gate, Kofi found himself waiting five minutes before school got out for his son to come out of the building and head to the bus. Like clockwork, Kofi saw the six-year-old who was his spitting image being led out of the same classroom by the same fine-ass teacher he had twenty years ago. Their eyes met, and Kofi smiled. He didn't know if his son recognized him, but he did see him get on the same bus to take him to the same suburban neighborhood.

Kofi fell out with his parents when they discovered he got addicted to pills and deviated from his studies at Wake Forest. Kofi was supposed to follow in his father's footsteps: pledge Kappa, get his undergrad in biology, get into University of North Carolina at Chapel Hill's dental school, and become an oral surgeon so they could franchise the dental clinic and become the first blacks to successfully do so.

Being at a large university, Kofi was supposed to have a tight grip on all his vices. It didn't work out that way. First, the Kappas found out he was pill popping and trying to sell weed on the side, so they dropped him from the line. Being that they loved his dad, the chapter president called his father, hoping that they could let bygones be bygones, overlook the transgression, and get him clean so he could pledge and preserve the family legacy the following year. His father agreed to hide the issue from his mother, but she would find out when he got tried and convicted of assault and battery on a female later that year.

It was when he was in jail that it was discovered that Kofi knocked up some stripper at Sugar Bares. He tried to deny it at first, but when DNA proved otherwise, Kofi's parents paid the stripper and her family a six-figure sum to buy his son, while working with a lawyer to strip him of his parental rights.

The round-trip back and forth to Columbus had been brutal because he hadn't lined up a hustle yet. He didn't want to fly into John Glenn Columbus International because he knew his father knew people at the airport who would report that Kofi was in town. The various airport workers knew his father well because he was a frequent traveler, flying in and out for conferences, classes, and fraternity meetings.

All Kofi wanted to do was see his son in peace.

Undetected by anyone he recognized, Kofi managed to sneak on the bus that went from Columbus to Greensboro, and he had hoped that he would be able to call someone to come get him once he got downtown.

Throughout the trip, Kofi sat next to a fat, bald-headed guy who kept looking him up and down. He prayed to God that the man was getting off at one of the stops. A few stops came and went, but the man stayed on the bus. Kofi tried to squeeze by him, but the inconsiderate jerk wouldn't move. He was a big guy, but not sumo wrestler big, and Kofi didn't understand why he couldn't step back an inch or two to let him by. Kofi sucked in some air and managed to squeeze by him. Feeling his fat roll and shift almost made him want to hurl. Once Kofi got past him, Kofi ran to the first seat available next to the bathroom.

"We are now in Greensboro. Please make sure you have all of your belongings."

Kofi grabbed his backpack and watched as everyone else began to grab their belongings. Kofi wished he made more than a few sandwiches, but he did the minimum to strike his parents' suspicion that he'd been in and out of their house. Kofi got up with the rest of the passengers and made his way off the bus.

"Did you enjoy the ride?" the bus driver asked him. Kofi saw his grill filled with yellow and messed-up teeth. He wanted to run, but instead, Kofi had to play nice.

"Yes," Kofi answered as he got off the bus; and when Kofi turned around, Kofi noticed the bus driver's eyes were focused on his behind.

"Take care of yourself, young man." He attempted to flash a winning Colgate smile.

"Believe me I will." Kofi played his role as he turned around and headed to the bench where he knew his pre-paid Boost Mobile smartphone would get the best Wi-Fi signal. He knew Leshaun's number by heart but didn't think she'd be in a position to pick him up. He couldn't remember Zay's number, and 9ine changed numbers more times than he changed his drawers. And Chasity wouldn't give him her number.

When Kofi got a good signal, he logged on to Instagram and sent Zay a message in his DM to come pick him up. He knew his young "brother" was vain and always looked to see who checked him out. For kicks, Kofi stood up, took off his shirt, and took a picture, pretending his arm was a selfie stick. He looked around and, when the coast was clear, he pulled his soft, thick chocolate bar out of his pants, squeezed it a few times, and took some more pictures for the Gram.

"Oh, shit, that's him," Kofi heard a woman yell as he quickly stuffed his junk back in his pants. He couldn't believe he'd almost got caught flashing. "Hey, baby." The woman was loud.

Kofi looked in her direction and vaguely remembered her. Something about her looked different. He quickly posted the pics and let his fans know he was in Greensboro. "Hey, girl, what's up?" Kofi gave the overweight white girl a hug. He still didn't remember where he knew her from.

"You remember me right?" she asked as Kofi pretended like he knew her from somewhere. He tried to look inside her open purse for a number or some clue as to who she was. None. "We hooked up at the Sheraton at the Koury Convention Center."

That narrowed down a few prospects. Kofi and 9ine fucked several chicks up and down Koury; it was a matter of remembering whether 9ine was with him. "Yeah, girl, it's been about a year right?" Kofi fished for information. He knew he had to put on an award-winning act if he was going to have some cash.

"Yeah, you remember." The woman got excited as she hugged him. She pulled on his six foot frame so he'd lean down to be closer to her size. "I got a room. Can you do that thing where you fold me into a ball, sit on me like a chair, and eat my ass while you finger fuck me?"

Ching! Ching! Ching! That's when it hit him that Kofi smashed her the previous Halloween. He dressed up like Allen Iverson and went tricking in the city. Leshaun had to beg him to cornrow his hair so they could add some weave to it so he'd look more like the NBA star. The outfit treated him to almost five grand. Two grand of it came from the girl standing before him, and he still couldn't remember her name. It didn't matter because Kofi hit the jackpot and couldn't wait to get some of her coins in his pocket.

"What room we going to?" Kofi asked.

"Look, my car is parked a few blocks away because my husband and I are here on business. But, listen, he should be back in my room in about an hour. You think you can shower and do that thing I like?" The overweight lover pulled out two Benjamins and a prepaid debit card with a receipt verifying a purchase for $500.

"Yeah, I can make it do what it do real quick. Let me check my phone, so I can let my brother know I'll be a little late."

Kofi saw Zay respond to his DM letting him know he and 9ine would meet him in three hours. *Perfect,* Kofi thought as he walked with his trick to her car hand in hand. He saw that eighty-nine people liked his pics and he had a few DM messages. Kofi figured he'd put in work with this girl and then maybe get on with the next one and get a few stacks. Shit, if the night went well, he'd talk Zay and 9ine into staying the night so they could help get Leshaun's money up together. Even though she supplied a large amount of work, she gave the men more freedom to freelance because they could protect themselves and they practiced discretion. Why miss money? If she didn't book it and they were able to get it through other means, they went for it. Her only thing was not to call her when shit went left on shit they'd gotten themselves into.

Chapter Nine

Leshaun looked at Tiana's smiling face as "That's My Best Friend" by Tokyo Vanity played on the ringtone. Excited, Leshaun swiped to the right.

"I found a good ringtone for your ass, too." Leshaun sang the lyrics to the song as she held the phone.

"Aww, I haven't heard that in a minute." Tiana smiled as she started dancing. "I'm glad I Facetimed you because Chasity was on her A-game last night."

"Oh, word?" Leshaun asked.

Tiana pulled up a thick stack of bills next to her face and gave a wide grin. "I knew the bitch could fuck, but her stick-up game is just as vicious. You should have seen how she left that white boy."

Leshaun's smile fell into a frown. "I don't want her sticking up people, Tiana. I got three niggas for that."

"And?" Tiana jumped. "Ain't nothing wrong with a bitch who can get her hands dirty."

"See, you not thinking." Leshaun put the phone down. "I don't want Chasity out their robbing people and shit. I need her to be focused on her schoolgirl act. And, by the way, I think the measuring tape is a bit overboard."

"The girl is good with her hands and likes to build things," Tiana pointed out. "In her short time with us, she's fixed a few of the outfits that the girls have outgrown so they could be passed around for the others to wear. She hemmed one pair of pants that was too long for 9ine, and you should see some of the creations

she made for Zay to model for his Instagram fans. She
made some underwear where the Magnums had multiple
compartments. Our boys will have no reason to come
back to us with anything."

"I want Chasity to focus on turning tricks and being a
schoolgirl." Leshaun wasn't hearing it. "I have older men
who want to get their peverted fantasies off, and Chasity
is the best one for the job. I can get fifteen to twenty
stacks a session just for that."

"And she can still do that!" Tiana raised her voice. "I
think you gonna fuck up your money being shortsighted
on this."

"And what happens if something goes wrong?" Leshaun
asked. She hated when her directions weren't being
followed. "Do what I'm asking you to do. I want her
tricking and improving her bedroom skills. Not trying to
be a fashion designer; not trying to stick up folks."

"If you don't let her explore her dreams, she is going
to leave you for someone who will," Tiana warned. "I
wonder if that's why Janae and Lysa left."

"Did you ask them?" Leshaun snapped.

"I didn't call to argue with you." Tiana exhaled. "I
thought you'd be happy to hear how resourceful Chasity
has become."

Leshaun picked the phone up. "No. I just want the girl
to make my money, and that's it. I'm not featuring her on
nothing else."

"Okay." Tiana put her hand up. She figured she'd put
the stacks of money down when Leshaun didn't have
the phone in her hand. "Maybe I need to come by later,
because you tripping."

"I'm not tripping," Leshaun insisted.

"Yeah, you tripping." Tiana hung up the phone.

Leshaun looked at her iPhone in confusion because
she couldn't believe Tiana ended the conversation with
her like that. "Girl done lost her damn mind."

Leshaun put the phone down and walked to the bathroom. She took out lavender and chamomile bubble bath and ran the water. The flowery smell soothed and calmed her immediately. She hadn't expected to get into an argument with Tiana. Leshaun stripped off her clothes and got in the tub, hoping to take her mind off the confrontation.

Leshaun could hear the door open, and it startled her. "Hello!" she yelled from upstairs in one of the smaller bedrooms. She looked out the window and didn't see a car in the driveway. "Hello!" she yelled again.

Leshaun looked at her surroundings and quickly gathered her thoughts. For one, she was in Prince's cousin's house. She'd left her room at the Grand Bohemian after the argument with Tiana, and she came to the house to escape. Prince had given her a key to the vacant home that he and one of his cousins maintained. It was considered a family home, and while Leshaun had free access to it, she didn't abuse it. Only Prince, Gogo, and Tiana knew that Leshaun would escape there every so often; and after the argument with Tiana, she'd gone to the residence to clear her mind.

"Hello!" Leshaun yelled one more time. After not getting an answer, she quickly ran to the dresser where she knew Prince had a .45 hidden in the drawer. She knew neither Prince nor the cousin was in the house because they always called her to see where she was at before they came by. There were news stories of some of the houses in West Asheville being broken into, but Leshaun didn't think she'd be in the middle of a break-in attempt.

She checked the clip to make sure there were bullets and that it worked correctly. Then she quietly made her way downstairs. Leshaun listened as she tried to figure out where the intruder was located. After hearing whoever it was rumbling in the kitchen, Leshaun quickly devised a plan.

I know this muthafucka heard me. I'm loud as hell, she thought as she cautiously made her way from the stairs across the living room. Leshaun leaned forward, hoping to take peek into the room with the gun at her side. The noise in the kitchen stopped, and she stepped back.

Did they hear me come down the stairs? she wondered. She started to call out again but decided against it. Leshaun aimed the gun in front of her and decided to charge and take the intruder by surprise. It was the only weapon besides the .45 she had. She ran in the kitchen and quickly let off three shots at the person she saw standing at the counter.

"Aahhh!" she yelled as grocery bags went in the air. "Oh my God! Oh my God!" Leshaun quickly made her way behind the counter and found Tiana lying on the floor. Her eyes were closed and her body motionless. She didn't have to feel her pulse to know that Tiana Hampton was dead. "How come you didn't say anything?" The smoke from the .45 infiltrated Leshaun's nose as she cried.

Her best friend, road dog, confidant. Tiana knew all her deepest and darkest secrets and helped her pull off some amazing heists. All that was left of Tiana was a small bullet to the head, leaking blood and brain matter on the hardwood floors.

Another bullet had entered above Tiana's abdomen and left a dark, crimson stain on her tight fluorescent orange tube top. Tiana's eyes stared off in the sky, her face motionless and shocked. If Leshaun could judge the look on Tiana's face, she'd assume that her friend probably was in disbelief that Leshaun shot her. As more blood oozed out of Tiana's body, it made a puddle under her and started to ruin the low-cut white jeans.

Leshaun gave Tiana a once-over and had to admit that, despite being shot twice, her friend was damn near flawless. She wondered where Tiana got the orange eyeshadow and matching nail polish that accentuated her five foot five, 169-pound frame. The blush still highlighted Tiana's full cheeks. The rust red lipstick brought out her full lips, complementing her shapely body.

"Oh my God!" Leshaun screamed as the water welled to her eyes. She could barely see as she wiped away her tears like windshield wipers. The gun still in her hand, she lifted it to her right head and, in her mind, she pulled the trigger. Leshaun was sure she was joining Tiana in hell, or wherever it was they sent the bad girls. She shook her head. Suicide wasn't the way to go, and Leshaun knew she was stronger than that.

A glance down made Leshaun believe that Tiana had moved. She seemed to have made her way a few inches to the left. Her eyes were still focused on the ceiling, and the only thing that was moving was the puddle under her that had gotten bigger. Leshaun knew her mind was playing tricks on her, but she wanted to be sure before she dismissed the thought.

Bending down, Leshaun put her gun on the floor and put her right hand over Tiana's face. "Lord, forgive me. I didn't know she was here," Leshaun prayed as she covered Tiana's eyes and moved her hand down her face, bringing her eyelids to a close. Even though she knew Tiana was dead, she put two fingers under her left chin. As suspected, Tiana had no pulse. The bullets had killed her friend instantly.

"If I could, I'd take it back." Leshaun's voice trembled as she moved away from the body. "How did an argument lead to this?"

Leshaun walked to the marble-covered island and reached for her white leather purse. Her hand sank to the bottom and crawled until it reached her iPhone. Manicured fingernails clicked like keyboards as she dialed 911. Even though she could've had a clean-up crew come and make Tiana's body disappear, she knew her friend didn't deserve that. Yeah, she was mad at Tiana's decision to undermine her; she wouldn't have killed Tiana just for that reason. Tiana deserved a proper burial, and she knew that if she told the truth—she did call out for someone in the house to answer her three times and they didn't—Leshaun would be cleared and the police would rule the murder as an accident.

"Nine-one-one, what's your emergency?" Leshaun was jolted by the deep masculine voice in her ear.

"I need an ambulance to 879 West Chapel Road. My friend . . ." Leshaun fought back tears. She wanted to confess and face whatever consequences came her way. "I didn't know she was using her key to get in my house and I killed her. Please, someone come right away." Leshaun dropped her phone.

The "I didn't know she was using her key to get in my house" part was true. After Leshaun and Tiana argued over whether Chasity should only be tricking, Leshaun took a bath at the hotel. Deciding to escape and to be in a new location, Leshaun made the fifteen-minute trek from the Grand Bohemian to the house in West Asheville. If Tiana had called, Leshaun would have told her where she was because they always made up and apologized to one another after an argument. Even though she'd given Tiana a key, she'd also instructed her to call before coming over. Leshaun had called out for Tiana or whoever was in the house to introduce themselves and the silence only heighted her senses and put Leshaun on guard.

"Ma'am, I need to you to step this way," a young lady in an Asheville police uniform grabbed Leshaun's arm and pulled her to the side. Leshaun was so lost in thought about her last moments with Tiana that she didn't hear the police or the paramedics entering the house. She didn't see them either as forensics were taking pictures of Tiana's body on the floor and dusting for fingerprints.

"I'm sorry," Leshaun apologized, more to Tiana's lifeless body than to the officer leading her to the couch.

"What happened?" The young, blond, blue-eyed officer addressed her more like a sister-girl than an authoritative figure.

"I heard someone enter the house with a key and, when I called to see who it was, no one answered. I panicked, grabbed my gun, and after I called out again for the intruder to announce themselves, I still didn't get an answer. I shot the first thing I saw moving, and I didn't realize it was Tiana. I'm sorry." Leshaun's voice shook as tears fell faster than water leaking from a faucet.

"So this is Tiana"—the officer pointed to the body as it was being covered with a white sheet—"didn't say she was coming over or let you know she was stopping by?"

"No," Leshaun insisted. "If she had said something I swear to God I wouldn't have been alarmed. I called out three times and got no answer."

If Leshaun had been thinking, she would've kept her mouth shut. It wasn't like this was the first murder she'd committed, but this was the first time she murdered someone who meant the world to her. Even though Leshaun was mad at her girl, Tiana Hampton wasn't supposed to die.

Not today.

"Well, let's go to the station and sort this out," the officer suggested.

Leshaun wasn't down for riding with 5-0 anywhere, let alone to the station. But her instincts told her to cooperate. She had told the truth and had nothing to hide.

Leshaun was relieved that she was being allowed to leave her house without handcuffs and enter in the back of an unidentified police car. She got in the back seat, strapped on her seat belt, and looked out the window as more officers and plainclothes police officers were entering her home. She could see the news reporters from the local ABC, CBS, and NBC affiliates rushing to the scene trying to get an exclusive.

"Let's leave before it becomes a circus," the young officer suggested as she got in the driver's seat and warmed up the car.

Leshaun thought about the posibility of her going to prison. She'd just murdered her friend, and she feared going to jail. It didn't look good that Tiana had a key, but the few times Tiana came over, she always called. *And groceries? What she'd buy groceries for? Maybe that's her peace offering but, still, Tiana should've called.*

I hope I don't end up in jail, Leshaun thought as the officer pulled off and she stared at the house she murdered Tiana in.

She just fucked up big time.

Chapter Ten

"Gimmie that ass, Cassandra!" Kofi commanded as he manhandled his overweight lover. He'd finally gotten a glimpse of her name after seeing her driver's license in her open purse she laid next to the television.

"Kofi! Kofi!" Cassandra panted as surging waves of intense pleasure spilled over from her pussy. She palmed his tight ass, her legs pushed back on his shoulders as his strenuous strokes rearranged the shape of her slit. For the past thirty minutes, the two had reacted to the strong sexual chemistry that linked them. He threw himself in and out of her wet hole with quick slides that left Cassandra dizzy.

"Pussy," he panted. "Sooo good!" He tried to crawl up in her guts, punching at her soaked pussy with no restraint.

"Do it!" she gasped. "Make me cum again! Yes, right there!"

Kofi stared at the erotic dance of Cassandra's heaving breasts. The tight and wet confines of her pussy gripped his column with each stroke. His balls slapped the back of her sweet chocolate, stroke after stroke after stroke. Filled with lust, he tried to assassinate the pussy with his curved dick thrusts. Deep and hard, he dug as her juices oozed out around his hammer.

The lights were left on as Cassandra melted under his forcefulucking. Above her and planted inside her moved a real man. His dick suffocated the pink walls of her squishy pussy. Tonight, she wasn't with a boy; a man fucked her, and the taste of it made her greedy.

"Oooohh, yeahhh!" She squeezed his ass with all her might and forced his balls deep.

"Rub my balls!" he grunted and came up on his arms to throw the long dick at her.

Their flesh collided violently below their waists. Sweat dotted Cassandra's forehead as her body experienced free-floating sensations. She crooned his name in rhythm with his strong and energetic movements.

Kofi took everything that was offered to him. He lost himself when her fingers reached his balls. He fucked her. Her pussy spoke around the condom, farting and smacking.

"Look at it!" he grunted with his hurried strokes. "Look at what I'm doing to you!"

Cassandra moaned and lifted her head off the pillow. Between her jerking tits, she caught a flash of his dick plunging in and out of her bald pussy. "Mmmmm, baby! You do it so good! You fuck me sooo good!" She dropped her head back down and circled her hips. "Ooohh, yeahhh, right there! You all up in my pussy!" She slid her hands up his sides until she reached his chest.

They raced toward the end. In and out, up and down, back and forth he tried to knock her pussy off the hinges. When it finally gripped them for the second run, Cassandra took the dick on all fours. She exploded all over his mature dick as it eased in and out at a steady pace. Kofi clenched her sweaty ass cheeks, threw his head back, and detonated inside the condom with no space between them.

The lights were too bright for Leshaun's liking. She looked down at her black Carolina Panthers T-shirt and loose-fitting gray sweatpants. They concealed her five foot five, 170-pound frame perfectly. The Carolina blue Tims felt heavy on her feet as she sat in a small interrogation room with a black plainclothes officer who looked like he could've gone to high school with her dad.

Leshaun caught her reflection in the large window that she knew at least one detective was watching her from behind. The R&B goddess Aaliyah stared back at her, and she liked that she thought of herself as the darker-skinned, thicker version of her. The way her bone-straight hair fell a little past her shoulders and the part down the middle of her head were nearly identical to the iconic singer's. Leshaun's face was slightly slender despite being a full-figured one, but her cheekbones were sharp. Her eyes were almond in shape and the color of rich milk chocolate. The only makeup she was wearing was the trace of the strawberry lip gloss she had put on earlier in the day.

"Ms. Gamble."

Leshaun's head turned when she heard the officer call her by her government name. She hadn't been called Ms. Gamble since her days as a daycare teacher's assistant. It felt funny answering to a name she always thought people should call her mom.

"Yes, sir." Leshaun extended the same courtesy. She didn't want to admit it, but she was nervous as hell. She fought to keep her eyes straight, her body from shaking like a leaf. She decided to tell the truth and answer any and every question the officer had about the murder she had just committed.

The thought crossed her mind as to whether the police may have suspected her in other shootings. She had at least ten bodies on her and, when she came to think of it, there was a body on that gun. But that body belonged to some sick pervert she and Tiana ditched in Toronto, Ontario after some old, middle-aged white man got mad that he couldn't force Leshaun and Tiana into a ménage à trois.

"So what were you and Tiana arguing about?" the detective pried. She'd forgotten his name that quick in the four hours she was in the room with him. Leshaun had already told him this information one time, but she repeated it, knowing she wouldn't get caught slipping in her answer.

"She said that she saw my boyfriend at the Walmart on Hendersonville Road with some ugly, flat-chested white girl," Leshaun answered truthfully and calmly. "I told her ain't no way Cam would go for some trailer-park trash because all he liked were big girls like me. She then tried to send me a pic in her text message, but I didn't believe her because, from behind, my man didn't look like the guy she was trailing."

"Who is your man?" the detective questioned.

Leshaun knew she needed to lie. She wasn't going to put Prince Boyd on blast. Prince knew how to disappear when it was convenient. Her birthday, their anniversary, Christmas: the important shit. Leshaun was confident that she wasn't the side chick because she knew his mom and his sister. She also got along with two of his ex-bitches, and she didn't lose any sleep over whether Prince was fucking them.

She knew that he wasn't.

And she didn't lose sleep over who Prince might or might not have been doing when he wasn't with her. He knew better than to cheat on her. He wanted it raw, and she made him get tested monthly, and she still made him wear a rubber. Sticking the head in was something he got to enjoy on special occasions: his birthday, their expensive date nights, Father's Day.

"Cam Newton," she lied, kinda. Leshaun had dated a man named Cam Newton who wasn't related to or bore any resemblance to the popular Carolina Panthers quarterback.

"Bullshit," the detective called her bluff.

"No, not the star. It's this white boy I'm seeing who used to be an investment banker." Leshaun continued to mix lies with truth. Cam was an investment banker with Morgan Stanley, and she did see him last week at Barnes & Noble. Saw him with an older black woman he married and the young black boy he was playing steppop to.

"Oh, okay." Leshaun watched the detective write down his name and possibly some fact she just told him. "I really hate that your girl didn't announce herself before helping herself into your home."

"Me too." Leshaun wanted to look down, and she did look away from the detective for a minute and glanced at the window. She knew they could hear her.

"When was the last time you saw Cam?" The detective added, "And do you have a number where I can reach him?"

"Yeah, I saw him last week with this other girl. He said they were coworkers and I've seen her at Morgan Stanley before, but I don't know her like that."

A knock on the door interrupted the interrogation and the detective left. She looked around the room. Once she found an imperfection in the wall, she focused on it as she tuned out the lights and anything else. She reflected to a happier time with Tiana when they first saw Prince. Leshaun remembered Tiana thought Prince was ugly until they saw him up close. Prince had a pretty boy face and a stocky frame with biceps that easily lifted 300 pounds or more. He had a slight pudge, but not an overlapping belly that screamed fat. And his calf and shin muscles were stronger than a horse's.

And his uncircumcised dick was hung like one, too.

He was wearing a fitted Johnson C. Smith baseball cap with an oversized Johnson C. Smith athletic shirt and some loose-fitting jeans. Prince would later tell them that between hustling, he studied economics. Let him tell it, the two went hand in hand.

"Ms. Gamble." The detective brought her back to reality. "Just wanted to let you know that we found your story checked out and we will not be filing charges at this time. While it is unfortunate that your friend died, you had reasonable cause to believe that the home you were staying in was being invaded because your friend did not announce herself."

"Thank you, sir." Leshaun was happy to hear the news, but she did not celebrate in front of the officer.

Instead, she got up, collected her things, and nodded her head. She was directed to processing where her gun and other possessions taken from her were returned. After she caught the complimentary cab home, Leshaun called and booked two tickets on a charter plane to Birmingham, Alabama.

For the next call, she made sure to make the Facetime feature on her phone available.

"Hey, baby," the man answered the phone.

"I need you stop what you are doing and fly out to Birmingham with me," Leshaun demanded.

"Fly out to . . ." Prince looked away, trying to gather his thoughts at the urgent request.

"I'm not Facetiming you for you to say no. This is an emergency." Leshaun grilled her phone like she was face to face with Prince.

Prince exhaled. "Okay. When do we fly out?"

"In an hour." Leshaun pressed the red button on her phone. She needed to get out of Asheville, and she didn't want to be alone. And the company she wanted, a female couldn't provide.

Chapter Eleven

In secret, Janae kept in touch with Bryson ever since that wild, passionate, sex-filled night. She woke up in his arms and received a thorough fucking that left her breathless before sunrise. Every night they spent hours on the phone, talking about life and each other. It pained her to have such a long distance between them. From Nashville to Asheville was a five-hour drive down I-40 West. Their flowing talks were based on true emotions and not the thrill of lust.

Times were still hard on Janae. She hated to lie to Bryson, starting with the bogus name she still went by. At the moment she had her legs tucked under her on the couch in Lysa's living room. For the first time in her life, she was engrossed in *Desperate Hoodwives* by Meesha Mink and De'nesha Diamond. Page by page she stared riveted, cheering for the main characters to overcome their issues.

"Whatcha doing, ho?" Lysa sauntered into the living room with a cigarette between her manicured fingers. The tight jeans hugged her thick curves intimately, and the white tiny tank top did wonders for her bouncy breasts.

"Reading this book I got from the library," Janae answered without breaking her attention from the novel.

Lysa took a pull on the cigarette and sat down on the loveseat. "I thought your ass didn't like to read." Lysa blew smoke from her mouth.

Janae marked a page and closed the book with a touch of reluctance. "Just trying something new I guess."

Lysa rolled her eyes. "Whatever. We 'posed to be hustling and trickin'." She laughed and slid the cigarette back between her lips. Janae placed the novel by her hip and adjusted the white-and-black bandana on her head. Lysa frowned. "You need to do something to that nappy-ass head of yours."

"What for?" Janae retied the bandana over her rough-looking hair. "Ain't got no man to look good for."

"And it's gonna stay that way if you keep rocking that nappy shit like it's in style."

Janae shook her head at the silly remark. Lloyd paid her for the work she'd done, but Janae chose to be stingy with it. She had enough to get her hair done, but she didn't have any bookings. Janae's mom taught her how to use a flat iron and curling iron, so she always knew how to do basic shit. When she wasn't working, Janae kept it simple. Since she typically knew in advance when she had an escort client, she'd set up her hair appointments in advance with a beautician she paid to come to wherever she was laying her head. And she tipped her well, so the woman didn't ask any questions.

"I've been on Facebook and Twitter all damn night!" Lysa complained as she reached for the ashtray on the table.

"Ain't been on mine's in three weeks," Janae replied as she picked *Desperate Hoodwives* back up, more interested in what the two authors had to write about than the mindless gossip conversation Lysa wanted to have. Janae wasn't one too much into girl talk; she used her words carefully and kept it moving. With Lysa, she made an exception and tried to do "normal female" with her.

"I bet Bryson been posting shit on your wall." Lysa leaned back so she could show Janae Bryson's Facebook page.

"Fuck him." Janae leaned back and yawned. "Damn, I'm tired." Janae wanted to end the pointless conversation nicely, but Lysa was persistent.

"I think I found our new lick." Lysa tapped the ashes into the ashtray. That devious glow filled her eyes.

"Who?" Janae settled back on the couch for another night's rest.

"Keshawn Valentine." Lysa paused to refill her lungs. "There's a post on his Facebook page about him doing a show at the Orange Peel next week. I swear, he the only rapper I know who can keep a flow while strumming guitar riffs."

"Lauryn Hill?" Janae looked at her confused. She remembered watching the *MTV Unplugged* special a few months before the World Trade Center attacks. Janae picked up the book again and read a few passages.

"She's a singer," Lysa countered, and Janae shook her head as she continued to read.

"And a rapper." Janae was disappointed that Lysa not only didn't know but couldn't appreciate Lauryn Hill or her historical significance to music. In her attempt to pay attention, Janae folded the page of the book and closed it. "What's the plan?" She gave Lysa her undivided attention.

"Same as before. Try to get close to 'im and do my thang. All I gotta do is get his fine ass up in a room and it's a wrap."

"Okay, you're gonna have to come up with something better then that." Janae put the book to the side and leaned forward. "We can't just think if we dress seductive and be quick to open our legs that these niggas not gonna be on their guard. Dudes film their sexcapades and leak their dick pics on purpose just to get attention. What he look like?"

Lysa smiled as she let Janae's warning go in one ear and out the other. Janae could see that Lysa wasn't heeding her warning and she wore her poker face to hide her disappointment. "Fine enough to give up the goods before I rob his ass. Just go check 'im out on Facebook. Pull up Keshawn Valentine."

"I'll do it tomorrow. I'm 'bout to carry my ass to sleep." Janae shifted on the soft couch and reached down by her thigh for the urban novel. At that moment, she glanced at the screen of her smartphone. "Shit!" she muttered.

"What's up?" Lysa snuffed out the cigarette.

"I was supposed to call my cousin at eight, and now it's damn near ten! Got caught up in that good-ass book!" Janae snatched the phone and began typing her cousin's name so she could make the call.

Lysa scratched her scalp. "I think we can really come off big if we can make a move on Keshawn Valentine."

"You gonna take his car?" Janae asked after she dialed her cousin and got the voice mail. She sent a text apologizing for not calling when promised.

Lysa shrugged. "Shit, he might catch a plane or something. What I really wanna do is to get that nigga to minus some major moolah from his bank account."

"The rape scheme?" Janae wanted to know if Lysa had put more thought into the scheme she told her about a month before they left Leshaun. At the time, Lysa thought if she could film the sex act and make it look like the man was forcing himself on her, she'd be able to blackmail him for what she wanted. Janae poked a hole in the plan when she told Lysa the plan wouldn't work if they had visual only. Plus, Janae reasoned the audio with the motion picture would make the scene believable. That would be harder to do.

Lysa nodded. "He got too much positive shit going to let something like a rape embarrassment fuck up his image. Even if I can't prove it, just the threat of rape would be enough for him to cough up the bands."

"What you planning to hit him for?" Janae asked even though she didn't see the plan working. She at least wanted to see if Lysa put more thought into her plan.

"More than eight bands! That's for damn sure! I knew like hell we were gonna get more for that if we stuck with Lloyd. He on that bullshit. We haven't had anyone who could buy us a three-year-old car, let alone a new one," Lysa vented.

"Better than nothing." Janae adjusted her bra strap under her shirt. In the back of her mind, she tried to convince herself that Lysa had a well thought-out plan. After she looked at Keyshawn Valentine's page again and read the information, she could see that Lysa picked the right mark and the right scheme. The question remained if Lysa could pull everything together and make it click.

"How much you got left?" Lysa wondered.

Janae sighed and stared at the ceiling. "Uh, 'round thirteen hundred."

"Well, at least you got your car back. As for losing your apartment, you know you're welcome here forever." Lysa was genuine.

"I know," Janae replied in a funk. She liked Lysa and, for the moment, they appeared to be cohabiting just fine. But Janae knew she didn't want to have a roommate forever.

"Oh, when's the last time you had some dick?" Lysa got nosy. "Not some paid dick, some pleasure dick.

Janae blinked and cleared her throat. "Why?" Janae had no intention of telling Lysa about Bryson. Lysa knew just about everything there was to know about her. She wanted to keep a few secrets to herself.

"Because you need some! You've been under my roof for a month and a half with no dick. And when you were up in your own shit I can't ever recall you having anyone in your bed."

"And how would you know?"

"Because these floors are thin as hell." She laughed. "I be hearing everything when you finger flicking."

Janae rolled her eyes and kept the truth to herself. Bryson gave her a hint of a better life. A life free of stress. A life that she badly wanted.

"So, what's up?" Lysa lifted her eyebrow.

"About what?"

"Some dick! Lloyd has a homeboy from—"

"Nah, I'm good," Janae replied with her mind on Bryson.

"I know you ain't tripping over Bryson."

"Hell no!" Janae turned on her side. "Ain't worried about that fool."

"Better not be." Lysa stood. "I got to go get me some green. You rolling wit' me?"

"Not with my head like this." Janae shook her head no, plotting on a way to end the conversation and get in the bed without hurting Lysa's feelings.

"Oh, yeah." Lysa cracked a smile. "I forgot about that Medusa hairdo."

Janae snatched her smartphone off the table when Lysa left for a weed trip. She quickly hit the speed dial for Bryson.

"Hey, sexy. You're late." His voice melted in Janae's ear.

"It's your fault." She giggled in the dark living room.

"How?"

"Because of that book you told me to read. O.m.g, that shit is fiyah, because I couldn't stop reading!"

"I knew you would like it. So, how was your day?"

She sighed, wanting to be truthful. "Just another day. Making it, I guess."

"Sounds like it's more than that. Anything you wanna talk about?"

"Nope. Not about no stress. But I do want to talk about seeing you again."

"That sounds like a good topic. For what it's worth, I've been thinking about you all day."

Janae closed her eyes and imagined she was cuddled naked in his arms. "Tell me about those thoughts," she whispered.

"I've been thinking about having you down here with me," he admitted. "Like I told you a few days ago, I don't think any less of you over the fact of what we did the first night."

"And morning," she reminded him.

He chuckled. "And that too."

"What we did was natural, baby. First night, second night, that shit don't hold much weight with me."

"What does?"

She rolled to her back. "Life," she answered. "Life holds a lot of weight with me."

"How?"

"Life is a one-time run. Gotta make the best of it."

"Do you think you're doing that now? Making the best of your life?"

"Sometimes I don't even know if I'm coming or going. Life has a cousin called Days and I sure as hell have a rough time dealing with life day by day." She couldn't hide the dejectedness in her voice.

"Tell me this: if you could have one realistic wish, what would it be?" he asked in an effort to liven her mood.

Realistic? Shit, I can't tell him about my money issues. "Um, I realistically wish I was down in the A and in your arms. Well," she said, giggling, "I really want to be on top of you."

"Doing what?"

"Mmm, you know. Stop being silly." She beamed.

"Tell me," he pressed. "I really want to know."

"Okay," she said with all intent to be blunt. "I want to ride your dick real slow while you suck on my nipples. And I want to feel your hands all over my body."

"Keep going."

"Boy! You ain't about to have me doing no phone sex."
She giggled.

"Why not? You in bed, right?"

"Yes," she lied. "But I really don't like doing that."

"My bad. I'm sorry," he said wholeheartedly. "But ah,
that's your realistic wish?"

"Yep. Do you like it?"

"I more than like it. In fact, I can . . ." He paused. "Uh,
let me call you right back. I got a call on the other line
that I have to take."

Janae wanted to snap. "Uh, okay." She ended the call
without a formal good-bye. *Nigga just mad I ain't doing
no stupid phone sex!* she reasoned for his sudden depar-
ture. *Motherfucka ain't shit!* She tossed the smartphone
by her thigh and sighed with a load of stress. She felt stupid for thinking a man like Bryson would be interested in
a chick from the hood. *Probably got him a white bitch to
be with!* Janae tossed and turned on the couch, stressed
and horny as fuck! There was no privacy inside Lysa's
one-bedroom apartment for Janae to get herself off.

Suddenly the idea of a second shower made sense. *Shit,
I can pop one off in the shower.* With her mind made up,
she placed her feet on the floor and slid her hands over
the outline of her breasts. Her nipples buzzed under the
tight halter top, yearning for a man's wet tongue. Just
as she stood, her smartphone chimed with an alert of a
new text message. She opened the message with a single
finger swipe across the screen. Word for word, her heart
hammered as she read the text:

Hey, sexy. Your realistic wish can come true. Sorry for
ending the call, but I had to b/c I had to surprise you with
this. I made the arrangements for you to be in my arms &
more tonight! All you have to do is catch the flight out of
RDU. Flight info is attached. Your move. You have your
wish. Your move.

Chapter Twelve

"I can't believe this!" Leshaun whispered as the airplane leveled off for its trip to Birmingham, Alabama. She couldn't believe her realistic wish to be with Prince would be a reality in few hours. All she had time to snatch up were a handful of clothes before she rushed out the door. Her heart hammered, pounding for the idea of being happy with one man. She didn't think about what she was doing. She acted on her want and need of a man who had her all the way twisted. She left Asheville without saying shit to anybody. Leshaun settled back in the seat and closed her eyes. In her life, she was sick and tired of being pretty and poor. If possible, she hoped to change the latter to be happy. Pretty and happy. She took that hope to Birmingham, nappy head included. But her true reality would come close to the fact that two wrongs don't make a right.

"Can't believe what?" Prince grabbed her hand, bringing her to reality.

Memories flooded Leshaun's mind of how Prince wooed her and how they began their illegal, but tolerated, love affair. One thing Prince brought out of her was the desire to see the world beyond Buncombe County. Prince was the one who took her to Charlotte on her fifteenth birthday to visit some of his Mexican friends who threw her a *quinceanera*. Even though she wasn't a daughter, the family wanted a reason to celebrate and her birthday was just as good a reason as any. The family even watched

9ine as she danced, pregnant with Ten, and acted like a fifteen-year-old for once.

For her sweet sixteen, Prince bought Leshaun her first plane ticket and they flew to Dallas, Texas. Truth was she didn't know where she wanted to go, so Prince laid a map in front of her, closed her eyes, and told her to pick a place on the table. Her finger actually landed on Fort Worth, but Dallas was close enough. There, she'd caught Janet Jackson's The Velvet Rope Tour and visited Texas School Book Depository, where she got to learn about the assassination of President John F. Kennedy. She also hung out at the Arts District and the African American Museum and enjoyed staying with Prince at the Howard Johnson.

"Just everything." Leshaun let go. She looked at Prince and couldn't believe he had a smile on his face.

"We are going to be fine," Prince promised.

"We?" Leshaun asked. "I didn't know 'we' existed."

"No matter where I lay my head, we will always exist."

Leshaun removed her hand from Prince's. She looked around. The plane wasn't packed to capacity, as the row in front of them was empty. They actually had someone who was supposed to sit between them but whoever it was never showed up. "You must think we're Cookie and Lucious Lyon."

Leshaun wanted to take out her phone and check on the progress made to the hotel. She and Prince had spent the past few days helping the patrons with their insurance claims and making sure any of the lingering refunds had been settled. Prince was always good for making sure Leshaun handled her legal business, and it felt good working with him on dealing with State Farm investigators and local law enforcement. Everyone wanted to make sure she didn't start the fire to collect a check. The lawyers were in and out of her face, making sure all the paperwork was signed and that she'd had her T's crossed and I's dotted.

"We came before *Empire*," Prince boasted as he stretched out in the seat and enjoyed the ride.

"I'm not going to go back and forth with you," Leshaun vowed. "Eventually, I will find a man who will appreciate everything I have to offer, can meet me financially, and makes me only deal with you when it comes to Ten and her children."

"You forget 9ine and Zay are my sons, too." Leshaun could feel the venom in Prince's voice. She didn't mean to imply that Prince was a bad father and she knew that wasn't what she said.

"I'd like to be married, one day," Leshaun admitted. She'd never spoken those words before because even with all the money and businesses, Leshaun never thought marriage was possible. Who would want a woman who'd given birth to her cousin at thirteen, had a daughter at fifteen, and was sleeping with the man who theoretically was her adopted son? For the longest, she wanted Prince to be that man.

"You can get married." Prince sarcastically encouraged her.

"I know you don't want to tie the knot, so I know not to ask you," she told him pointedly and then laid her head back onto the headrest and closed her eyes. "I didn't bring this up to argue. I'm just . . . I'm at an age and a stage when I'm starting to see that there is more to life than what I'm doing. I'm in my thirties, and I still don't know what I want my final result to be, other than to experience marriage." Prince reached for her hand again, and Leshaun rejected him. "A part of me just wants to ask Janae and Lysa why? I know some nigga was behind it all but why?"

Leshaun had long deduced that Janae and Lysa attempted to do her in. She didn't need the unanswered phone calls, being blocked on their social media sites, or the fact that they were keeping their distance to vouch for what they'd done. And, of course, she wasn't a snitch.

"Ain't no need for all that." Prince leaned and put his head on her shoulder. "You know what you need to do." He lowered the tone of his voice. "And I'm gonna help you do whatever it is that needs to be done to fix the problem."

Leshaun turned to the side. "How are you going to fix my problem?" Leshaun had some ideas, and she knew what Prince had in mind. "I don't want no shit, Prince."

"They started it." He pouted like he was a toddler. "But I'm going to finish it. Don't worry, you'll be happy with the result."

Prince continued resting his head on Leshaun's shoulder. She couldn't wait until he was on top of her. At the moment, she enjoyed the intimacy.

"The plane will be landing in thirty minutes," one of the flight attendants announced.

In an hour, Leshaun may get what she was craving. Most importantly, her feet would be on the ground, and she and Prince would have more time to discuss his plan in private.

Dom's Paradice was the ultimate hip-hop and reggae club in Birmingham, Alabama. This two-story club Leshaun owned was a perfect getaway spot from the drama Asheville had become.

In Dom's Paradice, Leshaun flexed her legitimate business skills. She knew she couldn't scheme or assassinate people forever. Dom's Paradice was supposed to be a getaway for women, but after studying some of the clubs in Charlotte, Atlanta, and Houston, she realized she'd make more money if she let the men have a little piece of the pie too. But she only gave them Friday nights. She kept Saturday and Sunday nights for the ladies and flew in as many top strippers as she could afford. Old-school hip-hop and club bangers could be heard on Mondays and Wednesdays, reggae and reggaton blasted the stereo on Tuesdays, and she hosted her "Throwdown Thursdays" where she brought in top R&B singers to give mini-concerts featuring their slow jams.

With the money she made at Dom's Paradice, she didn't have scheme or kill anyone. All she had to do was open the doors, and keep the bills paid and her staff happy, and the customers came on their own. Her addiction to the fast life kept a foot between her legal and illegal business activities.

"Good to see you back," Johntae, her business manager, greeted her when she walked in the door. Method Man was encouraging people to "Bring the Pain, " and she appreciated the Wu-Tang Clan member's word play and delivery.

"I need a drink. And, before you ask, bring it to my private office in the back. I need to unwind."

Johntae briefly stared at his boss before he replied, "Not a problem."

Unwinding was on Leshaun's mind as she headed upstairs to her private suite. Inside, she briefly admired the new leather furnishings. She took off her shoes and left them at the door. She walked past the kitchenette area and headed straight to the bathroom. Inside her bathroom was a medium-sized tub already filled with hot water and bubbles that overflowed at the rim. She smiled, knowing that she had trained her business manager well. Her strawberry mimosa was ready for her, and she dipped her hand into the water. Satisfied with the temperature, she took off her clothes and stepped in. The water soothed and freed her spirit of the day's events. She took a sip of the mimosa and put it back on the counter. Taking in a deep breath, Leshaun looked around her then closed her eyes, exhaled, and let her mind wander free as she sank to the bottom of the tub.

"You're gonna get started without me?" Prince asked as he opened the door.

Leshaun was startled because she hadn't let Prince in on this part of the club. Nevertheless, she enjoyed watching Prince undress. His slim body moved flawlessly as he walked to the tub. Dark fruit waited to grow and be aroused to its full length, yet it had her hypnotized as she still couldn't believe it was the darkest thing on his body.

"It's a good thing there's room for two." Leshaun moved forward so that Prince could get in behind her.

Prince stepped in and slowly lowered his body behind Leshaun, his legs enveloping hers and his broad chest providing the perfect body pillow for Leshaun to lean back into. "Me too." Prince leaned back in the tub and enjoyed the feeling of being in water with Leshaun on his body.

Leshaun rolled away from Prince's nude frame under the sheets when her smartphone chimed. She yawned and took notice of the time glowing on the touchscreen. *Shit! It's fucking ten minutes to midnight!* She glanced back at the man who had her mind and body twisted. All ideas of robbing his handsome ass were traded with a craving for more dick. *I'm tripping for real.* She kicked the sheets off and sat up on the edge of the bed.

"What's up, girl?" Leshaun kept her voice low.

"Bitches up! And bum-ass niggas down!" Gogo replied with loud music in the background.

Leshaun got up and took the call into the bathroom. "Bitch, where you at?"

"At the spot watching Lloyd and crew."

Leshaun eased the bathroom door shut and kept the lights off. "The chop shop?" she whispered.

"Yep. And you know what that means?"

"You hit a lick!"

"Shole fucking did! And, girl, I got on my bullshit fo' real. I couldn't text or call because I had to get up with Lloyd."

"Who did you get?"

Gogo laughed. "Girl, you won't believe this shit! But word on er'thing, I found Lysa and Janae!"

"How the hell you pull it off?" Leshaun asked.

"They not being careful. You know how these dumb bitches do. Lloyd all about the pussy so if he think an opportunity landed in his hands, he gonna take it."

Leshaun smacked her lips. She knew of Lloyd's hustle all too well. Admittedly, he taught her some shit.

"All that bullshit aside," Gogo interrupted her thoughts, "that muthafucka got some good dick. We should be trickin' him; what a fucking waste. But anyway, bitch, we came off tonight! Lloyd's people said I can get eight bands for the Benz!"

Leshaun breathed a deep sigh of relief.

"What's up with you and where your black ass at?" Gogo asked, hyped up.

Leshaun turned the vanity lights on over the mirror and sink. "Nothing," she lied.

"Laid up somewhere with Prince!" Gogo griped.

"Bitch, please. I needed some me time before I got into some crazy shit, so I bounced out of Asheville. I got a room in Knoxville," Leshaun lied again as she thought about the good moments she had with Prince before sex.

"So what's up? You staying there tonight?"

Leshaun wanted to spend the night in Prince's arms. She felt he could remain her secret since she had some money coming her way. "Yeah, but I'll leave in the morning."

"Okay, I'll have your half of the bread when I see you tomorrow. And, girl, I gotta tell you all the details about the lick. Well, I'll holla at you later. And um, you still got my spare key?"

"Yeah."

"Well, I have to go talk to Lloyd so let me get off this phone."

"Bye, girl." Leshaun ended the call and tried to justify the lies she told her bestie. All she came up with were warm feelings directed at Prince. The more she thought about him, the more she realized he was the oldest man she had fucked. Her pussy jumped, and a slickness began to dampen the soft folds between her legs.

Chapter Thirteen

Leshaun hadn't felt right since she pulled the trigger on Tiana. She tried to forget what happened, but watching the bullets entering Tiana's flesh and the failed attempts to reach Tiana by phone troubled her deeply. The nightmares of the blood exiting her pierced skin swam over Leshaun like eels, and her tears fondled her 2,000 body parts like a bar of Lever soap. Her guilt played tricks on her, making her believe that if she called Tiana one more time or messaged her on Facebook, her friend would come back to life.

The alcohol relaxed her, made her quit shuddering and, in some ways, made her more accessible to Prince, which she didn't mind because that made her feel like she was a woman. The first time she felt a buzz was with Prince, and it had been moments after they just made love.

She didn't have a hangover from the drinking, but the alcohol didn't make her feel right either. She hit that pipe and, for a moment in time, she felt like she was in heaven. No more thoughts of Tiana falling by her hands. No more thinking about how Lysa and Janae betrayed her. No more burned down hotel. No bad dreams about her parents spitting on her or beating her ass with broomsticks, extension cords or switches. No more Prince and his other bitches she knew he was still screwing even though she was wifey, main bitch number one. Being drunk was a temporary solution that allowed her to escape the cares of the world.

After the first time she got drunk, she couldn't believe that Prince was in the room with her masturbating as he watched a random female trying to get her off. The licks felt good, but she wasn't about to return the favor, and she'd rather see his face between her legs giving her that pleasure. Leshaun decided then that whoever the bitch was getting off on her would be the first and last chick she had that kind of experience with.

"What's going on with you?" Prince rolled over. It disturbed him that she was still up when his stroke game should've put her to sleep.

"Nothing. I'm just thinking about some shit."

Prince looked at her sideways like she might've been lying. Leshaun was about to throw him the finger because he was the last person to question her integrity, seriously. "I told you not to bug out on Lysa and Janae. Replace them bitches. I thought I trained you better than that." He continued to interrogate like he was 5-0.

"Train me how?" Leshaun sat up. She didn't bother to lift up a cover to conceal her breasts.

"There you go with this sensitive shit." Prince turned to the side.

"You rude muthafucka!" Leshaun was trying to decide whether she was going to kick Prince out of the bed. "I'm sensitive because I got a lot going on. You acting like because I fly you out here and you give me some dick, that solves all my problems. If your dick were so amazing, I wouldn't have any problems, bruh. I would rule the world. My hoes would have another hotel to work out of. I wouldn't have to flex my brain to remember credit card info. I would be set for life."

"Shit, if my dick did all that, I'd never leave the bed."

Leshaun tried to kick Prince out of the bed, and she almost succeeded. He grabbed on to the edge of the mattress and appeared to hover over the side. She tried to kick his arm, but that upper body strength was too strong.

"Bitch, are you crazy!" Prince still struggled to get on the bed.

"Bitch!" Leshaun repeated as she kicked him in the face. That was the magic combination as Prince lost his balance and fell on the floor. "Who the fuck you calling a bitch?"

Prince tried to grab her but, when he failed, he retreated and covered his face. His agony expressed itself through bloodcurdling screams and Prince gasping for air. She took a peek in his direction to see if he was leaking blood. That was not what she wanted to be paying for.

"Fucking crazy," Prince cursed as he struggled to get up but fell again.

"You better remember that." Leshaun reached over the bed and pulled out her .45. She didn't want to have to kill her baby daddy, but she would if she had to. And Prince needed a reminder. "You need to get out."

Leshaun watched as Prince stumbled to find his wallet, phone, and keys. He seemed to be getting his bearings together. She tightened the grip on her .45. A part of her felt like maybe she overreacted. But she wasn't with him calling her no bitch. Or being selfish when it came to her need to grieve.

There was the problem. She had yet to respond to any text messages from her "sons" or phone calls from her friends. And Leshaun was disappointed in herself because this was not how she conducted business. No one was supposed to see her break a sweat, not even Prince. Lately, the rules were a little bit past fucked up. If she wasn't trying to blow her brains out, she was making hasty and costly decisions.

The door slammed, and Leshaun bolted out of the bed. She walked cautiously, gun slightly leveled at her hip. Once she made it to the door, she turned the lock and put the bar over the top lock. A part of her felt guilty. Maybe she did overreact a little bit.

The phone rang, and she took baby steps to answer it. Seeing 9ine's name blink on her screen made her smile. Slowly, she picked up the phone and slid the button on her screen to talk. "Hey, baby." Leshaun tried to hide any worry or fear in her voice.

"Mom, where are you?" The inquiry was genuine, but she knew that Prince was notorious for using 9ine or Ten to relay information to her.

"Safe." Her answer was blunt and firm. It wasn't safe telling 9ine where she was at, even though Prince left her room.

"Okay, Mom. We just picked up Kofi from Greensboro. He thinks he has a way for us to get some more money to rebuild the property. Also, Dad mentioned something about a property on Tunnel Road that might be available. It's one story with about fifty rooms and an easy fixer-upper. Zay and I checked it out, and we think we can do the painting ourselves. Dad may know some people who'll drop what they're doing and make the hotel a priority. Also, word on the street that a bed and breakfast on Kimberly Avenue near the Grove Park Inn may be available. I know it's not what you're used to, but I like it. I've been to it a few times and, truthfully, I think you should get both properties now and fix the hotel later with the revenue from that."

Everything 9ine just laid out sounded like mumbo jumbo. Buy this, buy that. She thought she was in a time warp and went back to the days when all he, Ten, and Zay did was ask for things and triple-teamed her to work her nerves. "Now is not a good time to talk about this," she finally answered after making him wait a few moments. Leshaun still struggled to process what he said.

Buy this, buy that.

"A'ight, Ma, I can tell you and Dad got into it again. Is he where you at or are you beefing over the phone?" 9ine tried to get her to Facetime.

Leshaun shook her head to herself. Wasn't trying to face him, even over the phone. "We within a few miles from one another, but nowhere near Asheville." She told the truth, hoping to ease his mind.

Even in his twenties, 9ine acted like a little boy who hated to see his parents fight. Prince was the only father he knew and, even when they were at odds, 9ine always respected the fact that Prince didn't have to step up and be "daddy" to him too. And Prince never took his issues with Leshaun out on him.

"A'ight, I hope you feel better and that you and Dad stop beefing." 9ine had no idea how big this beef between Leshaun and Prince had just become.

"We'll be all right." Leshaun hoped she hadn't given 9ine any false hope.

"Let me see if I can go get this money real quick." 9ine tried to put a smile on her face the best way he knew how. Knowing him, 9ine legit may have had something lined up for him to get into. And if Kofi and Zay were nearby, there was a good chance the three of them were dishing out mayhem and heartbreak together.

"Go get it," she encouraged him as she hung up the phone.

9ine eased her mind and, after an hour, she realized Prince wasn't coming back. She sat back on the bed and put the gun under the pillow. Then she got under the covers, slid down in the bed until she got comfortable, and closed her eyes until her soul allowed her to rest.

Chapter Fourteen

Once Leshaun stepped foot back into Asheville, she knew she was going to have to make peace with Tiana's murder. The one she committed. It wasn't a regular mistake she could undo with an "I'm sorry," and she couldn't get with Tiana's father or any other man, get knocked up, and then push Tiana out of her pussy.

Sorry just didn't work like that.

Tiana was more than one of her little hoes. Next to Gogo, Tiana knew just about everything. And, despite opening her legs for any man or woman who had the time or the price, she had a good heart and things she cared for. Tiana gave money to random people who said they were homeless. Whether she believed them was another question. After she wore an outfit a few times, she donated it to Goodwill or gave it to another woman who could push it a few miles.

Tiana didn't have a lot of money, but the bitch thought she was rich. And though she didn't have Gamble money on the legal or illegal scale, Tiana wasn't a wasteful person, and she really put the "You can't take it with you so enjoy it now" mantra to heart.

"Leshaun, are you okay?" Gogo stepped out of a chocolate-colored 2012 Acura TL Leshaun knew belonged to whoever was paying good money to trick on her.

"I'm fine." Leshaun still sat on the hood of a modest silver 2012 Ford Taurus The BB&T bank branch Leshaun instructed Gogo to meet her at was only a block from

Haywood Road in West Asheville. She spent the past fifteen minutes watching young white people jog in bikini tops and yoga pants and men flex in running shorts. Dogs put in more work than some of their owners as they dragged them with their leashes. The smells from the Italian restaurant on one block and the authentic Mexican restaurant in the shopping center near it competed for her attention.

Gogo smacked her lips and rolled her eyes. "You not allowed to murder no more bitches."

"Damn, Cookie." Leshaun referenced her favorite character from *Empire*.

"I was Gogo before there were Lyons," Gogo retorted as Leshaun got off the hood. "I feel good about his mood, though."

"Well, aren't you generous?"

"You know," Leshaun replied, opening the door for Gogo, "I can't fix what I did, but I feel like maybe some good karma will come out of this."

"Do you have the money to fix your hotel yet?" Gogo stopped and crossed her arms.

"No, but I will." Leshaun kept walking until she found a vacant chair in the lobby. She took a seat and then pulled out her phone and checked Zay's, Kofi's, and 9ine's Instagrams. She was pleased to see that the boys were up to mischief and that the female followers were impressed with the latest pics.

"So how long do you think Tiana's story will receive media coverage?" Gogo asked as she looked over Leshaun's shoulder.

"I'm not sure but, right now, I just want to focus on setting up this charity in her honor. I know I can't bring her back, but this is the least I can do," Leshaun replied. "Plus, I've heard good things about Merri Baker, and I can't wait for her help with this."

"Leshaun Gamble."

Leshaun was surprised to see a tall, middle-aged black woman coming out of the account manager's office.

"I'm ready for you."

"Remind me to set appointments more often," Leshaun told Gogo as they got up from the couch.

Leshaun and Gogo followed the woman from the lobby to a large office all the way down the end of the hall. Glass windows reached from the top of the ceiling to the bottom of the floor. The white blinds looked homelier. Inside of the office, she could see Merri Baker's accomplishments. Degrees from Clemson University and South Carolina State University adorned her walls, and professionally dressed black figures marched and played on the edge of her desk.

"So, Ms. Gamble, I understand you want to set up an account for a DBA?" Merri asked.

Leshaun told Merri it was a business because she didn't have all her paperwork together. She knew it would take about ten days from the date she filed the paperwork for the business to be incorporated. She knew it would be another thirty days before her 501c3 status would be approved, allowing her to legally take donations.

"Yes. I want it to be Leshaun Gamble doing business as Outta Tiana's Purse until my paperwork comes back and my incorporation is legal. I want to sell some old clothes and other things to get the money for the business and establish a good habit of separating business from personal."

"I have a better idea." Merri leaned forward on her desk. "Have you filled out your paperwork yet?

"No." Leshaun was confused, not sure what was going on.

"I love meeting and interacting with women who want to own their own businesses," Merri bragged.

Leshaun didn't take offense to the fact that Merri didn't know who she was or the kind of business she ran.

"And this is what I'm going to suggest you do. I like that name, Outta Tiana's Purse. And I'm gonna walk you through the process now. Just go to the state Web site, and see if the name is available. If it is, take about five, ten minutes to fill out the paperwork and then go to irs.gov and get an Employer Identification Number. Then, once you get the number, I can help you set up a bank account that you don't have to change."

Merri's suggestion made sense; and, within a matter of minutes, Leshaun had taken a hold of an iPad that Merri slid her way, filled out the paperwork, and had a printed copy of her EIN to use to open the account. Merri handed her starter checks, and Leshaun passed her $250 to open the account.

"I think you shouldn't do a nonprofit organization, and I'm gonna tell you why." Gogo couldn't hold her tongue any longer, and once they were out of BB&T, she spoke her piece. "Don't raise the money. Use Outta Tiana's Purse as shell company instead. Merri was right: that name is catchy, and I'd want to buy some shit outta Tiana's purse too. What you do is build on the idea 9ine called you with last night and make it work. Either you start looking to acquire another hotel, or you buy some bed and breakfasts. Even though Montford Avenue is an ideal spot, I'd venture out and renovate some of the larger properties in West Asheville. With all these little thrift stores around here, rent a small storefront and sell used clothes and shit. After all, Tiana loved wearing something once or twice and then giving it away."

Gogo got Leshaun's mind spinning. "I knew there was a reason I like you."

"Damn right. If you do it as a nonprofit, and then say you doing it in her honor, her family can challenge you and have you wrapped up in court. Do it as a thrift shop instead. You know 9ine and Zay can boost some stuff and with all the women who give them shit . . . Girl, sell it," Gogo suggested.

"You are so right," Leshaun admitted. "I can profit, and then write off the money I give to Goodwill, Red Cross, and them churches. Plus, folks will be more willing to spend a little more money if we can prove that we give the money to a good cause."

It was settled. Plans to make Outta Tiana's Purse a nonprofit were scratched. But Leshaun would take some of the concepts she thought of and apply them to a for-profit venture.

"Ummm," Leshaun moaned under Zay as his thick-headed dick plunged in and out of her wetness. "Pussy good ain't it?" she breathed as she clutched his bare ass.

Zay kept stroking between her soft thighs, slapping his balls on the back of her ass. The tiny room smelled of sex, condoms, and weed. Leshaun stayed true to the deal and gave Zay extra lessons on how to work the goods. She ran her hustle on Zay by making him kick the fee for the room. His first nut flooded into the condom with Leshaun bouncing on his dick backward. She sorta felt sorry for him, so she gave him a second shot at the pussy. Her breathing sped up as Zay grunted above her.

"Yes!" she shouted. "You better tear dis pussy up! Ummm, almost there! Almost there!"

Zay couldn't last the limit that Leshaun needed. He stiffened and filled the second condom with her ankles up on his shoulder. The dick was rated sufficient in Leshaun's view, and a deal was a deal. She stood in the shower after he left. Life for Leshaun, she lived it to the fullest. There stood no regret over her head and yet she felt numb at the idea of fucking Zay. Her actions, she would keep them secret.

After the shower, she wrapped a towel around her thick frame and sat at the foot of the bed. She yawned and glanced at the two ounces of Fireball on the dresser. She grinned with Zay on her mental. Just as she reached for her iPhone, a knock rapped on the door.

"Who is it?" she shouted.

"It's me, Prince."

Leshaun jumped off the bed to answer the door. A part of her didn't want to answer the door since they hadn't spoken in two days. "You came back for more?" She pulled him inside.

"Damn, girl, chill," Prince replied as he tracked Leshaun's ass across the room. The shape of it was still prominent under the towel. "I come in peace. If I wanted to fuck you up, I'd have gotten at you and Zay while y'all was hot and heavy a few minutes ago."

"You got my money?" she asked when she picked up the two ounces off the dresser.

Prince dug in his front pocket and pulled out a thick roll of money. He peeled off $700 and handed it to Leshaun. "This your new hustle?"

She grinned. "Maybe."

They made the exchange and tried to ignore the sexual tension between them.

"What's up with the room?" He invited himself to sit on the edge of the bed.

Leshaun took the towel off and reached for a clean pair of panties. "Why you so nosy?"

Prince stared at her nude frame. "Why you putting those on?"

"'Cause I'm 'bout to go home." Leshaun's attitude reeked in her response.

"Word!" He looked stunned. "You saying I can't get no pussy?"

"Not tonight, buddy." She shimmied the panties up her wide hips and over her ass. Her teasing moves caused her bare breasts to jiggle and sway.

"You on some bullshit." He nodded as she turned and picked up her bra.

"Go fuck your girl." She laughed. "I know my pussy good. But damn . . ."

"I'ma remember this when you want me to lick that ass and pussy."

"Ha!" She turned back around with the bra draped over her shoulder. "If I tell you to break me off with some head, yo' ass gon' do it. And you know why?"

"Why?" He grinned with his dick rocked up.

"'Cause you love how sweet I taste."

Prince sighed and thought of another side chic he could call for some pussy tonight. He enjoyed pussy, but he was never pressed for it. "When are you gonna come through with some new wheels for me?"

"I'm working on something now," she told him as she stuffed her large melons in the bra.

"Was that ten stacks enough for you?"

She nodded and felt a twinge of guilt about being dishonest with Gogo. The $1,000 Leshaun kept to herself, and now the deed of fucking Zay had her feeling like shit.

"Did you catch up with Lysa and Janae?" Prince asked as his hopes for some pussy faded.

"I been caught up with them. I just haven't made my move yet."

Prince stood. "Well, I guess I better hit the road."

Leshaun nodded, looking like an urban model in the bra and panties. After Prince left, she finished getting dressed and finally checked her iPhone for any calls or messages she missed.

"What the fuck!" she exclaimed after she viewed the text from Gogo. She figured Gogo was under some serious stress to up and drive all the way to Asheville. On her way out the door, she noticed a shiny object partially hidden under the bed sheets: Prince's smartphone.

Chapter Fifteen

Leshaun wasn't expecting the phone to be ringing at 1:45 in the morning. Immediately, her senses became alert as she wondered which one of her whores ran into some trouble, or worse, if one of her "sons" had been arrested.

She was back in Asheville. If she could have, Leshaun would've stayed in Birhmingham and never come back. She could, but Leshaun didn't want to. One, she'd never forgive herself if something happened to 9ine, Zay, or Ten while she was gone. Two, Leshaun didn't run from responsibility. Most of the issues involving the patrons of her hotel had been settled. Monies were refunded and most of the $500 Visa gift cards she ordered for the patrons had been distributed. The employees of Price Street Hotel were still being paid and enjoying their "unplanned time off." Her whores stayed busy and found new homes in other motels across the county and in the neighboring county.

For her part, she enjoyed a suite in the Grand Bohemian, across from the McDonald's that featured a grand piano. Normally, Leshaun didn't do fast food, but listening to classical music while eating her fish sandwich combo surprisingly put her at east. Despite the luxury and accomodations, she hated being in a room she wasn't familiar with. In her master suite, she made it a point to make sure her .45 and other weapons were well hidden. An assortment of switchblades and pocket knives were strategically placed around the bed and on the dresser. Even the metallic pink flathead screwdriver she depended on to fix everything was sharp enough to be deadly.

The .45 wasn't enough protection in her eyes.

Glancing at the screen, she noticed the number was private. That pissed her off because she hated when people called from a blocked phone.

"Hey, baby." She recognized Prince's voice.

"What the hell?" Leshaun almost snapped. "Do you know what time it is?"

"It's time for me to see you," Prince replied, and the confidence oozed from his voice. "Where you at?"

"Where Sarah at?" Leshaun copped an attitude as she slipped the Under Armour tennis shoes off her feet. She lifted her feet off the floor and made herself comfortable on the king-sized bed. "You should be calling her at two o'clock in the morning."

"Babe, don't do me like that." The frustration in Prince's voice turned her on. She could picture Prince chilling in his car, leaning back in his cinnamon-colored Acura TL. The amplification of his voice gave his position away. "I was thinking about you."

"Nigga, please." Leshaun put the phone on speaker and placed it on the bed. She lifted up her Golden State Warriors T-shirt and flung it to the floor. The room lacked a dresser and a mirror, so she couldn't see her reflection. "Sarah told you no, and you couldn't pick up a young thing, so you decided to fuck with me." The bullshit Prince was feeding her was old. Leshaun knew this was a booty call and while she didn't mind some dick, especially his dick, she demanded Prince treated her with more respect.

"Come on, ma," Prince pleaded. "Do we have to go through this shit every time I want to see you?"

"No, because I'm going to stop picking up my phone. Callin' me from private numbers and shit." Leshaun let her body sink into the bed. She pulled up the cream-colored satin sheets she bought and washed earlier today and was pleased at how soft the threads felt on her body.

"A'ight, okay," Prince grunted, his anger not well hidden. "I'm gonna remember this shit when you try to lift another credit card number from my place of business."

"Fuck you, Prince," Leshaun let out in frustration.

"I want you to," Prince fired back. "Just let me know where you stay and you can fuck me all you want."

Chapter Sixteen

Despite having all the information on Sheila Goldfied's Discover card, she couldn't do much with the information just yet. Leshaun needed to figure out where the chick lived and, if she could get it, the last four numbers of her social.

"I see a bitch still know how to work." Gogo entered the room loud as hell, like she didn't have the sense God gave her. Leshaun looked her younger sister up and down. Her Kool-Aid red dyed hair bounced as she made her way into the Grand Bohemian room. Her strapless blue evening dress surely turned heads along with the red, white, and blue earrings patronizing this "great" country. Gogo pulled red laptop bag off her shoulder and let it drop on the king-sized bed. "I was able to get the laptop and a few other shit from your room while you were out of town."

"Thank you." Leshaun's voice was barely audible as she left the table by the window and pulled the Lenovo touchscreen laptop out of the bag. Leshaun moved her manicured fingers across the screen and pulled up the hotel's merchant account information.

"I'm good, how are you, you rude-ass bitch?" Gogo pouted, but she wasn't ready for Leshaun to grab her by her throat and toss her on the bed like a crumpled piece of paper.

"Listen here." Leshaun's hand was still wrapped around Gogo's throat as she climbed on top of her. "As much shit as I do for you, the word 'bitch' should never cross your lips in reference to me, understand?"

Gogo struggled to shake her head yes.

"I asked you to get my laptop so I can move shit around and get some of these bills paid."

"I said I was sorry," Gogo barely squeaked.

"No, you didn't." Leshaun let up. Truth was, she didn't want to fuck up her money because Gogo had to blow off one of the rappers who would be performing in concert. Leshaun seen the dick pic he posted a few years ago and said the rapper had something to work with. Gogo needed to be in top shape and choking the shit out of her wasn't going to get her there.

"Well, I meant to." Gogo straightened her dress out as she got up. She gently rubbed her throat. "Is there anything else you want me to do?"

Leshaun knew Gogo was trying to stay in her good graces. "See if you can find Sheila Goldfield."

Gogo smiled because she knew it was time to get that work. She slid Leshaun's laptop her way and went to work. Within seconds, she pulled up five different LinkedIn accounts and turned the screen toward Leshaun.

The second listing matched the woman Leshaun remembered being in the IHOP. She touched the screen and pulled up her whole profile. Then she hit up the online phone directory and found the address for Sheila Goldfield in a matter of seconds.

"You want me to try to get a card duplicate?" Gogo offered as she looked over Leshaun's shoulder. She was always amazed at how Leshaun's mind worked as she memorized credit cards, personal information, and other shit that most people couldn't process. Leshaun thought fast, and it seemed that her mind moved faster than her fingers as she moved from one Web page to another, incorporating information into a few programs she also had running simultaneously.

"No," Leshaun scolded as Gogo pulled up a profile she hadn't recognized. "I'm not using this card now. I have a few others I need to tap into first. Plus, this card and profile have to pass my screening tests."

Leshaun was meticulous when it came to her credit card fraud activities. She always was very selective in the cards she used and the people whose identity she stole. Leshaun didn't make it a regular habit to take card after card and use it for frivolous shit. She usually waited months, sometimes up to a year before she tapped a card in her database. She specialized in hitting growing businesses with extra expenses they were least likely to report. All companies wanted the tax advantages of writing off any- and everything possible and, in Leshaun's view, purchasing items from different department stores and residential care supply vendors and merchants made it easier to hide what she was doing.

Of course, Gogo didn't know that and, despite the fact that the two were sisters, Leshaun kept her secrets close to the chest. The fewer people who knew how she got her dirt in, the better.

"You need to get ready." Leshaun looked at the time. "Are you hooking up with him before the show or after?"

"After," Gogo replied as she looked at herself in the mirror. She loved the way her outfit looked and was thankful that Leshaun didn't mess up her hair. With the tips of her fingers, Gogo put a few misplaced strands in place.

"Good." Leshaun closed her laptop and, from the bed, watched Gogo prepare. "Remember to text me and 9ine the hotel information. We got to be extra careful because Zay just hit me up saying that he and 9ine were picking Kofi up from G-boro and they were going to be working there tonight. Chasity working in the Indigo not far from the US Cellular Center and I don't have no one working the streets. For the time being, I'm off, so it will be me and Prince if I can get a hold of him to reach you in case something pops off."

"Big sis, I'm good. Don't worry about me. It's not the first time I've hooked up with this rapper remember?"

Leshaun remembered, and she already thought about how Gogo was stuck on ol' boy for three days after they fucked silly for the weekend. The pregnancy and the miscarriage Leshaun remembered, and she didn't want her sister to make the same mistake she did when she got her first celebrity john. She knew that any misstep and Gogo's face and description would be on Media Take Out and all the blogs.

"Be careful," Leshaun pleaded like a mother letting her child go out on her own for the first time.

Gogo stared into Leshaun's eyes. She knew that no matter how rough Leshaun got with disciplining her, Leshaun genuinely cared for her. That was more than they could say for their own mother.

Chapter Seventeen

"You done being mad at me?" Prince followed Leshaun out of the State Farm office as she power-walked to her car.

"I'm not mad." Leshaun copped an attitude and unlocked the door to her silver 2012 Ford Taurus. She stared at Prince as he hopped into her car and slammed the door. Leshaun followed suit as she looked him up and down in his IHOP attire. *I should've made his ass walk,* she thought as she turned the key in the ignition. The South Asheville branch Leshaun went to was a good ten miles to the IHOP Prince worked at near the mall. "I'm just fed up with all the extra shit with this insurance. I thought everything was handled and I'm still having to come up with more money."

"You didn't expect them to cut you a check today, did you?" Prince asked as Leshaun focused on the rearview mirror and backed out of the space.

"No, I expected not to be dealing with all this bullshit," Leshaun vented. "What else can I do? I've refunded the money, I've given them gift cards, I'm taking care of my legal workers and my whores. Can a bitch get a break or what?"

Prince sat in silence. He'd heard the same news that Leshaun heard. The claim wouldn't be paid until the insurance company was convinced that the fire wasn't intentionally started by Leshaun or any of her staff.

Leshaun told the insurance claims representative and the police investigating the same story: she'd had a party, and Zay left the stove on by mistake. Zay told the same story about warming up some pasta and forgetting about it when Tiana distracted him with some sex. Tiana corroborated their story before Leshaun killed her. The police believed the fire was started by accident; why didn't the insurance agency?

What Leshaun didn't need was a delay in rebuilding her hotel. This was the middle of June and tourist season only heated up from here. Without the hotel, Leshaun was losing almost a quarter of a million dollars a month. Dom's Paradice made money, but Leshaun kept that operation separate and didn't comingle her Asheville and her Birmingham money. Leshaun had enough money saved to cover the repairs, but that's what insurance was for. The premium was too high for the policy not to come through when she needed it the most.

Leshaun knew she had to come up with a plan and fast.

The repairs to the hotel were going to cost almost a quarter of a million dollars. The insurance adjusters needed a few more weeks to investigate how the fire got started and whether their policy would cover the repairs. Leshaun struggled to understand why she bought the policy if the insurance company wasn't going to pay up.

Nevertheless, Leshaun had a business to run. She had ten whores who needed to be tricking and bringing in the dough so she could continue to keep up the lifestyle they were accustomed to.

With what little resources she had, she told one of her clients who was a member of the local Masonic lodge that she needed to rent the building for the night. Fortunately, the lodge was available, and they had everything they needed except access to the top floor. Leshaun benefited from having friends in high places.

The lodge wasn't hard to get to, and she found that the basement key she'd been provided a few years ago still worked. She halfway expected one of the Masons to be waiting for her at the door to collect payment. She took out her key and let herself in the door. She called him back and let him know she was inside but got no answer.

At least I can conduct business in peace, she thought as she turned the light on and appreciated the empty building. She took out her phone again and texted all her crew and gave them the address and instructions on how to enter the building. As she looked ahead, she found an empty room partially opened. Inside she could see a square table with six chairs gathered around. She knew from having been to a party in the building before there was a storage room that had extra chairs. Fortunately for her, there was another room with a table and some chairs around it as well. She took all the chairs out of one room and put them in the room she wanted them to be used in. As she went to setting up the room the way she intended to use it, she heard a knock on the door.

Leshaun opened the door and was surprised to see Bradley on the other side. "Well, thank you for letting me use your building." She looked at her john. There were things that she liked about the sixty-year-old man. Number one, he still had a handful of silver hair. He kept up his great shape, hitting the gym regularly. The evidence was hard to hide on his five foot eleven frame. His olive-colored skin still looked smooth, and the wrinkles on his face were at a minimum for a man of sixty. Hell, Bradley could say he was forty-five and she would believe it.

"Don't mention it at all. I'm glad that you were able to use the space." Bradley looked around at Leshaun's decorations. "I can tell you are ready to throw down and get that hotel of yours back in order."

Leshaun reached for her purse and pulled out a few Benjamins and Bradley held up his hand and shook his head. "Naw, it's on me."

"Take the money, Bradley," Leshaun insisted as she pushed the money in his hand. "I don't want you to be expecting any free rides." Leshaun had to draw the boundary between friendship and business. Experience taught her that if she didn't, her johns would be expecting all kinds of shit and free rides from her. "Don't get me wrong, I appreciate you coming through at the last minute for me; but I have to be consistent." Leshaun closed the money in his hand.

Bradley kissed her forehead. "Okay, baby girl. I respect your business. You got full use of the building until three a.m.; then you got to clean up, pack up, and be out by four. And if you're having that type of party, don't film outside the building and don't go upstairs. The whole bottom level is yours."

Leshaun nodded her head. She had every intention of following the rules because she never knew if or when she would need Bradley again.

"So this is where we partying tonight?" Chasity walked in with Zay, 9ine, and Kofi not too far behind her.

Chasity couldn't wait for the next assignment to come through. True to his word, Kofi never forced himself on her, and 9ine and Zay kept their distances too. She was making money with some of the johns Leshaun or Gogo sent her way. Even though she'd never had a pimp, she'd been tricking and looking up to Lil' Kim since the fifth grade. At eleven, she was giving blowjobs for Blow Pops. By the time she was sixteen, she'd had three abortions that her mother knew about, been treated for NGU and gonorrhea, and lost count of all the men and women she'd slept with.

"Ma, you should've said something. I could've brought my DJ equipment." Kofi looked around and sized up the lower level. "Ain't nothing wrong with turning up in here."

Leshaun smiled. She liked the fact that her whores used their brains for more than just giving brain. Kofi already had money on his mind so she knew within thirty minutes a plan would come into fruition on how she was getting her money back.

"Zay and I will get on Instagram, post some pics, and tell everyone we having a party here tonight in a few hours. Gogo and Chasity will go to the store and get some food." Kofi took out the prepaid MasterCard he got from the girl he pleasured last night. "I checked the balance on this card. Five hundred and twenty-five dollars oughta cover it."

"That will get us a few Gs tonight but, Ma, how much will it cost to get the building fixed?" 9ine asked.

"Almost a quarter of a mil," Leshaun answered.

"Shit" and "fuck" were the common responses. A quarter of a million was a lot of money, and it would take almost a million tricks to see that kind of money.

"Leshaun, it looks like you and I are gonna have to take it back to the old days," Kofi spoke up.

Leshaun knew what he meant. The fact that he tried to stick her up was how they met. Leshaun didn't want to have to get violent, bring in guns, and start ski-masking. Making money on her back and using her lips were so much easier.

"A'ight." Leshaun conceded that Kofi was right. For that kind of money, they were going to have to strong-arm some folks. Leshaun felt she was out of options. There was no guarantee that they'd get the insurance money. If she tapped her savings, it'd take months to replace the money, and she didn't want to lose what little income she had from getting the interest in the CDs and other savings products she purchased.

Gogo already planted the seeds in her head, and now it was time to water the garden and make it grow. "Chasity, you got you a ruler with the set of school supplies I told you to carry for your schoolgirl act?"

Chasity looked at her and laughed. She knew where Leshaun was going. A mischievous grin took over her face as she couldn't wait to participate.

"So I can see how I can work some of this plan, Kofi, 9ine, and Zay, I'm gonna need all three of you to drop your drawers so I can know who got the biggest dick." Leshaun's mind was spinning. She knew 9ine, Kofi, and Zay were all packing but she never thought she'd need to get an accurate account of who was packing what. Showing pictures was one thing, but for her plan to work she needed to be able to describe them in that way. In the back of her mind, if she could sell one or two of them as being ten inches or bigger, she could get them more opportunities and charge more money. Low-key, her three boys didn't bring in as much money as the women, and Leshaun never forced them to because they did other work to make sure the other girls got paid. With Lysa and Janae still missing in action, she needed to see what artillery her army was working with.

"Ma," 9ine yelled while Kofi and Zay wasted no time unzipping their pants, "I'm not showing you my dick."

"Boy, I'm not even trying to go there with you on that." Leshaun covered her eyes and turned around. "Chasity, get the measurements."

With Leshaun facing away from him, 9ine swiftly and quickly dropped his drawers. Chasity pulled out a measuring tape and went to work measuring the men both flaccid and erect, giving all three of them blowjobs in the process.

"Zay got 'em beat by like half an inch," Chasity announced as Gogo entered the building.

"Happy, cuzzo." 9ine was pissed as he zipped up his pants. "And, Chasity, you finishing this shit when you come back."

"Whatever." Chasity licked her lips.

"What I miss?" Gogo handed Leshaun a knot full of bills.

"Zay won the dick-measuring contest," Chasity bragged while she grabbed her arm. "We got to go to the store to grab a few things while Leshaun and the boys work out their feelings." Chasity escorted Gogo back out while Leshaun pulled out her phone and texted her instructions.

"A'ight." Zay got animated as he looked at his phone. "They want to know how much we charging."

"Tell 'em twenty-five dollars for males, fifteen dollars for single ladies, and thirty-five dollars for couples. Open bar, and wear their sexiest outfit," Leshaun instructed. "No tennis shoes, no boots, no flip-flops."

"Ma, your mind working fast," Kofi complimented her. "What you plan on having us do?"

"I plan on sending you boys all over the country. Some things will be done together; some will be done solo. Whatever differences you have will need to be put to the side so we can get this paper. And, let it be known, whoever brings Lysa and Janae to me are in for a treat."

Leshaun went to the supply room and picked up a broom and dustpan. She started sweeping, making sure the lodge was tight. "Kofi, you and 9ine go get your DJ equipment. I know it's short notice, but I only got access to the space recently. Zay and I will help Chasity and Gogo set up once they get back."

With Kofi and 9ine out the door, Leshaun continued to work while Zay entertained some people on the phones. "What you need me to do, Ma?" Zay asked.

"I need you to make sure you are ready to strip," Leshaun ordered as she reached in her pocket and pulled out three twenties. "Go to one of the sex shops, and get an outfit that shows as much of what you are packing as possible. If you got your security outfit, bring it. I'll be putting you on the dance floor tonight. Be ready."

Leshaun kissed Zay on the cheek and watched as he went out the door. She looked around the room once, and she knew it was showtime.

Chapter Eighteen

The lodge was lit and, just like she pictured, full of men and women ready to get down and freaky. Dark fluorescent images of women licking each other between the legs broadcasted across the walls. The women had turned out, and the men were turned on.

Leshaun made sure that Kofi was set up in the area that led upstairs, making sure she honored Bradley's request. The makeshift liquor bar was set up in another area that led to a hidden stairwell to the basement. With her end covered, she made sure that the party was jumping and that all her whores stayed busy.

The smell of sex invaded Leshaun's nostrils, and the beat of the music was in sync with her soul. The women were dancing on a raised platform and having personal conversations with men of all different nationalities and sizes. She was looking for Zay but couldn't find him.

While the rent going to the lodge took money out of her coffers, it made more sense to host the party at the lodge than at Dom Paradice. For starters, the party was low-key. No one knew she was the host except those who'd received invitations through Facebook or Instagram. Leshaun learned early on never to mix her business and pleasure.

"Hey, Elle, what do you have for me?" A john called her by her nickname. She remembered the straight-laced teacher who was single and lonely after devoting most of his life to taking care of his ailing mother. She took special care not to turn him over to one of her wild whores.

"What do you need? Where's Gogo?"

"She stepped away for a moment," the john whose name she could never remember replied. "I wanna try something different tonight."

"Okay." Leshaun thought quickly. She needed to get rid of him. "I believe I have someone who can be on your speed." Leshaun was about her business, and she wasn't going to turn down no dollar just because it came from some dork.

"Let me take care of him?"

Leshaun turned toward the masculine voice, unaware that he had been in her presence. She looked at the man. "Yeah, if the money is right!" she responded sarcastically. She didn't expect Lloyd to be so brazen as to show his face at her party. But he was here, and she wasn't going to make a big deal about it in front of her client. Leshaun needed to demonstrate she was in control of the situation.

"Hey, Leigh Ann, take this gentleman to that room over there." Lloyd took out two Benjamins and put them in Leshaun's hands. "Make sure you show him a real good time."

Leigh Ann grabbed the nervous man by the hand and smiled at Leshaun and Lloyd.

"When you're finished, come find me, and I'll show you what I have."

"Okay," Leigh Ann promised before pulling the man to one of the rooms.

"Muthafucka, you must think you slick," Leshaun mumbled as she and Lloyd made their way downstairs. The smell of naked women and men in drug-induced orgies made her nauseated. The money the party was raising to rebuild her hotel was worth it, and Leshaun liked that she could be trusted to help some of the region's most wealthy and professional people indulge and safely get their freak on.

"What's up, girl?" Lloyd called out. "You didn't think I was going to show up?"

"I'm not worried about you," Leshaun responded as she held up her hand to emphasize her point. She saw Lysa and Janae making their way around the lodge, and she cracked a smile.

"Let me see; how does this go?" Lloyd was as excited as a young child opening up a Christmas present from Santa Claus.

"Those bitches chose you. Yeah, I know." Leshaun was determined not to let Lloyd get under her skin. After all, he came to her spot to put in work. He was paying her taxes and, for the night, she was fine with that. On the small scale, that meant Lysa and Janae were back under her control for a moment but, ultimately, Leshaun got paid.

"I want you to come to my warehouse," Lloyd extended the invitation. "I got some tight gear that's going to have these tricks standing at attention the moment they lay eyes on you. I found a black silk top that would look good on you."

"You say that as if you want me in your stable." Leshaun was puzzled as she looked at Lloyd and gave him a stank look.

"I think we're stronger together." Lloyd laid out his proposition: "I got the women and a wide network of clientele. Your hotel is one of the best locations in Asheville and, admittedly, where the best men are being pimped."

"Well, it's good you recognize that," Leshaun responded. "You better keep Lysa and Janae in check."

"I'm not worried about them two." Lloyd leaned closer to him to whisper something in her ear. "I have a show in Houston, and I have some outfits with a lot of glitz. I'd like to personally invite you and your crew to come to the dirty and make money with me and mine."

"You got jokes." Leshaun looked at Lloyd and shook her head.

"What you mean? I'm always serious," Lloyd responded.

Leshaun pulled Lloyd in for a hug and a kiss. "After we take care of business, I'll show you what I like."

Leshaun kept her eyes on everyone in the party. Even with Lloyd and his hoes on deck, she was determined to prove that she was in charge and that he didn't faze her one bit.

"Shit!" Lysa muttered. "These Gucci heels are killing my feet!"

"Girl, hush!" Janae nudged Lysa through the crowd in front of the convention center.

"I told you not to get this pair!" Lysa complained as she brushed by a group of older women, all fixated toward the roped-off valet parking area. Lysa didn't get the buzz about what was so special about Bryson. She was only kicking it with them while waiting to see who Lloyd was gonna trick her off on.

"We need to hurry up and get up front so I can see who is all here!" Janae craned her neck over the crowd of mostly women who waited to catch a glimpse of Bryson. In Janae's case, she wanted to put a mark on tonight's lick.

The two looked their best on this warm summer night. Lysa's hair framed her beautiful face with blond highlights. The red body dress magnified her thickness, wrapped around her large breasts while embracing the shape of her hefty ass. She was on her diva shit tonight, and no bitch could tell her otherwise.

Janae rocked a black backless dress that ended high above her knees. It clung to her curvy figure, and tonight she would flaunt all her physical assets.

"Damn!" Janae stomped when she reached the red velvet rope. "They already started coming in."

Around them nearly everyone in the crowd held up a smartphone, taking pictures. A line of expensive cars and SUVs snaked in front of the lodge as Bryson and the other players for the Charlotte Hornets made their red-carpet arrival. They'd made the trek to the mountainous city to support a local charity that helped young black men thrive in mathematics and science and pursue STEM-related college degrees in several of the states historically black colleges and universities. The team received a lot of respect in Asheville for some of the various events they did for a variety of organizations across the Carolinas.

"Mmmm! Who's that fine brotha?" Lysa tapped Janae's shoulder as a tall, suited man stepped out of a black Mercedes-Benz SL600.

"Nobody for us." Janae shook her head. "He's rich, but he's gay."

Lysa rolled her eyes, thinking it was a waste of some good dick. "Who are we looking for?" Lysa asked as the valet drove off in the topless Benz.

"Anyone who's riding solo. Ain't no need to waste any time if any of these dudes got a bitch on their arm," Janae whispered. "These players got an ego, and that's how we pop dat ass tonight."

Lysa nodded as a pearl white Toyota Avalon with gold trim cruised up to the flashing lights and red carpet. "Yo, don't he play for the Asheville Tourists, whatever his name is?"

"Quincy Cisneros."

"Yeah, him. What if he has a date?" Lysa asked with her eyes on the Avalon.

"He's single." Janae grinned. "And you know damn well he wouldn't bring a bitch here when all this pussy is gonna be thrown at his feet."

"So that means I'll have to gain his attention."

"That's what this is for." Janae grabbed Lysa's ass and squeezed.

"Stop playing!" Lysa shoved Janae's hand away as a handsome, bald-headed black guy with glasses exited the Avalon. The sight of him caused Lysa to stare. *Damn, he's fine!* "Who's that guy?" Lysa asked Janae, hoping like hell that it was Quincy.

Janae adjusted her bra strap. "That's Brenton Guldenby. He's the son of the owner of the Hornets and the Tourists. In his own right, he's a tech nerd who's part of a small black-owned startup in the Research Triangle. Remember his face because he's on our list."

Lysa nodded as she eyed her prey. She wouldn't mind throwing her ass his way, and she hoped he'd be down to catch it.

After eight more basketball players arrived, Janae's impatience got under her skin. The lure of tonight's stickup made her palms itch, and tonight she was ready to do the damn thang.

"Let's go inside," Janae said as she smoothed her dress out. "I think we missed Quincy and, plus, we need to make our move before another thirsty bitch beats us to the punch."

"Let's split up and mingle with the crowd," Janae suggested once they were inside the convention center.

"Mingle?" Lysa frowned. "I don't know shit about any of these athletes or other wealthy guys up in here. What are you going to do?"

"I'ma go find Quincy Cisneros. I overheard some bitches in the bathroom talking about seeing him up on the second floor. If I find him, I'll send you a text."

"I hope this works," Lysa mumbled with little hope.

"It will. Now go and pop that ass and show these athletes the difference between cornbread and silicone."

Lysa had no idea where to start. Everywhere she looked sat a small booth with different athletes signing jerseys or other paraphernalia, and talking to their fans. Stacks of new calendars, souvenir books, and other goodies covered the tables from end to end. Shirts were sold, pictures were taken, and at one booth stood a line thirty deep, waiting to have a book signed. Lysa hadn't read a book since high school. *Reading is boring as hell! Fuck I look like reading a damn book!*

Lysa made her way across the packed floor on the prowl for a lick. Three times she was stopped by different folks handing out flyers and postcards. As soon as she left their sight, she dropped the promo items on the nearest table and kept it moving. She had no intention of buying anything. Her motive was to take what she wanted and it sure as hell wasn't a bunch of flyers.

A round of applause gained her attention as she entered a new section on the first floor. Her heart skipped a beat when she spotted Brenton Guldenby standing up on a small stage. Lust spun around Lysa's nipples as she thought about testing Brenton's dick game. She didn't see no wrong in tricking and licking in the same night. As she eyed Brenton's crowd of fans, she realized that it wouldn't be an easy task to gain his attention. She noticed a few attractive females who could steal her shine with little effort. Lysa's drive to get paid forced her to stay on point.

"You're a fan of Brenton?" a deep Southern voice caught Lysa off guard.

She turned and, from her five foot three stance, looked up at the man behind her. She blinked twice and took in every detail. *Damn! This muthafucka is fine!* Lysa took a step back to view all of him. She had a license in being hood. She didn't know how to appreciate the man in her sight. His tailor-made black and teal three-piece suit didn't appeal to Lysa. She couldn't relate to a man in a suit and tie, rocking gator shoes. Hell, the only times she saw dudes dressed up was in church or at court. She dealt with the gangsters, the goons, the rowdy thug hustlers who rocked the baggy jeans, Jordans, and fresh 'Tims". She didn't have the slightest idea that the platinum cufflinks on the man's wrist were worth $8,000.

"Uh, what did you say?" she asked with a coy smile.

"Are you a fan of Brenton?" He nodded over her shoulder.

Lysa fingered a strand of hair over her bare shoulder. "Not really," she answered as lewd thoughts kept jumping in her head. Going without any dick for two days had Lysa itching for some pipe. "Are you a software developer?" she asked, sticking to the lick.

"No," he replied after a moment's pause.

Lysa remembered what Lloyd told her a few days ago. The charity event would draw in athletes, local celebrities, a few hustlers, and unknown men with major bread. She eyed him up and down. "Do you have the time?" she asked just to see what kind of watch he had.

He slid his left sleeve back and glanced at his rose gold timepiece. "Six minutes to eight," he informed her.

"Thank you." She nodded, making sure to maintain eye contact. "Nice watch. Is it a Rolex?"

He grinned. "Nah. It's a Patek Philippe."

Lysa didn't show any reaction because the brand of his timepiece didn't click. If she'd known the worth of the Patek Philippe, she would have robbed him for it on sight. "So, what's your name?" she asked with her eyes on his suckable lips. *Mmm, I bet he could go ham sucking on my kitty!*

He adjusted his solid white silk tie and appeared to ponder for a second. "Liam Sachs. And yours?"

"Buffy," Lysa lied without blinking. *I can palm that head all night!*

He smiled and fought the urge to stare at the chocolate sea of cleavage in his face.

"Um, I assume you like to buy and sell stocks and bonds?" Lysa made an effort to get small talk started.

"Sometimes," he replied as he admired her curves. "I'm a darker, distant relative of the founder."

She nodded. "This is my first time at such an event."

"Really?"

"Yep. And it's okay."

"Got any autographs from any of your favorite athletes yet?"

"Nah. I'm just enjoying the positive vibes."

Liam made his move. "Uh, would I be out of line to seek your company for a drink? There's a lounge in the back near the meet and greet area."

Lysa had to let his respectful request sink in. She wasn't used to being treated like a woman. From her countless nights hitting the clubs, hustlers would step to her on some hood shit: "Yo, shorty! Lemme holla atchu!" or, "Hey, ma, whut you tryin'a get into tonight?" On looks alone, Liam could get it! Lysa's pussy begged for a nice big pipe to stroke it. Through the lust, she stuck to her predator instinct and placed a mark on him because he smelled like that item she had to have: money.

"That sounds like a bomb idea." She boldly reached for his hand to start the hunt.

"Excuse me. Are you a model?"

Janae lowered the souvenir book she pretended to read and turned toward the voice. To her surprise, it was the man from the motherland who owned the SL600. "Uh, no, I'm not," she told him.

"Maybe I can change that." He grinned confidently.

"How?" Janae lifted an eyebrow. "I gotta hear this."

He held his hand out. "My name is—"

"I know who you are." She smiled and accepted his hand. "You're Suwali Zaire."

"I guess my name precedes me." He chuckled.

Janae forced a fake smile. *Conceited ass!* she judged easily.

"And your name is?" he asked as he released her hand.

"Chanel." She threw out the fake name.

"Okay, you know who I am so I'll cut to the chase. How would you like to be featured in an ad for one of my stores in South Africa?"

Janae blushed, totally caught off guard. "Me!" she gasped. "Are you serious?"

"Yes! I need a new, fresh face and, when I saw you, I couldn't take my eyes off the sight of you."

Janae couldn't hide her excitement. "Stop playing!"

"I'm serious. My ad drops next season, but I have to be ready to show it to my marketing team in two weeks."

"Why me?" she asked.

He took a step back and held up his hands thumb to thumb. "Your face is flawless!"

"Well," she said, giggling, "I woke up like this."

"I bet you did." He lowered his hands and stared at her with a lustful intent. "Are you here with your boyfriend?" he asked like he had something to hide.

Janae kept it hood. "Nope. What about you? You here with your wife?" She went ahead and put it out there that she knew he was married.

"I'm solo tonight. My wife isn't much of a public person." He showed no shame about being taken.

"And I bet she'd be pissed to see you flirting with me, right?"

Suwali grinned. "Is that what you think?"

"No." She stared at him. "It's what I hope."

"And it doesn't bother you that I'm married?"

"What bothers me is if you're playing games with me. Be straight up with me and don't shoot me any bullshit. Now what's up?"

He sighed and slid his hands in his pockets. "Here's the truth. It's no secret that I'm married, and I have no shame of it. But here's my twist. I, uh, have a secret that I do have a bit of shame behind."

"And it's what?"

"I still enjoy doing certain kinky things my wife don't do from time to time." He shrugged and waited to see how his words would be taken.

Janae returned the book to the table and gave her full attention to Suwali. "What is this certain thing or things you enjoy women doing to you?"

"Can I be blunt without you going off on me?"

Janae crossed her arms. "Say what you gotta say."

"Domination from a woman has a certain whip appeal."

Janae smiled quickly. She found her lick, and it was more than she expected. The rape scheme wouldn't be needed on Suwali. Janae had something more devious for Suwali and his secret cravings. "So the model talk was bullshit?"

"No bullshit." He shook his head. "If anything, it will give me a reason to have you around as long as you can keep a secret." He winked.

Janae didn't give a flying fuck about being on an ad for some store in South Africa. Her mind raced with ways to take his ass down for everything she could get. Off the top, she would relax him for the keys to that drop-top Benz, his cash, and the PINs to whatever credit cards he carried.

"And what will our secret be?" she whispered, reeling him in.

Suwali slid his tongue across his bottom lip. "The secret of me tasting you tonight."

Janae tracked the path of his tongue and wondered how it would feel on her clit. The thought alone caused her pussy to heat up. *I'ma get paid and get some head. Damn, this shit is so fucking easy! I'll have to tell Lloyd good fucking job on this one.* She turned on the entice- ment by tugging at the hem of her dress.

"Can you meet me outside in five minutes without drawing any attention?" he asked.

"I can do it in two minutes, baby."

Suwali glanced over his shoulder, hoping his actions weren't too obvious. "Meet me near the front entrance. I'll be in a black two-door Benz."

"And our destination?

"I have a room at the Indigo down the street."

Janae parted from Suwali and headed for the exit. Along the way she sent Lysa a text message: I'm on the hunt. Will hit you back in an hour or so. Going 2 Indigo up the block 2 do my thang. I'll ride wit the Mark. I got dis. Jus be ready 2 roll when I hit you back.

Janae entered the hotel room ahead of Suwali to show off her luscious derrier. The practiced steps made her butt cheeks move like a seesaw under the snug dress.

"Can I get you anything to drink?" Suwali asked as he loosened his tie.

Janae stood at the foot of the bed, scanning the lavishly appointed room. "I'll pass," she replied as he removed his dress coat.

"Can you take a shower with me?" he asked as her fruity perfume filled the room.

Janae smiled. "I don't see why not."

Suwali tossed the dress coat on the bed and reached for Janae's wide hips. "I knew you were soft." He squeezed her hips.

Janae reached for the top button on his shirt. "I've never been with anyone famous." She fed his ego. "Maybe you'll write a book about me. And I know it will be the shit!"

Suwali licked her neck and slid his fingers to the hem of her dress. "You look so damn sweet," he moaned in her ear.

"You gonna taste my pussy?"

He nodded as he slid the back of the dress up the curve of her ass. Her bare ass filled his palms when the dress circled her soft waist. "Magnificent!" He clutched both of her honey-brown cheeks as she unbuttoned his shirt.

"Think you can handle all that?" she asked with her hands sliding under his tank top.

"It's so big and soft!" He tested the weight of her ass as his dick grew along his leg.

"You're making me wet," she whispered against his shoulder. "And when I get wet, I gotta have some good dick. And I like it hard! Real hard and rough!" She reached for his belt.

"All I want to do is taste you." He continued to fondle her ass.

"That's what you're saying now." She yanked his belt loose. "I'ma get some dick. Even if I have to take it!"

Suwali couldn't ignore the flood of blood that raced to expand his penis. The breath rushed through his lips when Janae gently stroked his erection. Her wet tongue raced around his ear as her circled grip moved back and forth.

"Mmm, I like this dick," she moaned. "I wanna cum all over it after you eat my pussy."

Suwali tried to fight the urge to stick his dick in some pussy. In his selfish view, oral sex didn't count as cheating. In a span of four minutes, he allowed Janae to strip him butt-ass naked. That thirst for some pussy had his dick rocked up as Janae peeled her dress off.

"Go and start the shower," she stroked his erection again. "I'll grab my condoms outta my purse in case you change your mind."

He cupped his hands under her breasts and lifted them up to his mouth. He kissed each nipple and licked the left one until she moaned. Janae squeezed her thighs as a heavy wetness formed. Suwali had Janae horny as hell! She had to shove her lust aside to stick to the plan. After stroking his dick a few more times, she playfully shoved him toward the bathroom.

"Make sure it's still hard when I join you." She rubbed his brown ass and sent him on his way. The instant she stood alone, she rushed into action. She grabbed a box of condoms from her purse along with her iPhone. The latter item she hid across the room, knowing it was programed to start recording in ten minutes. Janae would string his ass along for a wild ride in the shower. The bed would be the stage for her. Every act she did with him would be recorded. She joined him in the shower and teased him by brushing her big ass against his wood. The timing had to be perfect, and in ten minutes she would have him on the bed, recording things that he wanted to remain secret. Janae thought she had it all figured out and her thirst for the lick had her slipping before her first deceitful step.

Chapter Nineteen

Out of Asheville city limits and on to some personal shit, Lysa pushed the black Acura TLX down Tryon Street and made her way to the private gravesite owned by the Esmay family near the Sugar Creek Parkway intersection. The busy Charlotte streets weren't a deterrent from seeing and paying respects to the love of her life. She waited in line like the rest of the traffic trying to get on West Sugar Creek Road so she could use the hidden entrance into the memorial plot.

Unknown to many people, Lysa had a separate life outside of tricking and the occasional boosting. She got into the game to get away from the family drama in Charlotte. Asheville was two hours away, far enough to do her dirt but close enough for her to come home when she needed to. Her youthful appearance allowed everyone to think she was nineteen, and she played the role to a T. The truth was, Lysa Esmay was twenty-eight and the daughter of a crime boss in Nicaragua. She had access to money but, unlike her siblings and cousins, Lysa never could get with the lifestyle of the rich and famous. She didn't want maids checking in on her and watching her every move. Lysa liked cooking her own food and folding her clothes and being an independent woman.

Lysa wanted to make her own way. And tricking and hustling allowed her to come up on her own terms.

The two car seats in the back seat of the car were empty, as she'd left her two boys, Simon and Jamal, at her parents' estate in Managua, Nicaragua. Normally, the boys would've followed her here, but Lysa wasn't just coming to America for a trip to see family and friends. Lysa was here on business.

Her first order would be to follow up with the police department to see if they had any leads on the death of her lover and partner, Isreala Esmay. Isreala was the junior leader of the violent and wealthy Esmay family. Members of the dark-skinned Hispanic family were beautiful, with many of the members infiltrating the entertainment industry as singers, actors, football players, and models. Their skin tone and expensive education helped them pass for black, and they were black. But when they were around one another, their native heritage took root.

Isreala Esmay had been killed by Leshaun a year and a half prior over their dispute of "territory" for the space that had been known as Dom's Paradice. Isreala wanted the property on North Davidson Street so she could bring back the drug trade in the once profitable area in midtown Charlotte. Isreala held tight to the memories when her family fought over that piece of real estate and the two-year battle it took to get it and the seven-year battle they fought to retain it.

Leshaun saw the opportunity to grow what has become NoDa's art district and to use the Charlotte version of Dom's Paradice as a multicultural melting pot. Leshaun saw the business opportunity to keep her doors open as the crowd changed over time.

The fact that Isreala made a big push for the land and kept herself visible in Charlotte was also a bonus for Leshaun. Several rivals of the Esmay family had put up bounties as high as a quarter of a million dollars for the death of Isreala.

Leshaun planned on and eventually used some of that money to clean up the area around Dom's Paradice and make changes to the former three-story warehouse on the inside.

Lysa looked at herself in the rearview mirror. She was pleased that her giant Afro had held its asymmetrical shape. Her big, golden, triangle-shaped earrings were a nod to her unique style. Lysa was careful to wear Isreala's favorite red tube dress and red two-inch Christian Louboutin red bottom pumps. The outfit was Isreala's favorite, and Lysa took pride in wearing it.

The phone vibrated on Lysa's car mount. Seeing Liam's name flash across the radio dial brought a smile and a sense of peace on her face. She'd been trying for the last few days to reach the man who was the father of her children.

Without hesitation, she pressed the call button on her steering wheel. "Liam, what's up," she greeted him as she continued to look at herself in the mirror. She moved the few strands of hair she thought were out of place to the right side.

"Baby girl, I'm sorry I didn't get in touch with you," Liam started the conversation. "I was stuck in Tijuana trying to close this deal for my clients. It took the Santos family forever to settle on the price of the retail shopping center, but we finally got the deal done. I wanted to surprise you in Managua; but when I got to your parents' estate, the maid let me know you weren't here. I'm waiting on the nanny to get back so I can spend some time with Simon and Jamal."

"I didn't mean for our wires to cross." Lysa felt guilty about not including Liam on the trip. He'd expressed wanting to come and visit the grave, especially since he was on good terms with Isreala and she gave him her blessing to be her "man crush." Usually, Isreala didn't compromise on the sexuality of the women she bedded. Dicks were forbidden unless they were her plastic strap-on. But one look at Liam and Isreala could see how Lysa couldn't fight the temptation. Liam was a nice shade of Coca-Cola caramel, and his presence was alluring. At six foot three, 208 pounds, he was the perfect shape for a shooting guard in the NBA. Instead of using his muscles to move down the court, Liam used his brain to push real estate across half of the country and a few states in Mexico.

That kind of intellect attracted both Lysa and Isreala.

"I'm good. Maybe I can catch a flight to Charlotte," Liam suggested.

Lysa could hear the maids talking in the background and one of the cooks asking Liam in Spanish what he wanted for dinner. His reply in Spanish reminded her of another reason why she loved him: he spoke English, Spanish, and Portuguese with ease.

"I can get into that," Lysa replied. "Maybe we can enjoy a few moments without having to be Mommy and Daddy for once."

Flashbacks came to mind of the last threesome she, Liam, and Isreala had. As her panties got wet, Lysa felt a little guilty knowing that Isreala would never be able to physically make her do that again. Or that she couldn't watch Liam's backside as he stroked Isreala like she'd never been played with before. Enjoying the view of Isreala discovering and being turned out by sex with a man always turned her on and Liam never disappointed.

"That'd be nice. You need to find a spot in the Queen City where we can show off our talents on XTube."

Lysa giggled. It'd been awhile since she let anyone see her and Liam get freaky on cam. "Yeah, I'll do that. Bring your camera so we can get some good angles."

"Bet. Tell Isreala I love her."

Lysa nodded her head as if he could see her. "No worries."

Lysa pressed the END button and dismounted her iPhone from the dashboard. She opened the door and stepped out and made sure her dress was straight and hugged her curves in all the right places. In Lysa's mind, Isreala could see her from heaven, and she wanted to make sure her girl always had a good view.

She walked to the unmarked plot where she helped bury her lover over a year ago. The grass pushed up well over the burial ground, and Lysa still wanted to talk Papa Esmay into letting her plant a tree there. Isreala had always talked about wanting to be buried under or near a tree and, for Lysa, this was the only wish she hadn't been able to grant yet.

"Sorry I'm late," Lysa spoke as she knelt down to the spot where Isreala's head rested. "Liam was getting me hot and bothered." Lysa got comfortable as she stretched out above the ground. "Anyway, next time I come out here, I'll bring him so the two of y'all can talk."

Lysa exhaled, and a tear dropped from her eye. "We still haven't found who killed you yet. Even though I think Leshaun did it, I believe that the Poconos family may have had something to do with it, too. I wouldn't put it past them." Lysa laid her hand in her lap. "CharMeck is dragging their feet. I realize you had a lot of enemies but you had a lover and a friend in me and I think I deserve to see your murderer brought to justice.

"Portia's crazy ass still trying to find out who did it too and that has me concerned because you know Chica Loca. All them screws still loose and Loco and Marcos aren't doing nothing but eggin' her on." Lysa shook her head in disappointment. She could see Isreala doing the same. "I'll give it to her, though: next to me and Liam she was the most loyal to your ass. Portia worshiped the ground you walked on and the girl ain't been right since you been gone.

"You know she asked Papa Esmay to groom her for your spot and she been doing little things to show she got what it takes. Don't ask me because you know I didn't get into that shi—"

Before Lysa could finish her thought, she felt a gloved hand cover her mouth. Another person quickly pounced on her legs and began tying her up.

"Portia ain't got shit on me, bitch," Lysa heard a female voice bark. She couldn't figure out who was wrapping her up, but she did know that the two or more assailants were too strong for her to fight. She tried kicking and moving her arms, but they were overwhelming.

Lysa looked around, but it was no use. Her eyes were covered by some cloth, and her arms were bound behind her. She felt her dress being hiked up and she screamed all she could.

"Ooh, her pussy wet." She could hear a high-pitched masculine voice as she felt a thick finger tracing the outline of her vulva. "Let me find out she gets off talking to dead bitches and shit."

"Well, give her some dick then," the woman commanded.

Lysa heard a package being torn as her body was forced to the ground. She wanted to fight her attacker but, instead, she attempted to open her legs to give her rapist easy access. She hoped that by giving in, her life would be spared.

The latex-covered penis entered her warm opening and, soon, she felt a heavyset man pushing and grinding on her as he grunted. He pumped fast as Lysa struggled to figure out how to breathe in and out of her nose properly. Wheezing was the best she could do as he continued with his 345-horsepower pace. Wetness continued to leak from her vagina, but Lysa knew that some of that was blood. Her rapist was of decent length but had huge girth, thus expanding her walls farther than she was accustomed to.

"Ooo, wheee," the man let off as his body shook violently. Lysa had begun to figure out how to breathe again as she could feel the man orgasming, releasing himself in the condom while still inside of her. He got up, and Lysa was happy that the rape was quick and his weight was off of her.

"Was the pussy good?" the female assailant asked.

"Yeah, ma," were the last words Lysa heard before she heard a gunshot ring out and the man's body fell on top of her. "Ma" surprised her with her own form of revenge. She felt her left elbow pop and the barrel of the gun being pushed to her left side of her head and the bullet rushing through her skull. Her next vision confused her as to whether she was alive or dead.

Chapter Twenty

"Johntae." Leshaun stared at her iPhone that was on top of the coffee table in her suite at the Renaissance. She was on Facetime speaking to the manager of her club. "Thanks for coming to Charlotte on such short notice. I'll be in the club in about three hours. Go ahead and have my suite ready. I want my mimosa and a bottle of Kinky Gold at room temperature."

"Damn, boss." She could see Johntae passing a note to a new employee he'd just hired for security a few days before. "You throwing them drinks back a little too fast."

"Boy, do what I tell you to do," Leshaun ordered as she brought her face close to the screen. "I'm trying to get loose before Noreaga brings that crowd in tonight. He don't come to Charlotte that often and, when he do, I want to make sure I'm that baddest bitch winding and grinding to that reggaeton."

"You keep it up and your ass is gonna be on WorldStar and YouTube," Johntae warned as he walked around and did his midday club inspection. "Everything look the way you want it to?"

"Yeah, and don't worry about the line outside the door before the morning is over."

Leshaun got up from the couch and headed to the kitchen. She reached in the cupboard for a plastic Zaxby's cup to pour some lemonade in. "We tried that shit last year with the running man challenge, and that didn't work. But if I should happen to go viral then that means Dom's Paradice will be poppin' the next few days."

"Let them titties fall out and we'll be viral again."
Johntae smirked.

"Remind me to fire your ass when I get in the door
tonight. Let me find where Prince is and I'll be in later
tonight."

"Bet. I'll make sure VIP is ready for Noreaga and his
boys. Maybe I'll talk him into doing some of his classics
and get the club bouncing."

Leshaun shook her head as she hung up the phone.
Taking a quick sip of her lemonade, she put the cup down
when she looked outside on her patio and still couldn't
see her sister outside. "Dammit, where is that girl?"

No sooner than her question flew out of her mouth,
she heard the toilet flush and the water running from the
small bathroom near the kitchen. Leshaun took another
sip of her lemonade and entered the kitchen.

"If Johntae has your titties falling out of your shirt in a
club full of horny men and lustful women, I'm killing his
ass," Gogo vowed as she walked to the sink, washed her
hands again, and grabbed a glass from the dish drain on
the counter and filled it with tap water.

"Gogo, don't worry. I'm not going to have my titties out,
I promise." Leshaun had no shame in Gogo overhearing
her conversation. Then she realized that she was talking
loud in the living room and had Johntae on speaker.
"You know I'm trying to keep Dom's Paradice jumping. If
people aren't coming, then I'm not getting paid."

"Oh, you getting paid." Gogo arched her left eyebrow
up. "You still dealing with Lysa and Janae?"

"I took care of Lysa last night." Leshaun didn't lie. "Now
she's with the rest of her family."

"What's going to happen when someone wants you to
do something crazy in your club?" Gogo took a seat at
the dining room table. She placed her glass on top of the
glass-top table.

"I'm not going to let it get that far." Leshaun took a seat.

"All the best laid intentions have disappointed many," Gogo warned. "So, you finally ready to tell me what really happened to Tiana?"

"That was an accident." Leshaun pleaded with Gogo to believe her. She almost felt like she was nine years old again sneaking cookies out of the cookie jar.

"She knew better to enter your house without announcing herself or knocking." Gogo had no remorse in her response. "For one, I taught her better than that. And two, I feel like she had dishonor and disloyalty on her mind by coming at you like that to begin with. She crossed the line of y'all's friendship so to hell with her."

Leshaun wasn't surprised that Gogo was so blunt and heartless. They got it from their daddy. She looked at the woman who still looked like she could take on the female heavyweight champion on her best day.

"You think you gonna have some new bitches in the club tonight?" Gogo looked Leshaun in the eye and spoke as if that were a demand instead of a question.

Leshaun shook her head and caught an attitude. "You not getting no 'bitches,' quote unquote, talking about them like that."

"Look here, little girl, just because you're the oldest, that doesn't mean you're the sexiest." Gogo spoke the truth. "I can make a sixty-year-old's dick get hard without the aid of Viagra, and I can hang better than most of these young, new bitches. I ain't had no dick in a minute, and I'm giving you fair warning that I'm fucking one of the niggas who bring they ass to your club tonight."

Leshaun ignored Gogo's comment and gathered her things. The last thing she wanted was to have to check Gogo for being disrespectful. Gogo looked nothing like her and their father. She was light skinned with dark brown eyes, and she had the body of a video bitch.

Leshaun was several pounds heavier than she would have wanted but she was heavy in the right places. She loved her round head and soft features. Gogo had taken after their mother's side of the family once she hit puberty, but to hear them tell it, Gogo acted just like their daddy.

"You still gonna have the niggas in the club tonight?" Gogo asked as Leshaun was about to walk out the front door.

Leshaun wiped a tear from her eye and chuckled. "You get on my damn nerves."

"I'm coming up there, and you better have me someone fly, or I'm whipping your ass with a belt."

Leshaun closed the door and walked to her car. With Lysa out of the picture, she could focus her energy on making sure her "sons" were ready to discuss business. No one could afford to have a misstep, and she really wanted to hear everyone's plans for how they were going to make up this money to get the property up and running and how they were going to run these other businesses simultaneously.

Chapter Twenty-one

You got lost? WTF! Anyway, I'm gonna hit the road to visit my aunt in Charlotte. Just got so much shit on my mind. I'ma stay a few days, and yes, I'll be back for our next gig. Thank you 4 everything. Love ya!

Janae glanced at the message Lysa left. In her mind, she thanked Lysa for making it to the room Bryson set up for her at the Four Points by Sheraton on Woodfin Street. She had no problems following the directions that he gave. Janae stepped on the elevator and pushed the button for the fifth floor. As Janae rode up to the room, she took pride in the fact that, unlike Lloyd, Bryson was more low-key. Everything didn't have to be glitz and glam with him. She could see that, in the future, Bryson could overtake Lloyd and run everything when the timing was right. When Janae reached the room, she took out the card key and slid it through the reader to open the door.

"Welcome home." Bryson invited her in. "I've been waiting on you."

"Hold on, damn. It's worth the wait." Janae fought off a hug. She didn't want to appear to eager.

"Is it?" the guy from Leshaun's party asked. Janae was alarmed because Bryson didn't say anything about a dude being with him and if Janae had known that, she wouldn't have agreed to show up. A part of her felt stupid for beginning to believe that it was a possibility for Bryson to turn her hoeish ass from hooker to housewife.

"Girl, you outdone yourself." Bryson licked his lips. "How much do I owe you?"

Janae looked at the guy in the corner with a smirk on his face, and she felt uneasy.

"Give me two hundred and fifty dollars and call it a night." She mentally prepared herself to no longer see Bryson as an honorable and respectable man but just another john she could get one over on.

The man from the lodge reached for his wallet on the nightstand and pulled out a wad of bills he bought to make it rain on the strippers shaking their body parts. "That's fair; here's two hundred and fifty dollars."

As Janae counted the money, she began to look toward him.

"Janae, you know my dude thinks you're fine and—"

"I'm flattered." Janae had an idea where this was headed and decided to nip it in the bud before it could get started. "But I got to go!"

"Wait! What I'm trying to say is—" Bryson tried to reach for her and Janae snatched her arm away.

"I don't give a damn what you're trying to say. I'm not falling in love with you," she vented at Bryson. She fought hard to keep at bay the tears that wanted to fall from her being so stupid.

"Who said I wanted to be in love with you?" the guy butted in. Janae saw him place the gun on his lap. "I just want to watch you two fuck!"

Bryson walked up behind Janae and began to kiss on her neck. "I'm sorry. Don't resist. He will hurt us both!" His warning was a little too late.

Janae was shaken. "Look, I said I'm not fucking with you like that. Don't put your hands on me," Janae cautioned him while staring at the pistol. The pistol raised and Janae could feel Bryson cup her breast. She had to think of a plan and fast, but she had no idea where to begin. Janae began to give in to the feeling of defeat and ecstasy. Her head rolled back as Bryson began to explore her body.

"That's it," Bryson encouraged her. "Let go and enjoy." He leaned in and whispered, "We'll take it as far as we need to until one of us can snatch the gun from him."

Janae looked toward the bed where the guy was sitting, still trying to keep her composure. Janae noticed that he slipped his hands in his pants and started massaging himself. Bryson imitated his movements and, soon, Janae's panties were filled with Bryson's massive fingers tickling the lining of her lower set of lips. Janae moaned and grunted in a moment of ecstasy; her body shook uncontrollably.

"That's how it's done." The guy shouted excitedly, his hand movements increasing in pace. "Bitch." He smirked.

Once the guy got his excitement and Bryson left her body alone, Janae put on her clothes and grabbed the duffle bag while walking toward the door.

"It looks like to me you enjoyed yourself," he taunted as he continued to smirk and lick his lips.

"Did I?" Janae questioned as she reached for her purse. Janae dug out three one dollar bills and tossed them on to his lap. "Here's three dollars. I just paid for it."

"Bitch, you know that was worth more!"

He was right. Janae's dignity and self-respect were worth way more than the funky three dollars that she gave him. But the purpose in all of this was to show that he didn't intimidate her; at least, that's what Janae wanted him to believe.

Chapter Twenty-two

Inside a brick two-story Baptist church in Burlington, North Carolina, Kofi knelt at the altar on his knees, eyes closed. He couldn't control the sweating, even though he patted himself down a minute ago. He looked around and realized he was alone, almost.

"Dear Lord, I hope you forgive murderers and rapists, for I am both." Kofi's mind travelled back to a few nights ago. He, 9ine, and Zay staked out an upscale beauty salon. They were supposed to just catch the owner, and make him give up that night's deposit, which they estimated to be almost $10,000. During a scuffle with a man who was much stronger than anticipated, Kofi shot and killed the man. "That night wasn't supposed to happen, Lord, I swear. We were supposed to just take the money. We weren't supposed to take his life."

9ine grew tired of waiting for Kofi so they could be in and out. He walked up and knelt next to Kofi at the altar. "Unless you are doing a séance to bring back the dead, your time here is useless."

"Shut the fuck up," Kofi whispered. His eyes opened, and he looked to his right. "Somebody's got to pray for us."

"I'm gonna let that slide, but don't get too comfortable here. We have a job to do," 9ine reminded him.

Kofi rolled his eyes and scrunched his face. He didn't want to admit that 9ine was right. They were there to do a job. "Can I have a few minutes with the Lord before we rob Him?"

9ine moved in closer to Kofi. "You shoulda taken care of that last night. Now get your string-bean-looking ass up before I fuck you up."

"Where's Zay at?" Kofi got up and followed 9ine away from the altar.

"Where do you think he's at?" 9ine snapped.

Kofi was in pace with 9ine. He scanned down to his chest to see the fake law enforcement badge on his chest.

Zay could smell the clean sheets his client laid on the king-sized bed in the upscale hotel room she paid for. He smirked, knowing he was where Kofi wanted to be, but in order for them to pull this off, he had to play his position. Memphis, Tennessee was easily a seven-and-a-half-hour drive down I-40, but Gogo worked her magic and managed to get him a roundtrip, nonstop flight from American Airlines for about $300.

"Are you ready for mama?" the MILF he was waiting for asked.

Zay placed his head in his hand and posed naked. The only thing covering his front was a box of chocolates in a heart-shaped box with a cutout for his "candy." A wicked smirk was on his face. The MILF came out in a sexy black teddy set that highlighted her curves and defied her age. Zay moved around, trying not to let his hard-on show. "Hell, yeah!" he answered.

"Hmm, you're gonna have to show me." The MILF crawled on the bed, her fragrance reaching Zay before she did. He threw the box of chocolates on the floor. The MILF was pleased with what she saw. "Mmm, I like it."

"Well, all you gotta do is come get it." Zay licked his lips and blew her a kiss. "I got all night."

"You better." The MILF crawled on the bed seductively and straddled Zay. She lifted up slightly to unsnap the button on her crotch, giving Zay easy access. He quickly pulled out one of the chocolate decorations that held a compartment for the KYNG condom he secured there. The MILF moved fast to tear the condom and put it on her lips. She unwrapped it with her mouth and rolled it down his flesh. She pushed Zay on his back and hopped on top, lining his thick dick at her entrance. Once he was snuggly insider her, she moaned.

Kofi and 9ine headed toward the usher's office. "I should've gotten the job at the hotel," Kofi complained.

"You should've won the dick-measuring contest," 9ine snapped back.

"I didn't know Zay had an advantage." Kofi looked around to make sure no one from the church recognized him. "It's my dad's fault," he mumbled.

"That might have been your mom's fault." 9ine grew agitated. He didn't want to stay another minute in the church and Kofi's whining wasn't helping the situation. "Look, man, I don't want to talk about what Zay's sticking. We got somebody we need to stick."

9ine kicked in the closed door. Three ladies inside were startled as they were in the middle of putting the money they just counted into the bank bag. "Alamance police! Put your hands up!" 9ine yelled.

Kofi got behind a young lady and put some handcuffs on her. "You have the right to remain silent. Anything you say or do will be used to against you in a court of law. You have a right to an attorney—"

"What are we being arrested for?" one of the ladies asked.

"Want to explain this?" 9ine pulled out a small bag of snow white from one lady's purse.

The other two ladies turned on the lady with the bag. Her eyes grow big. "I, uh . . ." one of the ladies started stuttering.

"Hush," 9ine ordered as he and Kofi handcuffed the other two ladies, who had their heads down. Kofi led the ladies out of the room while 9ine snatched the bank bags containing the tithes and offerings collected for the day. 9ine and Kofi led the three ladies to a fake police car and shoved all three into the back seat. 9ine got in the front seat while Kofi put the purses he confiscated into the trunk of the car.

Zay worked a sweat as he power-drilled into the MILF. Her legs were over his shoulders, and he firmly pinned her arms to the bed. Up and down he went unmercifully as she screamed in ecstasy.

"Oh, fuck me!" the MILF panted as she wiggled and squeezed Zay's dick.

For his part, he was surprised that she got wet and that her orgasms were strong and powerful. He liked it just the same. He hated that the only thing separating him and her was the thin piece of latex, but it was necessary that he keep in mind that there was supposed to be as little evidence of his presence as possible.

Zay cursed himself for sweating, but he figured in a minute it would be all over. The MILF hung in there, but he noticed that her eyes were starting to droop. He smiled and grunted as he continued to pound inside her. After a few strokes, he stopped. He looked down and felt her pulse. She was breathing, but her mind was out of it.

Finally! The MILF was asleep, thanks to the drink she was drinking before she rode Zay. Zay got up quickly and reached under the bed for his bag, and he pulled out his non-latex gloves. Swiftly, he made a rope and some duct tape appear, and he went to work tying the MILF up and putting her in the tub.

Faster than Janet Jackson at a concert, Zay put on black ankle socks, black mesh boxer briefs, and some khaki-colored Dickies attire. Zay picked up the glass with the rest of the drink, and he dumped the rest down the toilet. He opened a small bag containing cleaning supplies, and he cleaned the toilet and wiped down the doorknobs. He entered the room and pulled the sheets from the bed and put them in the athletic bag. He grabbed the trash and the food and put them in a big trash bag. Zay grabbed the MILF's purse, pulled out the cash and the credit cards, and placed them in the suitcase. He looked back at the bathroom and didn't hear a sound. Feeling safe, Zay grabbed his bags, put on a baseball cap, and exited the room, escaping through the stairway at the end of the building and out the side door of the hotel.

Kofi and 9ine waited in a small, rank hotel room off of Smoky Park Highway. The old-fashioned hotel was in Candler, a small town next to Asheville heading toward the Smoky Mountains. The three-and-a-half-hour drive from Burlington to Asheville wore their nerves.

"We said eight o'clock." Kofi looked at the time on his phone. "He better not be late."

"Kofi, chill. You know Zay flew back," 9ine defended him as he surfed Facebook, fighting to ignore his stomach pains. Before he could say something back to Kofi, he noticed it was 7:59 p.m. when a knock was heard from the door. Kofi got up to answer it. Zay rushed in and threw a small athletic bag on the bed.

"Mr. Brown arrived on time. Had to book it in traffic." Zay looked to 9ine. "Good looking out, man."

9ine nodded his head. "I told you, man, in a few years, we gonna all be taking Ubers to get to and from everywhere."

"I gave him a fifty dollar tip for dodging that sheriff who set up a traffic stop right when we were supposed to get off at exit 37. We had to drive into Canton and come

back up Smoky Park Highway the long way." Zay looked
at Kofi. "Where do you find these spots, man? Seems like
you been everywhere."

"I can't tell all my secrets." Kofi chuckled. "You know I
went road tripping."

"Yeah; every time the car moved, you were on the
passenger's side," Zay replied.

Kofi cut Zay off. "So how much did we make?"

"We?" Zay questioned. "I'm the one who risked getting
herpes for this shit. You know that's incurable."

"True, but if it weren't for me giving you the lowdown
on my psychology professor, you wouldn't have been
able to find her. You wore a condom didn't you?" Kofi
snapped back.

"What you think?" Zay sneered.

Kofi shook his head. Zay unzipped the bag and dumped
the money on Kofi's bed. "There's ten thousand dollars. I
didn't think the old lady would be walking around with
that kind of money." Zay was excited.

Kofi picked up some of the twenties. "I told you I used
to break her off to make sure I got an A in that class."
The men laughed, and Kofi smiled as he eyed the rest of
the money as well as the takings. "She'll probably wake
up and forget your face. She'll probably be so ashamed
that she won't tell anybody. She's used to buying dick;
probably planned on getting some more from someone
else. Anyway, we got five grand from the church."

"So we each walk away with about five thousand dollars?" Zay verified. Kofi divided the money into piles,
separating the denominations. Then he gave everyone an
equal amount of each bill and put the rest up for Leshaun.
"What time you delivering papers in the morning?"

9ine looked up at him. "Same time I deliver them every
morning."

"I was thinking she could get me a route," Zay admitted.

"Mr. Master's Degree delivering the *Citizen-Times?* Not happening. Besides, I told you to get that cashier job in Druid Hills. What happened to that?" Kofi questioned.

"You didn't tell me I had to bang the manager to get it," Zay answered.

Kofi shook his head. "You're so fucking hardheaded."

"I'll take the job," 9ine offered.

"No!" Kofi yelled and grilled Zay. "We are in this together. Everything she tell you to do is because she thought it through. We need menial, minimum-wage jobs so we can keep this extra money we get under the radar. How we look with money in the bank, new clothes and shit, and we have no way to show how we earned the money?"

Zay and Kofi grilled each other.

"I guess I . . ." Zay was the first to look away.

"Next time, do what I ask you to do. Now we gotta wait a month before we get another job lined up for us. We gotta balance this tricking and robbery shit, man."

Zay picked up his cash and left.

"I should kill him," Kofi grumbled once the door closed.

"Why you say that?" 9ine wondered.

"Because he's about to be a problem, that's why. You didn't see that new 'fit Tracey rockin'? Cost at least five hundred dollars. That's why I told y'all: only get what you need to shit, shower, and shave. Nothing else. Give Leshaun the rest of the money. Help with a bill or two."

9ine let it go. He didn't want to argue with Kofi. All he knew was that, in thirty-six hours, they knocked down 5 percent of the dent needed to fix the Gamble property. He knew his mom and aunt had other plans and may have matched what they made tonight. 9ine loved when he, Kofi, and Zay were getting along and he hated when they appeared to be at war with one

another. Kofi and Zay were the closest things to broth-
ers he had, and he didn't really rock with Ten socially
once he got in his teens. Leshaun spared her from
tricking and deep down he was glad.

The thought crossed his mind to check on his mom to
make sure she was all right.

Chapter Twenty-three

Leshaun couldn't hide her excitement as she rolled through the streets of Asheville with Prince. He gave her a late-night tour of the city behind the wheel of his metallic black Jaguar F-TYPE coupe. She felt like a third grade student on a field trip. Prince wasn't a man of her lifestyle. He wasn't hood or a thug, and the challenge he presented tested Leshaun to stay on point. Her thoughts ran wild when they reached his yellow four-bedroom home under a full moon.

"Welcome to my home." He smiled as he drove into the two-car garage.

Leshaun waited until he slowed to a stop before she showed her gratitude. "C'mere." She motioned with her finger.

Prince leaned toward her and pressed his lips against hers. He tasted her mouth like a glass of aged wine. He sucked on her tongue and lips and slid his hand up her thigh with the engine running.

Leshaun caressed his face, kissing him and showing him the undeniable desire she had for him. She moaned against his sweet lips when his fingers stroked the side of her breasts. Each thump of her heart matched the whetting pulse of her pussy. In the height of her passion, she lowered a hand across the center console and down between his legs. She lightly bit his bottom lip when she discovered the lump below his waist.

"Help me," she moaned breathlessly against his lips. "Pull it out."

Prince spread his legs as she fumbled with his belt. He took her tongue back inside his mouth as the garage door lowered behind them. His dick strained under his clothes, waiting to spring free. He slid his hand up her arm when her fingers dove inside his pants. This was the best feeling in the world to Prince. Well, maybe not the best, but it stood in the top range.

"Hands on the wheel," she whispered with her fingers circled around his dick.

"Baby," he panted against her neck. "Let's go in—"

"Do it!" She squeezed his dick with all her strength.

He licked up her neck as he followed her command.

"Now sit back. And don't you dare take your hands off the wheel."

Prince sat speechless as Leshaun adjusted her position to lean over in his lap. She stroked his dick up and down, pausing to smear whatever drops of precum over the tip she found. He flexed his grip on the padded leather steering wheel as Leshaun lowered her wet mouth down his penis. The warmth from her mouth took his breath.

"Leshaun," he groaned as her head bobbed up and down over his lap. "Ooohh, baby, this feels so good! Mmmm, your mouth is so wet! Lips so soft."

She maintained a controlled pace and massaged him with her soothing wet lips. His flavorsome dick stretched her jaws as she tried to swallow all of him. She couldn't restrain herself to stop. Up and down she sucked, constricting her lips on the upward trip.

"Leshaun, please don't stop!" he blurted with a concentrated grip on the wheel.

She sped up, sucking fast, slurping at her own spit and the overflow of precum. Her mouth tried to consume the solid flesh over and over. She lost her rhythm for a moment when his ass shot off the seat, pushing more of his dick up her throat. No complaints rolled from her mouth. Her tongue flicked up and down his shaft; she needed this. She took him back inside her mouth, mad with a thirst for him.

Prince wriggled inside the cavity of her sensual mouth. He chanted her name as she bathed his dick with her warm and wet tongue. "Leshaun!" His foot hit the accelerator, revving the engine. "Leshaun!" he shouted, fucking upward into her mouth. The RPMs rose. She kept sucking as the growl of the engine bounced off the walls.

Leshaun sucked piggishly on his lubricious hammer as slobber ringed her bobbing lips. His climax raced up and into her mouth without warning. She surprised herself by the raw reaction she treated him with. She swallowed his warmth, and cuddled him against her face while kissing it.

Prince eased his foot off the pedal when Leshaun sat up. "Why . . . why did you do that?" he asked in a state of shock.

Leshaun wiped her mouth as it sank in. She shrugged. *Damn! I'm tripping for real!*

He sat in silence for a moment. "That was the best!"

She forced herself to look at him. "I don't know why I just did that," she explained. "But FYI, I don't regret doing it and—"

"It's natural, baby."

She had to smile at his use of her own words. "Um, I'm in need of a shower because I'm like, really soaked from sucking your dick."

"How about I tend to that? And then we can take a shower together."

She glanced at his wet, limp dick. "That's what's up."

Seconds later she stepped out of the Jaguar and wondered what awaited her inside his home.

***

Sated to the point of falling asleep, Leshaun had that feeling after she squirted her fifth wall-climbing climax from Prince's handsome face.

"I noticed you didn't bring a bunch of clothes," he called from the shower.

Leshaun rolled to her side and admired his silhouette through the green frosted shower glass. Her body tingled at the sight of him. "You had me under a deadline," she replied from his large bed.

"I'll take you shopping tomorrow. And it's not up for any debate."

"Yes, my king," she joked. "So, what is it you do again? Your career?"

"I work at IHOP, and I pimp these hoes."

Leshaun rolled her eyes. She hated that he took her occupation as a joke sometimes. "Then you must be good at it to live like this."

"I get by," he replied modestly. "Oh, yeah! Guess what's buzzing on YouTube? It hit the scene and went viral just a few minutes before I got off work."

"What?" she asked with little interest.

"Well, this lesbian basketball player got caught cheating by her partner with a man and the girl robbed them."

Leshaun sat up. "When did it happen?"

"At the DoubleTree Hilton on Hendersonville Road. It's crazy because the girl got put on blast by her partner for not being all the way gay."

None of that shit mattered to Leshaun. Her concern sat with Zay not getting caught up. "Uh, did they catch the girl who robbed them?"

"Not that I know of. If you want to view it, you can you use my iPad on the dresser. It's already online."

Leshaun shot from under the covers and crossed the room naked. She had to view the clip to make sure Zay hadn't fucked up in any form or fashion.

"What time is it? My watch is on the night table," Prince asked.

"Four fifteen." She read the time off the iPad as she carried it back to the bed.

"I'll set the alarm for noon because you're wearing me out."

Leshaun ignored his comment as she sat cross-legged on the bed with the iPad on her lap. "What's the clip listed under?"

"Uh, 'Busted My Cheating Bitch,'" he told her. "It's about a five-minute rant."

Leshaun viewed the YouTube clip from start to end. The WNBA star's lover put her on blast for the world to see. There was no mention of Zay's name or nothing that could lead to an arrest. From what she viewed, the basketball player's lover was simply and deservingly so pissed. Relieved, she left YouTube and pulled up her Facebook page while Prince continued his shower. She was shocked that Lloyd sent her an instant message. Leshaun rolled her eyes at one of his posts on her wall.

Hope we can work our issues out. I do miss you!

She scrolled down the page, deleting Lloyd's posts because she knew he wasn't talking 'bout shit! In truth, no one on her page earned a reply. She glanced toward the shower to check on Prince. *Damn, he take showers longer than me!* With time on her side, she typed in a name to search: Zay Brown.

She wanted to check the status on the next lick. "Damn!" she muttered when she discovered his page was private. After a few seconds though, she sent a friend request and left the next move up to Zay.

By the time Prince exited the shower, Leshaun was done with the iPad. She greeted him with a sultry tongue kiss when he rejoined her under the green satin sheet.

They touched each other intimately, her hand gently stroking his dick, his fingers fiddling the slippery folds of her pussy. She lay under him, shocked at her need of more sex. They took separate showers to avoid fucking again. All it did for them was a period to rest.

"You smell so good!" He licked between her plump breasts as his new erection filled her hand.

"Let's do it one more time," she gasped. "And then we'll call it a night."

"I can't get enough of you," he moaned as his dick brushed up the length of her sopping wet pussy.

"Grab a condom right quick." She squirmed as she gripped his penis like a joystick.

Prince reached blindly for the box of condoms on the night table. He took her left nipple inside his mouth as he flipped his watch aside.

"Hurry, baby." She rubbed all over his chest and shoulders.

Prince reached back and hooked her right leg in the bend of his arm. "Shit!" he blurted.

"What?" Leshaun stared up at him.

Prince rolled from between her legs with a heavy sigh.

"Prince, what's wrong?" Leshaun sat up quickly with her titties swaying.

Her answer came when he dropped the empty box of condoms between them. "We used them all."

"For real! How many was in it?"

"Uh, six."

Leshaun laid her hand on his hard stomach. "Please tell me you have some more."

"If I did, I would have it on."

"Well, you need to go out and get some."

"At four in the morning?"

"Yes, at four in the morning. Now get up and get going."

Prince came up on his elbows. "You serious?"

She nodded and slid her hand up and down his stomach. "Yes," she whispered just before she leaned in for a kiss.

Four minutes later he backed out of the garage in his Jaguar to meet the needs of his younger mate.

Leshaun fought and won against the urge to snoop around after Prince left. The house was strange and unfamiliar to her, so she remained in bed. *Think I might suck his dick again,* she thought as she lightly rubbed her clit. She closed her eyes and tried to think of something kinky to surprise him with. Her mind focused in on his deep attraction to her breasts. In nearly every position, he either had his hand or mouth on one or both of her ample breasts. She grinned. *I'll let him titty fuck me. And then I'll—*

Her thoughts were stalled by an alerting tone from her smartphone. She threw the sheets back and rolled to Prince's side of the bed to grab her smartphone. The familiar tone alerted her to any new activity on her Facebook page. To her shock, Zay accepted her friend request. *That was quick!*

She lay back down with the smartphone with a strong, compelling urge to check out all the hype on his page. She viewed his pics, mainly the ones that came from Instagram. From what she saw, quite a few of them had to be removed due to the content. Chasity flashed across her mind. Seconds later she viewed his friends list and came up on Chasity's fake Facebook profile. Even on her real profile, no pictures could be found. *Let me see what this nigga looks like.* She went to his pictures and lost her breath when his face appeared on the screen.

Prince sighed and shook his head as his smartphone buzzed. A block away from his crib he slowed to a stop near a fire hydrant. If he didn't answer the call, it would make his issues worse.

"What do you want, Sarah?" he asked without masking his ill mood.

"Why have you been avoiding me?" she begged.

He squeezed his eyes shut. "Sarah! I'm one inch from taking a restraining order out on your ass! I'm pleading with you to back off!"

"But—"

"This is your last warning! We both have our careers to think of and yours the most. Things just didn't work for us!"

"That's how you truly feel?"

"Yes," he answered, full of regret over choosing his former boss and business partner over Leshaun.

To his joy, she ended the call without a single word. Pushing Sarah from his mind, he pulled from the curb to head back home.

"Baby!" he shouted when he later stepped through the door. "I'll be sorta disappointed if you fell asleep on me." He dropped his keys on the kitchen island along the way to his bedroom. "I got a surprise for you."

Oddly, the only reply he got was silence.

"Leshaun?" He tossed the box of condoms from hand to hand. "Please don't be asleep." He smiled as he nudged his bedroom door open. He came to a halt at the sight inside his bedroom.

"Why the fuck you lie to me!" Leshaun shouted, fully dressed with her hands on her hips.

Prince stood in the doorway. "First off," he said, his voice staying level, "you need to lower your voice and talk to me without all the drama."

"Drama!" Leshaun frowned. "You're the one causing all the drama by all the fucking lies you've been telling me."

Prince shoved the box of condoms in his pocket. "What did I lie to you about?"

"Everything!" she shouted even louder. "How the fuck can you explain all this bullshit you dropped in my ear!" She stared at him with fire in her eyes.

Prince took two steps toward her then stopped. "Again, what did I lie to—"

"How come you didn't tell me you *knew* Zay was your cousin? I mean seriously. It's bad enough 9ine is my son, and his father is one of my cousins. And then I find out this shit and his family, including you, could've taken him in and didn't! This is past fucked up!" Her nose flared. "He's your fuckin' cousin!" she shouted in his face. "FYI! I just got off your Facebook page!"

"I can explain everything if you'll just calm down." Prince sat at the foot of the bed as Leshaun kept her distance.

"And why should I believe anything that comes out your mouth!" Leshaun snapped. "The first day we met, I fucking asked who your family was, and you said you weren't related to too many people here! A fucking barefaced lie!"

Prince sighed. "Look, I didn't lie. I didn't find out the truth until later on. Zay is my *distant cousin*. My . . ."

Leshaun smacked her lips. "That's some bullshit! When you knew the truth was when I should've known the truth. I raised that boy and did his family a big fuckin' favor. What the hell!"

"Is that how you see it?" He kept his calm because he understood her anger.

"What I see is a lying-ass muthafucka! I can't believe this!" She threw her arms in the air. "I'm like, really pissed at you right now!"

Prince nodded. "I can understand."

"Anything else I need to know about?" she asked with her face fixed with a frown.

He shook his head. "Do you want to leave?"

She blew hard through her nose. "If I wanted to leave, I would have done so!"

"So you're staying?"

"I don't know!" She crossed her arms. *Fuck! I'm digging this dude, but he always got some shit with him.*

"I'd like you to stay with me." He stood. "I was wrong to not tell you, and I'm sorry."

Leshaun averted her eyes to the floor. "I bet you were," she mumbled.

"I promise to be fully honest with you from here on out." He closed the space between them and waited for her reply. "Don't stay mad with me."

She smacked her lips and looked at anything other than the man in front of her. Even if she wanted to, she couldn't stay mad at him. In the back of her mind, she thought of the mass of her own lies that she stood in. For a split second, she felt moved to keep it real with him, but her common sense kicked in. *All he wants is some pussy.* She unfolded her arms while doing her best to conceal her smile.

"I knew you wasn't mad."

"You don't know shit!" She playfully shoved him in the chest. "And don't lie to me no more."

"I promise." He took her in his arms, easing his hands around her waist. "Now, will you stay with me?"

She circled her arms around his neck. "Maybe." She kissed his lips.

"Why maybe?"

"Ummm, because I can't let you lie to me and get off with a free pass."

"Punish me then. I'm down for whatever to make up my wrong toward you." He slid his hands down to her juicy ass and squeezed.

"Mmmm, you squeezing my ass like it belongs to you," she purred as she pressed her breasts against his chest.

"That's because I want it to." He kissed her with a brief tongue action. "In fact, I want all of you to belong to me."

"What are you trying to say? No games. What's up?"

Prince pulled her against his throbbing erection. "I can show you better than I can tell you."

Leshaun wanted this. She wanted him and more. "Show me," she whispered. "Show me right now."

Leshaun started the next morning like she ended last night. She clawed at the bed sheets as Prince drove in and out of her slippery hole from the back. She gasped with each thrust that had her ass clapping and jerking back and forth.

"Prince!" she shouted as a wave of pleasure surged in her stomach. "Get up in it! Get up in my pussy!" She suffered under his lengthy strokes with her ass billowing.

"My pussy!" He smacked her juicy ass without changing the pace of his mild strokes. "Who pussy is it?" he puffed with sweat trickling down his chest and abdomen.

"Yours!" Leshaun shouted with her face on the pillow. "It's all yours! All yours! Mmm, you fucking me soooo damn good!"

Prince fell into a hypnotic daze at the sight and sounds of her ass clapping back against him. He stood at the edge of the bed, fucking her efficiently with his measured stabs.

Leshaun bit the pillow when her pussy abruptly clenched in midstroke around his penis. The pressure rushed out from her body like a tsunami. It took her breath away and curled her toes.

"Prince!" she whined as she popped her pussy hard on the length of his veiny dick.

"Cum, baby!" He tightened his grip above the flare of her jiggling hips. "Cum all over my dick and balls. Show me how good this dick is!" He closed his eyes and threw his head back.

Leshaun had no control over her body as her climax fired off like a string of firecrackers. Again she allowed him to show how much he wanted all of her. As she came up on her elbows, she begged him to cum. She circled her pounding pussy with his strong, long dicking strokes. "Mmm, I love it like this!" She bit her bottom lip and put a dip in her back. "Come on, baby. This your pussy now. Tear it up!"

The loud applause caused by Leshaun's big ass was too much for Prince to enjoy. All of his thoughts ran with the woman in front of him. He slid a hand to cup and fondle her soft breasts as his fourth discharge spewed from his erection.

Leshaun shivered on his dick, grinding back against him, taking all of him inside her. The proof of their new stage sat on the night table untouched and unopened: the box of condoms.

Chapter Twenty-four

"What the fuck are you doing here?" Janae stared at Bryson with her pretty face twisted. "It's nine o'clock in the morning!"

"I came to see Lysa." Bryson held up a Bojangles bag. "And I got some breakfast for her." He grinned at the sight of her bare titties under the intimate apparel.

Janae snatched the bag. "She ain't here!" She turned from the door and stomped toward the living room.

Bryson stared at her phat ass cheeks under the see-through green teddy. He invited himself in without taking his eyes off Janae.

"You got some shit with you!" she snapped from the couch as she pulled a sausage biscuit from the bag. "How the hell you gonna all of a sudden pop up after we just got fucked over?"

He shrugged. "It's our secret." He grinned. "Like you said about the—"

"Boy, shut up!" She unwrapped the biscuit.

"Where Lysa?" He sat across from her on the loveseat so he could look between her legs. *Mmmm, that pussy phat as hell! I gotta get back up in it!*

"Gone to Charlotte," she forced between bites of the sausage biscuit.

"For what?"

She shrugged and spread her legs a little just to tease.

Bryson rubbed his chin, sat back, and adjusted his dick. "Uh, what about last night? I—"

"That was business, Bryson. Please don't be on no feeling me type shit. He wanted a freak show, and you got to cop a feel of the pussy. It was that simple, okay?"

"So you saying it'll never happen again?"

She sighed and chewed hard. *This nigga pussy whipped al-fucking-ready!* She swallowed.

"Not even for the same deal we made last night?" He made no further effort to hide the swelling between his legs.

Janae froze with the breakfast biscuit in her mouth. *Now he's talking my language!* She bit into the biscuit and chewed slowly. *Can't front like the dick wasn't good. If I do this, I have to be on my 007 shit and keep it on the down low.*

Bryson had an eyeful of what he wanted again between Janae's healthy thighs.

"Why you and Lloyd switch girls and shit?"

"Huh?" He blinked from the trance of staring at her chubby pussy lips.

"You heard me!" She kept her legs open.

Bryson licked his dry lips. "We both freaks and we like women who down to do some freak things in bed."

"Like what?"

Bryson frowned. "Why we talking 'bout this shit? What's up with our—"

"Just answer the fucking question before I get pissed!"

"I like to raw dawg bitches in the ass!" he blurted. "And I ain't got no shame in eating it, baby."

Janae rolled her eyes. "If we do this shit, I want the weed up front. Ain't no bullshit talking 'bout you have to wait on somebody to do this or that. And it has to be that good shit!" she stated.

He nodded. "Twice a month is all I can swing." His eyes lusted over her tits and pussy.

"I can rock with that." She smiled and lowered her gaze at the lengthy print along his leg. "When will you re-up again?"

Bryson stood and reached up under his baggy shirt. "I got two ounces right here." He produced the product and laid it on the living room table.

Janae dropped the half-eaten biscuit in the bag and set it on the floor. "You really tried to lick Lysa's ass and she wouldn't let you?"

He nodded. "You think it's nasty?"

She wiped a few chunks from her lips and shook her head. "You wanna lick my ass?"

Bryson stepped around the living room table and reached for her hand. When she stood, he turned her around and filled his hands with her well-rounded butt cheeks. "Wanna jump in the shower?"

"Ain't needed. My ass and pussy stay fresh like roses, baby," she whispered over her shoulder.

Bryson lifted the back of the thin teddy over her ass. "Damn it's so soft and phat." He rubbed all over her ass and hips while kissing along her shoulder. "Get on the couch and hold it open fo' me."

Janae couldn't front on Bryson. He had her entire body buzzing. Nipples, pussy, and ass. She slipped her thong off first and swallowed a moan when he reached between her legs.

"Pussy wet as fuck!" He roved a finger up and down the line of her pussy while mashing his erection against her pillowy ass.

"Let's get one thing straight. I ain't . . . Mmm, that's my spot, boy!" She jerked her pussy from his dancing fingers. "Ain't sucking your dick. Don't ask and don't put it near my face," she asserted.

"I'm cool with that." He leaned his face against her ear.

"Good." She moved toward the couch.

Bryson leered at her well-built hood thick frame as she slid the teddy straps off. His dick jumped when the teddy circled her feet. She took her position and knelt on the couch, her titties swaying beneath. Her hands gripped the back of the couch when Bryson spread her butt cheeks open like the Red Sea. Her body responded to the touch of his tongue. She gave him her ass to eat. But just breaths before she could tell him to stick his tongue in her ass, Lloyd kick the door off the hinges.

"What's your muthafucking problem!" Janae shouted at Lloyd without bothering to cover her nakedness. Lloyd was furious as he made his way from the door to the bed.

Lloyd glared at Bryson. "You might wanna bounce, homeboy."

"Who the fuck you think you is!" Janae got up in Lloyd's face. "Kicking my gotdamn door in like you own some shit up in here!" She shoved Lloyd and watched him stumble a few feet back. "What the fuck is wrong with you!"

"Put some clothes on!" he said, gritting his teeth.

"Ain't putting shit on!" she shouted in Lloyd's face.

Bryson swallowed his pride and made his exit. Whatever beef she had with Lloyd, it didn't mean shit to him. "What the hell you do that for?" Janae gestured toward the door as soon as Bryson left. She really didn't want him to leave, and that fueled her anger even more.

"You fucking know why!" Lloyd turned and tried to fit the door in place as best he could. Once he got it situated, he sighed and turned to face Janae. His eyes roamed over her honey-brown D-cups and the pointy brown nipples. He felt little remorse for cockblocking Bryson. As he looked her body up and down, he fell into a trance.

"Lloyd!" Her voice broke the spell.

Lloyd cleared his voice. "Why you playing games with me? I don't want you fuckin' wit' no one else!"

Oh, God! I should've stayed with Leshaun! Janae couldn't believe this possessive, weak-minded nigga thought and treated her as if she was his exclusively. Lloyd definitely had her confused with Leigh Ann. "Nigga, bye! Ain't no muthafucking way."

"There is a way! That bullshit game you running is gonna get yo' pretty ass hurt!" Lloyed flexed by balling his fist. Janae looked at his hand then looked at him. She knew he lost his mind.

"By who? I wish a muthafucka would!" Janae lost all respect for Lloyd. She got in his face to see if he'd make good on this threat. Lloyd tried to hold back his smile. "Ain't shit funny!" She shoved him again. "You kicked my door in. And now you saying I'm only to fuck with you exclusively! Fool, you ain't making a bit of sense to me. Wait." She examined his face closely. She sniffed the air around them. "You high? That weed you smoking got you tripping like a—"

"I'm not high!" He grabbed her wrist.

She yanked free of his grip. "Ain't fucking with your dumb ass like that! And yo' black ass gonna pay for my door and I mean that shit! Busting up in here like you paying my rent—"

"Janae!" Lloyd towered over her. "Will you shut the fuck up!"

"Boy!" she fumed. "You are pissing me off fo' real! Muthafucka, we even! You forgot about my door?" She rolled her eyes and suddenly noticed he had on the same gear from last night. "Why you ain't wash your ass? Dirty-dick-ass nigga."

Lloyd sat down and kicked his feet up on the table. "Can I chill here for a few days?"

"Hell to the no! Better go get a room or something. You ain't fixing to be getting on my nerves all damn day!"

"Wanna hear some crazy shit?"

"I'm seeing a lot of crazy shit by looking at yo' silly ass!"

"Nah, for real for real. I don't give a fuck 'bout the bread I lost."

"Then why the hell you kick in my door!"

"'Cause I was jealous."

Janae gasped. "Seriously?"

He nodded. "You know that pussy is the best." He laid his hand on her bare thigh.

"And it's true." She smiled. "But you ain't getting none until you fix my door." She shoved his hand away and looked back at the door. "Damn! You tore my shit up!"

"Gimme your phone and I'll get it fixed today."

Shit. Might as well give 'im his phone back. "Use your own shit!" She frowned.

He shook his head dejectedly. "I lost it last night."

"You better be glad I like your crazy ass." She stood. "You left your phone in the room. It's in my bedroom." As she walked by him, he grabbed her around the waist and slammed her face down on the couch.

"Stop playing, boy!" She tried to turn and shove him away, but suddenly she froze when his lips tickled her bare ass. "Lloyd, if you don't stop—"

"What?" He licked her left cheek while rubbing and squeezing the right.

"We can't do it." She closed her eyes and arched her butt against his face.

"Why not?" He softly bit all over her ass as his dick woke up.

"The door," she moaned. "Aaahhh, I love it when you bite my ass like . . . Oohhh, shit! Lick my sweet ass. You know how I like it."

Lloyd worked her body to a boiling state before he jumped up and slid the kitchen table against the front door. In no time he joined her in the nude to take a shower. They fucked hard and fast in the bedroom, going through two condoms before their bodies shut down. Janae figured she could use Lloyd for her gain. His dick and fetish of eating her ass were just the type of benefits she could rock with.

Lloyd kept his word and had the front door fixed by 2:00 p.m. Later that evening, he sat back, relaxed, on the couch with Janae watching TV. Janae made looking sexy so easy in a loose shirt and thong. She hummed the latest Chris Brown song while applying a coat of pink nail polish to her toenails.

"Where Lysa at?" he asked with the aroma of her ass and pussy on his mustache.

"Minding her business," she replied as she dipped the nail brush in the bottle.

"Always gotta be a smart ass." He grinned.

"Boy, shut up."

He reached for the remote and changed the channel. "What up with that new lick you and Lysa working on?"

"Boy, bye!" She laughed. "Don't try to butter me up because your ass is homeless."

"You find it funny?" he asked with a straight face.

"Damn right I do. And if yo' ass wanna stay with me tonight you betta show a bitch some respect," she joked.

"I got your respect right here." He grabbed his dick and shook it.

Janae put the polish down and slid across the couch. "Why you wanna know about the lick?" She pressed up close on his arm and lusted at the dick print under his boxers.

"Maybe I can help you." He slid his hand up her juicy thigh. "My people can set up a bank account."

She slid closer and shoved a hand under his boxers. "Maybe you can." She squeezed him. "But right now I wanna ride this stick and then I'll tell you what's up."

Chapter Twenty-five

Zay moved the blue and white roses and bottle of Grey Goose to his left arm as he reached into his right pocket and pulled out the card key. As he tried to enter with his card key, he was frustrated that it didn't work after two attempts.

"Gogo, let me call you back. My guest is here." Leshaun sat on the couch in a royal blue Victoria's Secret negligee as she looked at her nails and tried to rush her sister off the phone.

"I thought you were gonna stop messing with Zay," Gogo could be heard saying.

"I like trouble sometimes," Leshaun admitted as she rolled her eyes at the phone.

"Whatever," Gogo replied.

"Look, get you a man, and not one attached to someone else; then you can talk to me about what I need to do about Zay." Leshaun pressed END on her phone as she saw Zay trying to come into the unlocked door. His efforts were blocked by the chain.

"Open the door, Leshaun," Zay yelled as he bumped into the door. "I gotta go."

"Put it in a jar and make lemonade!" Leshaun yelled.

"Why you got to be so difficult? I got something for you." Zay tried to keep calm while holding it in.

"I don't need you, Zay, or what you think you got in your pants." Leshaun still refused to get up and unlock the door.

"What I think I got?" Zay lost his cool.

"It's barely there," Leshaun replied nonchalantly.

"Really?" Zay knew this game already and decided he was going to wait it out. He knew Leshaun wasn't going to leave him outside of the room forever.

"Yeah, really. You need to call Dr. Oz and see if he can hook you up with an implant." Leshaun decided to stop playing with him and quickly undid the chain and took a seat on the couch. She reached behind her and pulled an object out.

Zay scowled as he quickly switched the items from the left arm to the right arm. He grabbed the doorknob tight, stepped back, and barged his way into Leshaun's room. As he stepped in, he was surprised to see Leshaun aiming a Glock at him.

"If I wanted you in my apartment, I woulda let you in." Leshaun gave Zay attitude.

"Then why'd you undo the chain?" Zay asked.

"Maybe I changed my mind," Leshaun suggested.

"You gonna put that gun away?" Zay tried to figure out how he was gonna stop Leshaun from playing games with him.

"Why don't you come get it?" Leshaun toyed with him.

Zay moved toward her and Leshaun got off the couch and stepped to him. Zay looked annoyed when he lifted the flowers and the alcohol.

"Ooh, for me! These are my favorite colors." Leshaun got excited.

"I know," Zay answered.

Leshaun put the gun on the table, and she took the roses and the Grey Goose from Zay. Leshaun smelled the roses then put them in the empty vase on the table and placed the Grey Goose next to it. Zay took a seat.

"And you gave me the headache," Zay sarcastically replied. "Got some Aleve?"

"All day strong. All day long." Leshaun walked to where Zay was sitting, and she straddled him on the chair. Leshaun wrapped her arms around Zay and gave him a kiss. "You know I be messin' wit' you."

"Umh-humm. I'm gonna stop messing with you since I'm barely there," Zay grunted.

"You know I was just teasing." Leshaun slowly ground on Zay's lap.

Zay and Leshaun continued to kiss as Zay lifted Leshaun up and put her on the table. Zay continued to kiss her neck as Leshaun reached down to unbuckle Zay's pants. The pants fell, and Leshaun tugged and pushed Zay's boxer briefs down. Zay was kissing and sucking on Leshaun's breasts through her negligee.

"That tickles," Leshaun whispered. Zay moved his fingers to her sides and tickled her as he continued to bite and suck on her neck. "Ooh, man."

"What's my name?" Zay asked.

"Zay. Your name is Zay," a voice in the hallway replied.

Zay and Leshaun stopped as they look at the lady in the hallway who was watching them through the door.

"I guess the neighbors know my name." Zay chuckled.

"Whatever, Trey Songz. Go close the door." Leshaun pushed Zay off her.

Zay quickly reached down to pull his boxer briefs and his pants up. He reached in his pocket and pulled out a Fire & Ice Trojan condom. Leshaun took the condom as she followed Zay to the door.

Leshaun sat up and watched Zay breathe from the bed. She looked around the room and then looked back at Zay who was mumbling incoherently. "Zay, wake up." She nudged him. Zay turned over away from Leshaun, and she nudged him again. "Zay, wake up."

Zay opened his eyes, turned his head to face Leshaun, and lay on his back. "What you wake me for?" Zay rolled his eyes.

"I'm concerned about you." Leshaun sat up so she could face him.

"What brought this on? You been watching *Scandal* again?" Zay rubbed his eyes so he could wake up.

"No. I heard you talk about killing Jerome again," Leshaun told him.

Zay sat up. "What?"

Leshaun coughed. "Your exact words were, 'I killed Jerome, and now you can go to hell with him.'" Leshaun imitated his voice.

Zay shook his head. He wanted to hide the fact that was in his dream/nightmare last night. "I'm not going to kill Kofi."

"You say that, and I want to believe that. I don't know what y'all are into, but y'all need to fix it, whatever it is," Leshaun ordered.

"We're not into anything. We just don't see eye to eye right now," Zay admitted.

"What did you do this time?" Leshaun pestered. The worst thing about raising Zay was that she knew him well enough to know when he was hiding something or fixing to lie. Zay sat up and glared at her.

"I didn't do nothing," Zay insisted.

"Okay." Leshaun didn't like or trust that answer.

"I'm serious," Zay said. "Everything is all good between us. You know you disagree with your girls some of the time."

"Yeah, but I don't dream about knocking them off either. When are you going to tell me what the three of y'all been up to?"

"We getting your money; that's what we're up to."

Leshaun had to remember he wasn't the young child or teenager she raised anymore. Zay was a grown man with the magic stick she crossed the line with. "Remember Gina?"

Zay bit his lip and Leshaun could see his anger rising. "Not this shit first thing in the morning." Zay stormed out of the bed.

"No, I'm serious. Gina used to always have my back, but we fought like cats and dogs. You broke up some of those fights," Leshaun pressed on.

"Really, by crying?" Zay was sarcastic.

"When I got raped, she was the one who not only taught me how to shoot; she helped me find that nigga and we killed him and his crew. I'd give anything for God to bring Gina back." Leshaun couldn't hide her feelings.

Zay leaned over and held Leshaun tight. "I know you miss my mom."

"Your mom used to sleep with my men, leftovers, 'cause she was insecure about her looks. That's beside the point. She was there for me when I needed her and Kofi was there when you needed help," Leshaun told him.

"So what you saying, Leshaun? I should call Kofi and put together an OutKast reunion? Not gonna happen." Zay walked around looking for his clothes. They'd had sex in every room imaginable and in the hallway. No telling where his stuff was.

"I didn't say call him today, but I do think the two of you should sit down and talk. Whatever is bothering you is going to eat you up until the two of you talk." Leshaun soothed him. She didn't need her men fighting among themselves while they were trying to take care of business.

"A'ight, whatever. I'm not calling him now," Zay answered.

Leshaun wrapped her arms around his neck and kissed him on the cheek. Zay's hardness melted and, slowly, he kissed Leshaun back. Leshaun walked him back to the bed, and she pushed him down and straddled him. "When are we going to quit telling everyone that we're not sleeping together?"

"When I'm sure 9ine is not going to try to whoop my ass," Zay answered as he kissed Leshaun again.

"Tell me what the three of you are up to." Leshaun knew they were doing more than screwing old ladies and running scams at bachelorette parties. They'd amassed fifty stacks in a short period of time, and she wanted to make sure their bases were covered.

Zay moved Leshaun off him and headed to the bathroom. Leshaun got up too. Their rendezvous was over.

Chapter Twenty-six

Living a lie didn't relate to Leshaun any longer. Two nights ago she broke the chain of lies and told Prince that she and Zay were sleeping together. She told the truth about her issues about killing Tiana and coming up with the money to get Price Street Hotel back up and running. He didn't trip when she mentioned her days of stripping and hustling weed to get by. In all, she was straight up and revealed herself as a pretty chic from the hood. No lies stuck to her, but she simply didn't speak on Gogo and the plot they had lined up to rob and kill Lloyd. In secret, Leshaun and Gogo still needed to work out the kinks, but it was a job that needed to be done.

They spoke on a future of being together. They had sex, fucked, and made love all over the house. Each time he threw his seed in her, he begged her to stay, to move in with him. For Leshaun, the reality of the bond she had with Prince came in a whirlwind of events. The lifestyle he showed her wasn't the hood. He took her shopping in his second ride, a cobalt blue Maserati Quattroporte and she couldn't stop thinking about Gogo. Leshaun knew she couldn't cut all ties from Asheville, no matter how easy it felt doing. For now, life seemed simple with Prince. He lavished her with affection and treated her with the highest degree of respect. He opened doors for her and turned her pussy to a frothy split during their countless moments of lovemaking.

"What are you doing, baby?" Leshaun strolled into the study in a pair of pink Victoria's Secret panties and matching bra. Her walk was mean in her stylish name brand stilettos.

"Working on this book," Prince replied from the desk.

Leshaun slipped her arms around his neck and kissed the side of his face. "Write books? I didn't know you were into that."

"How you think I got the money to get these cars? IHOP don't do that. And I'm not tricking like that. I sell the work to some of the biggest names in street lit and, as long as my money comes up, no one comes up missing. It's what I do." He turned his head and gave her a deeper kiss. "I'm about done."

She smiled. "So if your books is doing all that, why you work at IHOP?"

"Because I'm not into working a desk job every day, all day," Prince answered. "I like to cook, and I like getting out of the house. Plus, working at a restaurant allows me to meet all kinds of people, and I use them to model for characters in the books I write. Plus, I don't like to depend on a check from an author or a publisher. I like to see money every day, which is why I work so hard at IHOP."

Leshaun had no choice but to accept his answer. She knew people had many hidden talents and she knew he liked to write when she met him. Leshaun didn't know he continued with the writing and made something out of it. She wondered if all the times she thought he had another woman Prince was really locked in a room somewhere, letting his emotions out on the keys. Thinking about the bookshelf she had, she wondered if Prince had written for any of her favorite authors. "Don't let me rush you," she encouraged him.

Prince inhaled her peach-scented body spray as he closed the Word program on the laptop. What he felt for Leshaun wasn't lust. "Sit on my lap for a second."

Leshaun circled the chair he sat in and eased down across his lap. Again she slipped her arms around his neck and slid her tongue inside his mouth. She welcomed the tender caress of his hands on her lower back and inner thigh.

"What time are you coming to bed?" she asked moments later with her head on his shoulder.

"Not long. I have to call my client before it gets too late." He rubbed her warm chocolate thigh. "I need to make sure everything is in order for this book I gotta send the publisher later this week."

Leshaun bit her lip as she tried to figure out a solution. "Do you have to go?"

"Of course I do, baby. It's part of my contract that I visit the place I'm researching, and it's a free vacation on my end. Why wouldn't I go?"

She shrugged. "How long will you be up there?"

"Two days. After I finish researching, I'm scheduled for a meeting with one of the clients in Las Vegas. And after that, I'm back on a flight back home."

"Can I go with you?"

"You changed your mind?"

She nodded. "I can pick up a few of my things from home."

"How about ya get everything, because this is your home now. And I mean that, Leshaun."

"That's a big move you're asking me to make."

"I know." He lowered his lips and kissed the swells of her breasts. "You're so damn sexy!"

"What if I get pregnant?"

He traced the waistband of her panties as her question forced him to face a consequence. "We already have a daughter. And I'd be a very happy man."

"You really mean that? Like, what about Sarah?"

"Of course I mean it. And I'm done with her. I know the risk we're taking without a condom. And I don't care how fast things are moving between us. What I feel for you starts right here." He pointed at his heart. "And you're special because you're you. I guess it was love at first sight for me."

"I've never been loved before," she admitted. "Everything about you now is a new experience for me, and it don't have anything to do with you being rich." She giggled. "But I do like how you are spoiling me."

"Anything for my sexy chocolate cake." He filled his hand with her hip and squeezed.

Her heart wanted him, and she listened to it. "Take my bra off." She licked up his neck and took his earlobe between her soft lips.

Prince couldn't get enough of Leshaun and her high sexual drive. When she asked for it, he rose to the stage each and every time. His erection drove up against her ass as he eased the bra straps off her shoulders.

Leshaun kissed him when the bra fell to the floor. Her tits wobbled against his chest as their passionate kiss drew on. She pulled from his lips and cupped her breast to his mouth. Like a newborn, he sucked gently on her nipple. "Mmm, that feels so good!" She licked his bald head and rained kiss after kiss on it.

Prince slid a hand up her inner thigh until he reached her center. He wasn't surprised to feel a wet spot on the panties.

"Let's do it in here," she gasped and spread her legs.

Prince licked her nipple and slid her panties aside. Her pussy lips popped free, swollen and wet. An intense ring of pleasure raced up her dark legs as he pushed his middle finger inside her.

"Prince, yesss!" She jerked herself on his finger. "Touch my clit, too! Ooohhh, yeahhh, baby." She stuck her tongue in his ear, breathing hard.

His want was his need of her. With patience, he lifted her toward that peak with his fingers in her pussy and his mouth on her breasts. With each strum against her clit, her pussy leaked and coated his hand. He tasted her by licking and sucking on each of his slippery fingers. "Stand up and bend over my desk."

Leshaun stood and lifted his hands to her bare titties. "I know the difference now." She grinned down at him as he admired her freshly shaved pussy.

"About what?" he said, rubbing her nipples in a circular motion with his thumbs.

"With you, I know the difference between sex, fucking, and making love."

"And what's on your menu tonight?"

Leshaun bit her bottom lip as he squeezed her breasts together. She rubbed his face. "If you're up to this, fuck me in here, have sex in the living room and, last, make love to me in the hot tub. And I want you to cum inside me each and every time."

Prince stood, proudly showing off the lump under his pants. She covered it with her hand while sucking on his bottom lip.

They never made it to the hot tub due to Leshaun tapping out from the dick. After he hammered her for nearly an hour nonstop, she jokingly asked if he was using any sex enhancement drugs. He promised his stay up in her pussy was pure. Before their night ended, she took a relaxing bath with him by scented candlelight. He pampered her soapy breasts from behind while whispering his promises of devotion to her. She wanted this lifestyle with him. A lifestyle of love.

The next morning, she woke up alone under the sheets. "Prince?" She sat up and rubbed her tired eyes. Just as she started to slip from under the sheets, she found a written note on top of her smartphone on the night table.

Morning, Beautiful

Relax. I got called into work to cover a shift for a coworker running late. Didn't want to wake you, so I left you in dream land. I'll be home by noon.

Prince xoxoxo

Leshaun smiled and figured she would surprise him with a home-cooked meal. She got up and got dressed and was in the kitchen ready to show her skills to Prince. Just as she started to search for something to cook, the musical doorbell chimed. She went to the front door in a pair of high-cut boy shorts and one of Prince's shirts. Through the glass portion of the French door, she saw an attractive, sophisticated-dressed white woman in heels. She opened the door. "Uh, what's up?"

The lady slightly raised her eyebrow. "Who the fuck are you? And what are you doing in my husband's house?"

Prince sped down the two-lane road to his home with Leshaun heavy on his mind. The meeting lasted longer than expected and his calls and texts to give Leshaun a heads-up went unanswered. He felt they were meant to be because being without her for the past few hours was torment.

"Baby girl," he called out when he stepped through the door. "I got some good news about the option to turn one of my books into a movie." He loosened his tie as he entered the living room, expecting to see Leshaun. To his surprise, he saw a Post-it note stuck to the flat-screen TV.

Let's do something different today. Go to the bathroom.

Prince smiled, totally in the mood to do anything new with Leshaun. He made his way down the hall and found a second Post-it note on the bathroom mirror.

Get naked for me now. Next step is in the kitchen.

Prince removed his suit and stripped down to his boxers and socks. He paused in the doorway and took off his socks and then his boxers. His dick led the way on his trip to the kitchen. The third note drew his attention to the stainless steel refrigerator.

Grab some wine and bring that dick to me. Your bedroom.

Prince snatched a bottle of chardonnay out the refrig-erator and hurried to meet Leshaun in his bedroom. He tried to imagine the "something different" she had in store for him. His dick jumped when he saw the fourth Post-it note on the bedroom door.

Close your eyes and let me take you to paradise.
No talking.

Prince stuck to the game and closed his eyes. A breath later he heard the door to his study open behind him. He wanted to turn and take Leshaun in his arms, but for now, he followed her rules. A rush of excitement filled him when a blindfold slipped over his eyes. He inhaled quickly when a hand eased down the length of his dick. He clutched the neck of the chardonnay as Leshaun licked the mushroom tip of his penis.

Before he took his next breath, his penis slid inside her mouth. Behind the blindfold, he tried to picture Leshaun bobbing her lips back and forth on his taut erection. Without sight, it made him focus on what he felt and heard. He felt her soft lips encircled his dick and he heard the wet slurps. He felt her hands working in sync with her lips on his shaft. In and out, his bulbous tip popped between her lips. The wine nearly slipped from his grip when she lightly raked her fingernails under his balls. Just as his body settled in for a ride to a climax, she stopped.

He moaned when she licked all over his tip, slowly with the tip of her tongue. Next, she took him inside the bedroom without releasing her hold off his penis. She took the wine from his hand and guided him to the bed. Prince went to his back, aching for her to use her wet mouth again. Her actions were in fact "something different, " and the excitement showed itself between his legs. A new twist sped up his heart rate when he felt a leather strap being secured to his wrist. Once in place, he could only lift his hand an inch or so off the bed. He willingly gave her his other wrist to the leather strap, placing him in bondage.

His legs were spread apart, and his ankles were placed in the leather straps, leaving him naked and spread-eagle.

Prince broke the rule and moaned Leshaun's name when he felt a feather skimming up the rise of his dick. "Please don't tease me, baby." He strained at the straps, wanting to break free so he could fuck Leshaun. His needs were met when he felt her lift his dick up to her lips. For the next four minutes, she jacked and sucked up and down on his dick while lying beside him. He chanted her name and gave praise of her special talent with her mouth. His breathing raced when he felt her getting on top. A shift of her weight come to no surprise that she planned to ride him. He jerked his ass off the bed when she pulled his dick toward her pussy. It slid in, raw and deep.

"Ooohhh, Leshaun. Ride it, baby. Bounce that sweet pussy on my dick." He yearned to see her chocolate breasts jumping and that sexy look that changed her face.

He moaned under her as she forcibly bounced her soaked womb on his penis. Her nails left marks on his chest. She reached back and felt how his long dick slid in and out of her.

"Yesss! Pussy sooo good!" he moaned. "I'm gonna cum, baby! Aaahh it's so good!"

She sped up. Throwing herself up and down, her hands braced on his chest.

Prince shouted Leshaun's name as his dick shot its climax inside her. In the height of his release, the blindfold came off. To his uttermost reach of shock, he stared up at Sarah biting down on a cloth to muffle her moans as she took the dick. His body went against his mind. He hated her even as his dick blasted off again and again. Sarah spat the cloth out and swirled her pussy on his dick. Prince closed his eyes in defeat, powerless to stop Sarah from taking all she wanted.

A rage burned inside him as Sarah eased off his lap. He squeezed his eyes shut as she licked him clean. His will to resist her stood no chance.

***

Gogo rolled from under Lloyd when she heard the shower running. She rubbed her tired eyes and took notice of the time on her iPhone: 3:45 a.m. Without waking Lloyd, she got out of the bed and cursed when she hit her toe on the leg of the night table.

"'Bout time you come back." Gogo walked into the bathroom.

Leshaun snatched the shower curtain open with her face twisted.

"What's wrong with you?" Gogo closed the door and leaned against the sink with her arms crossed. "You haven't answered any of my calls since your ass left."

"Shit just fucked up right now!" Leshaun replied from the steamy shower.

"That ain't new. And that sure as hell don't explain why you've been MIA on me. I've been worried sick about your ass."

"I just need to get my life together, and I want to . . . I just . . . Shit!"

Gogo sat down on the toilet. "Something we need to talk about?"

"Promise not to get mad?" Leshaun asked timidly.

"I promise. Now tell me what's bugging you, girl."

Leshaun stayed under the shower and told Gogo all about her encounter with Prince and with meeting his bitch of a ex-wife.

Gogo took a moment to let everything sink in before she said anything. "Did you tell this nigga about me?"

"Fuck no!" Leshaun turned the shower off and reached for a towel. "He's still coming up here, so I hope you got your shit together."

"Are you sure," she stressed, "that you didn't mention shit about—"

Leshaun sucked her teeth. "Ain't no fucking snitch!"

"Didn't say you was."

"Well, stop asking me the same damn question over and over. No means no, okay?"

Gogo bit her words to avoid an argument. "Everything is in place. Even with your ass MIA."

Leshaun slid the shower curtain open with the towel around her neck. "I feel so damn stupid!"

Gogo nodded. "Uh, you might wanna go and take some tests and stuff to make sure he ain't give you any STDs. That dick musta been fire!"

Leshaun rolled her eyes and kept her comments silent. The dick was more than good. That thang was Frosted Flakes great! "You can cancel your plan to steal his car because he's catching a plane up here."

"Damn!" Gogo stood as Leshaun stepped out of the shower. "I was looking forward to driving his shit to the chop shop."

"Lloyd here?" Leshaun asked as she tied the towel around her naked frame. "I saw his ride outside."

Gogo nodded. "And would you believe his girl kicked his black ass out?"

"That's what he get," Leshaun replied.

"And guess what else? I got him to help me with this next lick."

Leshaun sighed as she stood at the door. "I just want all this shit to be over with. Real talk. I'm tired of being stressed out."

Gogo hugged Leshaun and dealt with her guilt on the things she did behind Leshaun's back. Fucking Lloyd and short-changing Leshaun ate at her conscience on the low.

"We'll get through this," Gogo promised. "Even if we have to rob every crew and john."

Leshaun wanted to believe in Gogo. Whatever happened with Prince, she didn't give a fuck. Her broken heart pushed her mindset to a driven purpose, and it was all about the money.

Chapter Twenty-seven

Janae couldn't believe she was inside Bryson's bedroom. Not a hotel, bed and breakfast, or some other place to fuck. She'd made it inside his massive bachelor pad. Fitted caps from every ATL team lined the sturdy top frame. Pictures of Bryson and various females took up the outer perimeter of a mirror she couldn't stand to look at anymore. Janae sat up in the bed and saw her clothes lying in a pile against the wall.

Bryson surprised her, entering the bedroom with a breakfast tray. "Rise and shine, sleeping beauty. I made you some breakfast. Turkey bacon, egg and cheese wrap with hash browns and bell peppers."

Janae reached up and took the tray and placed it in her lap. "Thank you, babe. I'll be down in a minute."

Bryson smiled. He walked over and gave her a kiss. "I left the black card on the table. The keys to the Mustang are on the key hook. Go get a new dress. The dealership is having a ball tonight, and I want you to be in something brand new. I know you can pick them out."

"I thought you were going to get the day off?" Janae was a little concerned. The royal treatment Bryson had been giving her as of late was nice, but she knew somewhere there was a cost.

"I thought so too, but the owner's son called out, and I got to close this deal personally," Bryson insisted. "You know Lloyd and I do what we got to do to keep our clients happy."

Janae threw on a smile. "Okay, babe, I'll get something nice to wear. What's my limit?"

"What limit?" Bryson acted like he was insulted. "Girl, you playing. I told you pick something nice. I expect you to spend a couple of stacks. And with the deal I'm about to make, I'll pay it back." Bryson gave Janae another kiss. "I got to go. I'll send the limo to pick you up by six."

Janae shook her head as she watched Bryson rush out. *I wonder if the poverty I exchanged for extravagance was worth it? Don't get me wrong, I like the money; but I have no man at home to share it with.* Janae picked up the phone and went through her pictures. She admired the pics of her, Lysa, Lloyd, and Bryson and her and the other girls in their stable. But she got to the few private pics Kofi sent during their courtship, and she licked her lips. She put her hand down there for some finger play but quickly changed her mind. She picked up the phone, went to the messages app, and clicked on the last conversation she had with Kofi before everything went down.

"I wish he could come over for a minute," Janae mouthed to her phone as she set the phone to the side and went to finish her breakfast.

Kofi sat in the dining area of the bed and breakfast they were working out of. He was enjoying a homemade bowl of grits, sliced cheese, and bacon bits. Zay's cheap Android phone buzzed and danced. Kofi looked up and saw Leshaun's number and shook his head. "There she go, texting for some sex again. Go give boss lady some dick."

Zay stormed into the kitchen and snatched the phone. "Why I gotta give her some dick, Ko?"

"It's eight thirty in the morning. You still don't have a job, at least not a legitimate one. She don't have a job.

Prince probably pissed her off again. So she wants you to go over there and put in some work. What are you going to do, son?" Kofi stated the obvious.

"Let me get that paper when you're done with it. Maybe I can find something this week." Zay sat at the table, opened the phone, read the text, and deleted it.

"You said that last week. And we're still here," Kofi reminded him.

"I'm still looking. Trying to get up out of here comfortably," Zay assured him.

"Trust me, I'm starting to become content with being a deadbeat father. No responsibilities or a mouth to feed, praise Jesus." Zay and Kofi stare at one another. "You were always a sensitive one. Keep breaking her back so she'll keep calling back. Maybe this time you'll make a baby with her. 'Sides, you don't have nothing better to do than to plot our next crime and go lie up with the boss."

"I'm not laying up like that with Leshaun," Zay denied.

"You better go lie up with Leshaun. Maybe if you were getting some on a regular, you could get and keep a job. That's motivation. If it were me, you'd have another little brother or little sister by now. Because I would have lain all up in that girl."

"Thanks for the unsolicited advice," Zay offered.

"It's okay to ask for help," Kofi offered, "to not know what to do. To seek out guidance from someone who's been there, who knows. It's not okay to continue to lie in a state of helplessness because that's all you know."

"I'm not going to go lie up with that girl," Zay insisted.

"Tell me another lie. You gotta come up with some better ones," Kofi replied.

"I'm not lying. I don't want to keep robbing people forever." Zay sounded motivated.

"Robbery is like crack. You'll always keep chasing that first high. The thrill will never be same as it was the first time," Kofi warned as he watched Zay get his things and head out the door.

Zay agreed to meet Leshaun in the food court. When he saw her, she had a few shopping bags from some of the big-name department stores. Leshaun set the bags down in a seat next to them.

"Thanks for meeting me here." Leshaun looked him over. "How come you didn't get anything to eat?"

"I wasn't hungry," Zay lied. His stomach was growling, and he hoped she didn't hear it.

"Well, I'm going to get some Chinese food." Leshaun reached into her pocket and pulled out two twenties and handed them to Zay. "I can't be the only one eating, so go get you something."

"Okay." Zay took the money and went and got their food. He hated when she chose to treat him like he was a toy in her dollhouse. Always convenient, always there.

The line was short, and he kept it simple with chicken fried rice, vegetable eggrolls, and Sprite. Zay waited until Leshaun came back from washing her hands before he sat down.

Zay dug in his pocket to pull out some money. "Here's your change."

"I'm good. You might need that to catch the bus home or something." Leshaun put her fork in without blessing the food.

Zay stared at her, opened his mouth to speak. "But . . ." He started to address the comment, but Leshaun kept eating her food. "Thank you." He slouched in the chair.

Leshaun paid him no mind. "Even with this fucked-up situation I've been delivered, I'm working on making this experience better for my good. The lesson I learned is not to put all my eggs in one basket." Leshaun finally looked up from her plate. "I have different things going on, but everyone can't see my hand."

"I see I need to take after you." Zay bowed his head to say a small prayer over his food.

"Really." Leshaun scrunched up her nose.

Zay leaned over the table. "Hopefully now that I'm in your face you can hear me. I might be down on my luck, but I'm not going to let you or anyone else walk on me and treat me like shit."

"Zay—" Leshaun tried to change the subject because the last thing she wanted was a fight with Zay.

"No, you listen," Zay cut her off. "I'm not in need of your approval of what I do and how I live my life. When I lived with you, you couldn't stand the fact that I wasn't your top-producing whore. That I downsized myself to the types of clients I'd consider just so I could pay my bills. Now that you live from hotel room to expensive hotel room, I'm good enough to do what Prince can't or won't do. So I tell you what. The next time you want some of this"—Zay stood up and grabbed his crotch—"you gotta pay for it."

Zay pushed his chair and walked away from Leshaun, ignoring the multiple times she called his name.

Chapter Twenty-eight

After the blowup with Zay, Leshaun was inside Torrid the next day. She had on her Ann Taylor suit with her hair pinned up, holding a few blouses, ready to try out the Discover card she had lifted. She had linked the information to a dummy card she intended to present to make the purchase.

"Can I help you?" A sales representative approached her as she was walking around the lingerie section.

"Yes, you can. I'm looking for lace panties. Can you point me in the right direction?" Leshaun put on her act. In reality, she knew where she was in the store, but she couldn't let him know.

"Sure. Down the aisle on the right."

"Thank you." Leshaun walked toward the aisle near the dressing room, scoping the items she was about to grab. She walked in the dressing room, put her purse down, and took a breather.

Hit and move, hit and move! Leshaun kept telling herself to get ready to take more stuff. She quickly picked out items and occasionally looked around as she walked to the dressing room.

"Miss!"

Leshaun stopped suddenly and panicked. She knew she hadn't made a mistake but hearing the assertive tone the sales representative was carrying made her second-guess.

"Yes!" Leshaun responded.

"You dropped your bracelet," he pointed out.

Leshaun turned around. "Thank you!"

Leshaun was messing up. What the hell did she need with a fake bracelet? Leshaun told herself that she had been in the store too long, and she should get the last of the things and go. Leshaun came out of the dressing room and handed the remaining undergarments to the sales representative.

"So, would you like to purchase any of the items?" the sales representative asked.

"Yeah, I'm on my way to the register now," she answered.

The sales representative nodded his head and took his place behind the register. "Would you like to add—"

"No, thank you." Even with a straight face, Leshaun was frustrated and nervous. She prayed for a smooth transaction. The items cost $365 in total. Not a lot of money in the grand scheme of things, but a large enough transaction to test the waters with the card. Making too large of a transaction would've alerted Discover, and she didn't want to do that.

The transaction cleared without a hitch, and Leshaun quickly made a beeline to the exit. Once she made it out of the door, Leshaun pulled out her phone and called Gogo.

"Hello," Gogo answered on the first ring.

"Hey, girl, where you at?"

"I'm about to go meet up with Lloyd. What's up?"

"Is that right? Come to my room first. I'll be there in about twenty minutes."

"Yeah, where you at?"

"I'm at this yellow bed and breakfast in the Montford area I'm thinking about buying. I'm gonna send you a text with the address in a minute."

"Okay, I'll see you in an hour. Bye."

"Um, I'm going to be someone's company tonight."

"Who?" Leshaun sat up.

Gogo blushed as she rearranged the *Essence* magazines on the brass and wood living room table. "Lloyd. Duh."

"Oh, yeah. Humph! I see you found your way into his inner circle." Leshaun was pleased to hear the news.

"Wasn't too hard," Gogo stated. "All I had to do was act like all I wanted was the dick. Ain't got time for no drama-filled relationship. Fuck that!"

"Aarggh!" Leshaun lay back on the sofa. "Life sucks!"

"Hey! You still got my green teddy with the sheer front?"

"Yeah. But it's at the cleaners."

"Damn!" Gogo stood with her hands on her protruding hips.

"Go hood on his ass." Leshaun giggled. "T-shirt and panties."

Gogo's mood went up through the roof to see Leshaun back in good spirits. "Put that gun up before Lloyd gets here. Don't want him to think we on no grimy shit." Gogo winked.

Leshaun smacked her lips. "He ain't caked up like that."

"True. But the dick is hellafied mmm-mmm good."

"Bitch, you crazy!" Leshaun laughed.

Chapter Twenty-nine

"Don't answer it," Gogo whispered against Lloyd's ear when a new text buzzed his phone.

Lloyd risked his fight with temptation by inviting Gogo aka Liah to his hotel room. He stood at the end of the teal leather sofa as Gogo flaunted her body for his pleasure. She reached for his hands and smiled up at him.

"I'm good at keeping secrets," she whispered.

Lloyd dared not to look at the rise of her cleavage and prominent nipple prints.

"You seem a little nervous," she said when he didn't reply.

"It's been a rough week," he admitted.

"Ummm. Maybe I can change that." She squeezed his hands and pressed her ample breasts against his chest.

"How?" Lloyd regretted his reply the second it spilled through his lips. He clearly saw her game of seduction, and yet he still risked the chance to play.

"I can think of a number of ways." She released his hands and trailed her fingers up his arms. "We're both adults, and I'm sure you have me in this room for a reason. "

Lloyd was mindful of women who approached him because of his career. With Gogo, her stunning looks were rated as mind-boggling. In his opinion, she could grace the cover of a magazine. He admired her looks, and his lust teased him into wonderment on the sight of her nudeness. "What do you want the reason to be?" he asked with his hands on her waist.

Gogo circled her arms around his neck. "Sex," she cooed softly. "I want to be the reason your dick gets hard. Can I see it?"

Lloyd pulled her against his throbbing erection by the belt loops of her jeans. "Do you know the difference between sex and fucking?"

Gogo felt his hammer below his waist and her thirst to see it grow. "Sex is . . . It's done for a goal. Two people helping each other toward that climax."

"And fucking?"

"It's raw and greedy. Fast and nasty and just . . . Mmm, you're making me wet, Lloyd!" She squeezed his shoulders. "I feel it. But I want to see your dick," she gasped as the friction of his dick stirred her pussy.

"What do you plan to do with it?" He brushed his lips across her ear.

"Anything you want me to." Her dulcet voice flowed into his ears and pushed him across that line. Gogo bit her bottom lip and clung to Lloyd as his hands took a firm hold of her ass. Dizzy with lust, she kissed his cheek before she nibbled her way to his lips. As bad as her body called for sex, her greed of money came first. She swirled her tongue in his mouth as she lowered a hand between his legs. She caressed the lump under his pants until he moaned against her soft lips. Her fingers traced the print before she undid his belt. She yanked it loose and sucked his bottom lip into her mouth.

Lloyd palmed her ass as a surge of blood raced to the tip of his dick. He couldn't catch a grip on the moment as Gogo worked her fingers through the front of his pants and inside his boxers. A groan rolled from his chest when she pulled his dick out like a rabbit out of a hat.

Gogo broke free from his lips to stare at his protrusion that filled her hand. *Damn, it's big! No wonder he had Lysa and Janae tripping.* "Nice," she cooed as she gently stroked it.

Lloyd closed his eyes as Gogo jacked his dick. It felt too good to even think about asking her to stop. He knew he was in trouble when she smeared his precum all over the tip with her thumb.

"Looks yummy," she whispered as she sat on the edge of the bed. Her new position placed her in the perfect spot to closely admire his thickness. She used both hands to massage his dick to its fullness until it bumped her chin. She smiled up at him and licked her lips.

Just another groupie. Lloyd tried to justify his lustful actions. With no care for tomorrow, he laid his hand on top of her head and parted her soft lips with his dick.

Gogo squeezed her breasts as his dick inched deeper in her mouth. Her plan of seduction was on schedule and Gogo went to work, devouring him with her hands, lips, and tongue.

Down in the lounge, Bryson sat alone at the bar with a glass of Henny. He wanted Lloyd to relax, and he figured his new whore would do the trick. Just as he reached for his drink, his smartwatch chimed with a text message alert. By voice command, he checked the text and saw he had a new message in his inbox on Facebook: **Da Baddest Bitch**. He frowned because the name wasn't familiar. He settled back in the chair and read the message that sped up his breathing. By the last word he shot to his feet and hauled ass for the elevator.

Lloyd had his eyes closed and his head tossed back as Gogo slid her soft lips back and forth on his dick. "Feels so good," he groaned with a hand fisted in her hair. "That's how I like it. Nice, slow, and wet."

Gogo lost herself in the promiscuous act. The more she sucked, the sweeter his dick tasted. She sat complaisant on the bed, moaning and sucking at his flesh. Her pussy turned soggy, and she had a burning desire to fuck him. She kept her hands circled around the root of his penis while she skated her lips across the rest.

Lloyd shivered when she groped his balls while sucking hard on his tip. "Ooohhh, shit! Work it just like that! Don't stop!"

Gogo circled her tongue around his sweet bell head and got on her porn star acts by slapping his wet dick against her cheek. She licked him up and down with her fingers still playing with his balls. When she took him back inside her mouth, she reached down to unbutton her jeans. She sucked him fast for a length of ten seconds before she stopped. "I want this in my pussy," she panted with his dick against her face. Before he could say anything, she stood and wiggled the jeans down her phat ass and wide hips.

Lloyd followed her rushed actions and removed his clothes. When he stepped free of his pants and boxers, Gogo dropped to her knees to lick his balls. She raked her nails up and down his hard muscular stomach. In a lusting blur, her remaining clothes were removed until they stood stark naked.

Gogo crawled back on the bed with her eyes locked on the stoutness bobbing between his legs. She bit her bottom lip and slid two fingers up the length of her slippery pussy. Her heart thumped as Lloyd tore open a condom with his teeth. She fell back on her elbows and spread her legs to display her phat-lip pussy. The lick could wait. She stared at him rolling the condom down to the root of his erection. Her pussy throbbed and leaked as she thirsted for his deep thrust.

Lloyd moved between her splayed legs and inhaled the aroma of her pussy. Her body, every inch of it, was favorable to him. He bathed her raised nipples with his tongue as her nails dug into his shoulders. The warmth of her meaty legs slid up his sides.

Boom! Boom! Boom! Lloyd tried to ignore the loud knocks as he continued to suck Gogo's nipple.

Gogo had déjà vu as Lloyd sighed between her breasts. "Damn!" He looked toward the door.

"You expecting someone?" Gogo managed to say with her pussy throbbing for his dick.

"It has to be my brother." He closed his eyes and slowly eased from between her legs.

"Mmmm." Gogo shivered. "I was hoping you wouldn't answer it."

Boom! Boom! Boom!

Lloyd frowned. "Stay in here and let me go see what's up." He reached for a towel.

Bryson barged into the room with a crazed look on his face. "Where is she?" he whispered.

Lloyd closed the door. "Where do you think she is? And why the hell are you talking so low?" He crossed his arms and waited for an explanation.

Bryson threw a worried look toward the bedroom door to his left. "Did you, ah, did you have sex with her?"

Lloyd sighed and shook his head. "Man, you are really tripping right now."

"We need to leave!" Bryson ordered under his breath.

"Leave?" Lloyd answered confused. "For what?"

"Because it's not safe! Trust me on this, and I hope you used a condom with that girl. We got to get out of here!"

Lloyd wasn't convinced because his body still yearned to get back inside Gogo. "I'm not moving until you tell me what the hell is going on!" he demanded.

"Remember what happened to Shyne? Well, stay your black ass here and you're gonna be just like 'im!"

Lloyd stared at Bryson as his warning sank in. "Are you saying—"

"We have to leave! That's all I'm saying!" Bryson started for the door with the intent to drag Lloyd with him.

"Ain't nobody going nowhere!" Gogo eased out of the bedroom in her bra and panties with a .22. "Both of y'all need to put our hands up and step away from the door!"

Bryson glared at Lloyd with a hard "I told you so!" expression.

Lloyd raised his hands in disbelief. *This what my dumb ass get!*

"You should have listened to your brother." Gogo smirked with the .22 aimed at Lloyd. "But it's too late now."

"How much do you want?" Lloyd asked. "That's what this is about, right? Money."

"Correct, baby. And I know you got that paper and I want a nice chunk of it."

Lloyd nodded toward the bedroom. "I don't carry much, but it's all—"

"I wanna touch that bank account, honey," Gogo interrupted. "Before I leave this room, I'ma need you to do a money transfer to an account I got."

"How much?" Lloyd asked with his eyes on the gun.

"Fifty bands! And don't front like you don't got it 'cause I know you do. Hell, fifty bands won't hurt your stash so let's get this shit over with."

Fifteen minutes later Gogo had forced Lloyd to subtract $50,000 from his savings account. Lloyd made the transfer happen by sending money to the offshore account Gogo had instructed through the app on his phone. Gogo could feel the phone buzzing in her pocket, notifying her the transaction was complete.

"Toss your phone on the bed," she told Lloyd. "You too." She nodded at Bryson.

Lloyd glared at Gogo from across the room after he tossed his phone on the bed. "I assume your name isn't Liah."

Gogo rolled her eyes. "Does it fucking matter?" she snapped. "It don't! But this is what I want to know." She pointed the .22 at Bryson. "Who warned you about me? And don't lie because I heard every fucking word!"

"Uh, somebody sent me a message on Facebook." Bryson looked up from the floor where he sat beside Lloyd.

"What it say?" Gogo shouted.

Bryson winced. "Said you were going to rob Lloyd and try to blackmail him with a rape charge."

"Who sent that shit?" Gogo panicked.

"Da Baddest Bitch!" Bryson told her.

Gogo's mouth dropped as she tightened her grip on the .22. "No," she murmured. "You telling a gotdamn lie!"

The truth punched Gogo in the stomach after she read the message on Bryson's smartphone. She began to think fast as to who would betray their trust. Leshaun had a snake in her circle, and she needed to figure out who it was and fast. She blinked her tears away and turned her anger on Lloyd. "Does that name mean anything to you?"

He nodded slowly.

"Shut up, asshole!" Gogo held her tears in check. "Don't say shit else to me! Not one fucking word and I mean it!"

Chapter Thirty

"Stop fucking playing!" Chasity shouted as she shoved an unwelcome hand from her soft ass. "Next muthafucka who touch me is gonna get fucked up!" She forced her way through a group of young hustlers inside the warehouse on Riverside Drive. "And it stank up in here." She frowned. "Smells like y'all been tricking one of them rotten pussy bitches all damn day! Where Ron Ron at?" she demanded in a sexy bowlegged stance that had every set of eyes locked in on her perfectly round ass.

"In the back," one of the hustlers answered.

Chasity turned and exaggerated the sway in her hips to make her ass bounce. Her effort was rewarded by the slick sexual remarks that chased her down the darkened hall.

"Ron Ron!" She barged into the room like a DEA officer on a bust. "I need something to put in my lungs."

Ron Ron jumped up from the corner desk with his hard face twisted. "Fuck you ain't knock!"

Chasity smacked her glossy lips and closed the door. "Miss me with that attitude. I ain't playing neither. And you need to holla at your crew about touching my ass!" She stood with her hands on her hips. "And why you looking at me all stupid like?"

Ron Ron blinked and stared at Chasity's large breasts sitting high under the skintight tank top. "You need to learn how to knock!" he managed to speak.

"Whatever!" She rolled her eyes. "Whatcha bagging up?" She nodded at the mound of weed on the table. "Hope it's that good shit."

"Sour Diesel," Ron Ron answered.

"How much for two ounces?"

Ron Ron rubbed his goatee and admired how the tight jeans highlighted the thickness in her upper thighs. "Uh, for you?" He smirked. "Gimme six."

"Six what?" she asked with a neck roll.

"Six hunnit and don't act like that ain't no deal!"

"Ron Ron!" She pouted and stomped with every intent to make her breasts bounce. "How you gonna charge me like that?"

Ron Ron tore his lusting gaze from her big titties. "You can kill that shit right there." He shook his head. "Six is a deal. Hell, I normally charge seven and you ain't 'bout to get it for no less!"

"But it's for me and Janae," she whined, hoping he still had a soft spot for her.

"Shiiit, in that case, gimme eight."

"You ain't shit!" She crossed her arms as the smell of the potent weed ran up her nose.

Ron Ron stared at how the jeans sliced up into her pussy. *Damn! She thick as fuck!* "I'm just fucking wit' you. But for real, you gotta give me six for two ounces, Chasity."

"I only got four," she lied. "You know how hard it is."

Ron Ron shrugged. "Can't give you two for four."

"I really, really need it." She crossed the dull brown carpet and grabbed his hands. "Please. Just this once."

Ron Ron knew Chasity well and not once had he tried to fuck her. His relationship with Shauntel kept his lust in check. "I can't do it yo," he replied as her breasts sat just a few inches from his face. "This is my hustle. It's business." He pulled his hands free and turned back to the table.

"Rooonn," she whined again. "Let me get two for four and do an IOU for the rest," she suggested, knowing good and damn well that she wouldn't honor the IOU.

"Not happening. Six is the deal." He flopped down in the chair with his back facing Chasity. He had to sit down to conceal his dick print.

"Why you tripping?" She stuck her lips out.

"It's business, Chasity, and you know it. I can't cut you a better deal on this." His words hit a roadblock when Chasity gently eased her hands across his shoulders. A breath later he felt her warm and soft breasts pressed against the back of his head.

"I never told Leshaun," she whispered.

Ron Ron closed his eyes and used her breasts like a head recliner. "What you talking 'bout?"

"Remember that cookout we had last year?" She slid her hands over his hard shoulders and down to his chest.

He nodded. "I remember it."

"I saw you peeking in my bedroom as I was drying off from my shower and—"

Ron Ron jerked up and tried to stand. "Yo! It—"

"Chill!" She pulled him back in the seat. "It's all good. Really, it's nothing to cause any drama about."

Ron Ron slid a hand down his face and sighed. "I know what you're trying to do." He stared at the wall. "And you know it ain't right."

"What ain't right is the fact that your dick is hard. Now call me a liar!"

Ron Ron dropped his chin. "What do you want, Chasity?"

She lowered her lips beside his ear. "How about I put a new deal on the table?"

"Six for two." He stuck to the original deal.

She licked his hear. "One for two."

Ron Ron twisted and slid from under her hands. He stood and turned to face her. "You done lost your fucking mind! One for two! Ain't no gotdamn way I'm fixing to let you cop two ounces of Sour Diesel for one hunnit!"

Chasity bit her bottom lip and caught Ron Ron off guard by grabbing his dick print. "I'm not talking about money." She squeezed him. "We can go to a room, and I'll let you get one nut up my pussy for two ounces of that Diesel. Now, what's up?" She saw the indecisive battle in his face. She kissed him and mashed her breasts against him. The battle was tilted in her favor when she felt his hands circling all over her phat ass.

"You win." He nuzzled against her peach-scented neck. "I'll take the one for two."

Chapter Thirty-one

Janae was in a deep sleep, the room quiet, cool just the way she liked it. The smartphone rang, startling her out of a deep sleep. As she tried to get her bearings and rubbed the sleep out of her eyes, she reached for the phone. Still disoriented, Janae managed to knock the stack of paper and other items on to the floor. When she picked up the cell phone the first thing that stood out was the time: 2:32 a.m. She become paralyzed with fear. Janae focused on the floral ion light as she tried to sit up in the bed. The name. *Leigh Ann. What the fuck, man? How the hell did she get this number? She knows not to call me at this hour!* In slow motion, Janae touched the TALK button and put the phone to her ear. "Hello."

"Janae, Janae, she's trapped! They found her. She's trapped!" Leigh Ann was screaming and hollering into the phone. Janae's heart dropped because she couldn't comprehend what Leigh Ann was saying at the time.

"Leigh Ann, stop screaming and tell me, who's trapped?" Janae ordered.

"Lysa!" Upon hearing the name of her partner in crime, Janae jumped up.

"Lysa is trapped how?" Something in Janae's spirit didn't seem right with the whole story, but she went along with it.

"Lysa was in a car accident, and she's trapped against a building."

Janae had tried to remember the last time she heard from Lysa. She wasn't the girl's mother, but she figured Lysa had found her a sugar daddy and was milking him dry. "Leigh Ann, where are you? Where's Lysa?"

"Not too far from the warehouse."

"I'm on my way!" Janae jumped out of the bed and put on some clothes she'd gotten with Bryson's black card. That's when it hit her that he hadn't been around for a few days either.

The thought crossed her mind to call Kofi, but she held back. She hadn't spoken to the man in weeks and, by now, the betrayal had to have him feeling some type of way about her. The betrayal was serious and big enough for Kofi to kill her over. She wondered if Kofi was up to whatever happened to Lysa. Doubt set in with the thought that if Leshaun saw both of them at the party, why didn't she come after them?

Once Janae got to the accident site, she jumped out of the car before it was able to come to a complete stop. There were two fire trucks, eight police cars, and an ambulance. Janae's eye fell on the truck that was wrapped around the tree on the passenger's side: the side that Lysa was sitting on. She ran up to the truck, but a firefighter held her back.

"Lysa, Janae's here. You're going to be okay," Janae attempted to assure her, but Lysa's body was disheveled. Her face was puffy and beaten beyond recognition. Janae knew it was her because of her A-symetrical hairstyle and the earrings and she was still in the clothes she'd worn when they last saw each other.

"We will do the best we can," the officer assured Janae, but it was no use.

Lysa was dead, and she didn't die in no car crash.

When Leigh Ann approached the scene, it felt like Janae was having an out-of-body experience. She approached her and gave her a hug.

"We gonna find out who did this. Lloyd and Bryson gonna set them straight," Leigh Ann vowed.

"Speaking of, did you call them?" Janae wondered. The crowd got bigger, and she could only imagine the circus that was getting ready to ensue.

"Can't get either one of them on the phone."

Before Janae could put two words together, the rescue team finally got Lysa out. They placed her corpse in a body bag and put her on a stretcher. Janae knew she was going to have to face Leshaun for everything sooner or later and the stakes of the game she was playing were high.

Janae sighed and looked at the time on her phone. "It's damn near five o'clock in the morning! I can tell this day is gonna be fucked up," Janae complained.

"Aren't you the least bit worried about Lysa?" Leigh Ann snapped.

"She's already dead!" Janae snapped back. "I know what I need to do, but it would help if I could get in touch with Lloyd and Bryson."

Janae scrolled through her phone and got to Lloyd's number first. She slid a hand down her face, knowing she was about to put her life on the line. Janae took a deep breath to soothe her nerves before sent the call. "Hello?" Her voice broke as her heart threatened to jump out of her chest.

"I really don't know what to say."

Hearing Gogo's voice caught Janae by surprise. Her heart raced as she thought about Lysa paying for the lick they made with her life.

"I got your message," Janae said.

"I'm glad you did. We need to meet up real soon."

Janae breathed a sigh of deep relief. "Where?" Silence. Janae tried to ear-hustle to see if she could hear where Gogo may have been, but no clues emerged. "You still there?" she asked.

"We really need to talk and, if you can, I'd like you to come see me."

Janae gripped the phone. "Do you think it's a good idea?"

"Look, let's talk about this face to face. Just the two of us. I'll text you the address."

The next sound Janae heard was the dial tone. The game had changed for her and not in a good way. She reflected on the position she found Lysa's body in, and she knew that unless she came up with something quick, her fate wouldn't be that much different. The phone chimed, and Janae looked at her message.

"You need me to come with you?" Leigh Ann offered. "I can see if Ron Ron—"

"That worthless muthafucker can't do shit!" Janae barked. "I need to face my troubles myself and, if you want to live in the next few hours, I'd suggest you stay far away from me."

Chapter Thirty-two

Gogo stood behind Bryson with the .22 jammed against the pillow, pressed hard to his head. "Your girlfriend's on the way."

Lloyd laid his phone down and locked eyes with Gogo. "She's on her way. Now please take the gun from his head. I did what you told me to do."

Gogo returned his stare as Bryson knelt in front of her. "Did you love 'er?"

Lloyd blinked. *I can't try this bitch. She got that pillow to hide the sound in case she pulls the trigger.*

"If ya did, you have a poor way of showing it."

"Why are you doing all this? You got the money and—"

"Don't fucking worry about it! Just sit your ass down and stop talking to me!" Gogo nodded at the chair. "I swear to God I'll pop this nigga!" She jabbed the .22 against the pillow and nearly caused Bryson to lose his balance.

Lloyd flopped down in the chair as regret ate at him.

"Just wait here," Janae told Zay as she hurried out of the car.

"Yo! Ain't sitting out here forever!" Zay warned.

Janae froze with one foot out the door. "Then leave!" Janae was regretting calling Zay and telling him that she had information that she knew he needed. Janae was lying, and she knew it, but it was about survival.

Zay punched the top of the steering wheel as Janae closed the door. He tracked her across the parking lot as she headed toward the front entrance of the hotel. "Fuck this shit! I bet them bitches trying to cut me out!" Zay snatched the key from the ignition and jumped out of his ride to follow Janae.

"Come on in and close the door, bitch!" Gogo gestured Janae inside the room as she stood behind Lloyd with the .22.

Janae closed the door with her hands shaking. "Look, Gogo—"

"You snitched me out to this muthafucka!" Gogo spat. "I can't even respect you right now! What the fuck!"

"What Lysa and I did was fucked up." Janae's voice broke as she came to grips with the situation she faced.

"Fucked up?" Gogo frowned. "You call this a fuck-up? After what we did for you and this is how you betray us? You must not give a fuck about you or me! FYI, Bryson's bitch ass is tied up in the bathroom!"

Janae gasped.

"Yeah, ho, and before everything went down, I sucked his dick and he loved it!" Gogo bragged as she rolled her neck.

Janae darted her eyes around the room for a weapon. "Why are you doing this?"

"Why did you betray us? You the one who's on some Benedict Arnold type shit. All that and neither one of these niggas love you!"

"Why do you care?"

"I don't! What I do care about is this nigga knowing too much about me!" Gogo kept the .22 to his head. "I got fifty thousand dollars from his ass, and your dumb ass ain't getting shit but a bullet!"

Janae studied Lloyd for a few seconds as he sat motionless in the chair. His impassioned expression tugged at her heart. "So you're a killer now?"

"Stand there long enough and your ass gon' see!" Gogo asserted hotly.

Finally, Lloyd and Janae made eye contact. She saw his fear and helplessness. "I can't let you do this," Janae said with a straight face.

"Ha! And just how do you plan to stop me? You so much as take two steps and I'ma turn them bed sheets red with his blood. Now try me and see if I'm fucking playing!"

The former friends stared at each other. Silence stood between them for a period of ten seconds.

"You ain't built for this," Janae said, breaking the silence. "We both been on some bullshit and it is what it is. But you don't want to do this."

"I'm not going to prison so you can kill that dumb talk about letting this fool live!"

"Ain't nobody going to prison," Janae stated calmly.

"And how the fuck do you know?" Gogo shouted.

"Because I love Janae and I'm willing to let all this shit ride," Lloyd blurted.

Gogo's eyes bugged after Lloyd spoke. She didn't know what to think or say.

"You got the money." Janae saw the indecisive look on Gogo's face. "Leave me with him. No one is going to call the—"

"Bitch! You must think I'm stupid!" Gogo's anger twisted her face. "I'm not gonna fall for this bull—" Gogo's heart dropped to her stomach when Zay slid into the room with his Glock. He moved in silence and caught Janae completely off guard. He turned the odds in his favor by pressing the Glock against Janae's cheek.

"What the fuck are you—" Gogo started to protest.

"Shut up, bitch!" Zay pointed at Gogo. "I heard enough and both y'all bitches done fucked up!" Zay thumbed the safety off and shoved Janae toward the sofa. "Sit down and don't fucking move!"

Gogo loosened her grip on the .22 as Zay forced Janae to sit. The broken .22 wasn't helping her none in the shit she stood in.

"Toss that gun on the bed and bring your grimy ass over here!" Zay kept the Glock on Gogo as she followed his orders. Once she was seated next to Janae, Zay moved toward the center of the room so he could cover all three at gunpoint. He paced in front of the wall-mounted flat-screen TV with his face tight. "Ain't here to play no games! First muthafucker who gets outta line is dead! And that goes for you too, Gogo. Now, you know the deal so let's make this run real smooth. I want you to get back online and clear out your entire account and transfer everything to the same account you sent the fifty bands. We clear on that?"

Lloyd nodded.

"How much is in the account?" Zay asked with the Glock held along his leg.

"Around ninety-eight thousand." Lloyd realized he could gain nothing by telling a lie.

Zay nodded greedily as he pulled a silencer from his back pocket. "You got ten minutes to make the transfer. And if it's a penny short, Janae will get her shit split! Time is running out."

Chapter Thirty-three

Janae shook her head. "This is fucked up," she mumbled.

"Karma is a bitch, huh?" Gogo rubbed her knees to stop her hands from shaking.

" We ain't no gun or nothing and I ain't 'bout to try Zay. Maybe he'll bounce when he gets the money."

Gogo looked like she was about to cry. "I can't believe this shit!"

"Uh, where is the .22?"

"On the bed. But it ain't gonna help because Zay knows it don't got a firing pin, because it's the same one that Leshaun took out his car." Gogo hung her head with heavy regret.

"Maybe we can tell—"

"What the fuck y'all whispering 'bout?" Zay shouted. "Try something stupid if you want to!"

Gogo and Janae had kicked their beef aside to face a common threat to their lives. They knew too much of the joys of life to simply give up. Even in silence, the two agreed to go out fighting. Gogo reached for Janae's hand.

"I'm sorry," Gogo mouthed with tears welling.

Janae squeezed her hands together and nodded.

Zay paced behind Lloyd with his attention locked on the iPad screen. "Is that the only account you got?"

Lloyd shook his head. "But it ain't no need to waste your time because I can't take any money from the other one."

"Why not?" Zay pressed the silencer tipped Glock behind Lloyd's ear.

"It has a joint owner, and it takes both of us to be online to make a withdrawal."

Zay rubbed his chin. "You're not as stupid as I thought." He lowered the Glock. "How much time is left before the transfer is finished?"

"Three minutes," Lloyd answered.

"Good! Now I hope you will . . ." Zay whipped the Glock up when Gogo stood. "Bitch, I told you not to fucking move!"

"I got to use the bathroom," Gogo whined as she clutched her legs.

Zay sucked his teeth. "Hurry the fuck up!" He lowered the Glock. "And don't lock that door!"

Janae waited for the bathroom to close before she made her move. "I know how to go into his other account," she whispered.

"What the fuck you talking 'bout?" Zay flexed his grip on the Glock and stared at Janae.

"I know the access information for his joint owner," she lied. "I went through his computer one day while I with him."

Zay bit the hook. "How much is in it?"

"Close to a million."

"Is that true?" Zay shoved Lloyd in the back of his head.

"Yeah," Lloyd replied through his teeth, knowing Janae was up to something slick.

Zay grinned at Janae. "Well, I guess you want something in return for that access info, huh?"

She nodded, buying time for Gogo to do whatever she planned to do in the bathroom with Bryson.

"Okay, what do you want?"

"Half," she said, knowing he wouldn't agree.

"Bitch, you crazy! How about I let your black ass live?"

Janae stared at the floor for a few seconds. "How you gonna take everything?"

"You can dead any thought of me feeling sorry for yo' ass," Zay answered. "You know how the game goes: rob or get robbed. Now, what's up? Your life for the access codes."

Janae saw the light blink under the bathroom door. *Shit! I hope that's a signal that she's ready.* "Uh, what about Gogo? If I give you what you want—"

"Gogo!" Zay shouted, having forgotten she was in the bathroom. "What's taking you so long?"

Silence.

Zay raised the pistol and rushed for the bathroom. He barged inside, banging the door against the wall. "What the fu—" He glared at Gogo on the toilet.

"Damn! Can't I at least use the got—"

"Bitch, don't play wit' me!" Zay jammed the silencer against her temple.

"Zay, please don't shoot me! Please." Gogo cowered and moved from the pistol.

Zay glanced over his shoulder at Lloyd and Janae. "Either one of you move and I'ma bust this bitch wide the fuck open!" Zay stepped farther inside the bathroom with the shower behind him. "Hurry up!" He pressed the black silencer against her forehead until the back of her head hit the wall. "This ain't a game. I'll leave yo' ass dead and stinking right on the toilet!"

Gogo closed her eyes as the fear of death gripped her. *Please, God. Let me make it through this mess. Please!* "You fixed it?" Her voice broke at the realization that she could've followed her original plan and been gone. *Instead I'm about to be gone.*

Zay frowned. "Fix what?"

"The .22."

It took him a few seconds to clear his mind. "Yeah, I had it fixed. What about it?"

Gogo opened her eyes. "Why didn't you tell me?"

This bitch up to something! "Where is it!" he shouted.

Just as he started to shove the silencer in her mouth, Bryson slung the shower curtain open. Zay spun, caught totally off guard at Bryson in midswing with the .22.

Smack.

Bryson's first hit with the .22 against Zay's face dazed him. Gogo kicked Zay in the back as Bryson pistol-whipped Zay to his knees. Lloyd rushed in and tried to grab the Glock as all hell broke loose on the floor.

"Grab the gun!" Janae shouted in the doorway. "Get it! It's on the floor!"

Gogo fell hard on her bare ass after tripping over Bryson and Zay scuffling on the floor. Lloyd joined the fray in a three way fight over the .22. Gogo tried to scramble to her feet with her panties and jeans around her ankles. As she reached to pull up her clothes her eyes fell on the Glock under the toilet. She snatched it only seconds before she was kicked in the side.

"Shit!" Gogo rolled toward the wall as Zay elbowed Bryson in the jaw.

Janae stood speechless as Gogo aimed the Glock at the threesome on the floor. She noticed the crazed look in Gogo's eyes and right then she knew what would happen next. "Gogo, nooo!" Janae shouted. "Don't do—"

Spat. Spat. Spat.

Gogo gasped and dropped the Glock, her heart pounding in her ears. The smell of blood, death, and gunpowder hit Gogo like a backhanded slap to the face.

"Have you lost your mind?" Bryson argued with Lloyd. "There's a fucking dead man in the bathroom, and you don't want to call the police!"

Lloyd sighed and shifted his gaze toward Janae and Gogo sitting on the bed holding each other. "Let me think about this."

"What's to talk about?" Bryson said. "This is real fucking life! Which means a real gotdamn prison that I'm not stepping one foot in!"

Lloyd turned from Bryson and made his way across the room. He dropped to one knee in front of Gogo and Janae. Gogo blinked her tears away as she rocked slowly in Janae's arms. Lloyd closed his eyes to gather his words and thoughts.

"We have to call the police," Lloyd said in a gentle tone.

"Noooo," Gogo cried, clinging to Janae. "I can't go to jail or prison. I can't."

"You're not going to either," Lloyd said, trying to calm her. "But if you leave this room you're on your own. Both of you need to trust me because—"

"Why?" Janae said. "Why are you helping us after what we tried to do to you?"

Lloyd laid a hand on Janae's thigh. "As crazy as it sounds, I care about you, Janae."

"And what about Gogo?" Janae hoped he would speak the truth.

"If you can work with her I can too. Now listen to me because we don't have much time. You have to trust me for this to work."

Janae fought back her tears. "This is real. Just like Bryson just said."

"I'm aware of that, Janae. But I'm good at thinking things through, and I see a way I can help your friend and rebuild whatever bond you and I have."

Janae wiped her eyes. She wanted to believe in Lloyd but her years of doing bullshit had her unable to see any good in anyone. "Lloyd, I swear to God I'll make you regret this if you're trying to run game on me and my girl."

Lloyd stood and motioned Bryson to his side. He calmly laid out the lie they would all stick to once the police arrived. The four placed their differences aside and stood as one. Ten minutes later, Bryson called the police.

Two weeks of turmoil left Janae and Gogo at their wits' end. The investigation into the shooting stayed defined as such and not a murder investigation. Lloyd's statement to the police held up solid:

On the date and time of the shooting, I met Gogo King at my friend's book signing event at Goldie's bookstore. We spoke briefly after the event was over and I invited her to my hotel room. Along the way, she told me about her possessive male friend who had been stalking her for the last few days. She also told me that he kicked her door in and made a few threats against her life. I went ahead and invited her to spend some time with me, thinking the issue she had wasn't that serious. When we got up to the room, we spoke more about books and had a friendly talk. After thirty minutes or so, I headed out to get some ice, and on my return, I bumped into my friend . Said he had to run an idea by me about a new book. When we returned to the room, we overheard a shouting match in the bathroom. Bryson and I listened for a moment and realized that Gogo was crying and begging the guy to leave. We rushed in the bathroom and took quick action once we saw the gun. A fight broke out between us, and the guy was shot by Gogo with his own gun. It saved my life because the guy had a second gun, a .22 that he tried to use.

Bryson wrote a statement that stood up as well. When the police found more ammo for the Glock in Zay's ride, that proved the gun was his. It wasn't viewed as snitching; he was simply helping Gogo out of a truly fucked-up issue. The DA in Wayne County decided not to press any charges against Gogo. Based on the statements, Zay aka Jeff Woodhouse had stalked Gogo and followed her to the room with the intent to kill. The silencer on the Glock played in Gogo's favor.

Silence suffocated Gogo's small living room as she sat on the couch watching TV with Janae.

"What a month it's been." Gogo lit her third cigarette in the last twenty minutes.

Janae shrugged. "Could've been worse," she mumbled.

"I know, girl. Shit got real crazy because I swore up and down I was gonna get arrested and thrown in jail. I was 'bout to haul ass and get missing!" Gogo took a long pull on the cigarette.

"I'm just glad it's over." Janae shifted as her stomach started to ache.

Gogo exhaled a billow of smoke and leaned back in the corner of the couch. "And here we sit. Still pretty and poor."

"Hey, when you grabbed that gun, I thought for sure you were gonna pop all three."

Gogo closed her eyes with the cigarette resting between her lips. Truth be told, for a split second she filled her mind with killing everyone. Had she done so, she would have all the bread from Lloyd's account. Gogo opened her eyes and sat up. Money had no meaning in relation to her bond with Janae.

"Uugghh." Janae grimaced and held her stomach with both hands.

Gogo dropped the cigarette in the ashtray and rushed to Janae. "Girl, what's wrong with you?"

"Stomach hurt like hell! Feel like I'ma throw up!" Janae groaned.

"Not in my living room you ain't. C'mon, get up and I'll help you to the bathroom."

Janae stood weakly, leaning heavily on Gogo. "Probably that damn lasagna you made last night."

"Shit, I told yo' ass not to eat as much as you did." Gogo shouldered the weight of her friend.

"Aahh, this shit is killing me!" Janae dropped her chin as vomit bubbled in her stomach.

Gogo tried to hurry her cumbersome steps to reach the bathroom before Janae puked. As her sour luck stood, Janae lost it and, in the process, Gogo's grip slipped.

Down in Miami, Lloyd took the news of no charges being filed against Gogo with mixed emotions. He sat alone in his study with a shot of whiskey. Facing common sense, he knew it was in his best interest to leave Leshaun alone. Bryson made sure every dime of his money was returned to his accounts, but Lloyd felt empty. The last time he spoke to Janae was three days after the shooting. He told her it was best to end their bond because of the issues that would haunt them. Though it happened, he tried to forget that pleasurable moment inside Gogo's wet mouth. Today he wanted to forget about them both.

Janae woke up with a funky taste in her mouth. When she tried to lift her hand to her face, her motion was restrained. She panicked, thinking she was handcuffed.

"Girl, calm down!" Gogo grabbed Janae's wrists. "It's okay. You're in the hospital so relax."

Janae blinked and saw Gogo told the truth.

"Your crazy ass almost tore the IV out. You okay?" Gogo asked with a concerned expression.

Janae closed her eyes and took a few breaths. "What happened?" Her voice sounded weak.

"First, yo' ass threw up all over me. And uh, I sorta freaked out, and you slipped outta my arms and hit your head on the floor. You had me scared to death!" Gogo said as she rubbed Janae's arm. "You gotta little bump on your head. The doctor said it's a contusion and you don't show any signs of a concussion, so that's good news."

"How did I get here?"

"Ambulance."

Janae sighed and stared at the ceiling. "How am I gonna pay for this shit?"

"Girl, chill. You know I'ma help you." Gogo smiled. "FYI, the ambulance driver is fine as hell, and I got a number. You know I'll figure out a way to clear your bill for the ambulance ride."

Janae managed a smile. "And what about my doctor bill?"

"Sorry." Gogo laughed. "I don't eat coochie."

"My doctor a chick?" Janae said with a slight headache.

Gogo nodded. "Girl, you don't need to be stressing no bills right now, and I mean that," Gogo stated as she sat down. "You want some water?"

Janae nodded, thankful for having a true friend in Gogo. They both had their faults but, in the hood, friendship had the power to overcome all odds.

"What did they say is wrong with me?" Janae asked after downing two cups of water.

"Still running a bunch of tests," Gogo answered. "And being we from the hood, them muthafuckas think yo' ass is on drugs or some other bullshit! I had to show my ass with one nurse who kept asking me if you had used any drugs in the last twenty-four hours."

Janae rolled her eyes. "How long have I been out?"

"'Bout three hours."

Janae turned her head on the pillow and gazed out the window behind Gogo. "What's really hood?" Janae whispered with her thoughts on the aspect of her troubled life.

Gogo blinked and thought about the question. "I guess being poor. Don't nobody in their right mind would willingly live in the hood. Yeah, we are fools at times by glamorizing our lifestyle while each day we hustling like hell to get up out the hood."

"To go where?" Janae said as she restrained her tears. "We are who we are, Gogo. A new address won't change us. All we've been doing is running to go nowhere."

Gogo agreed with Janae, and she, too, had to struggle with her own tears. "Where do we go from here?" Gogo blinked, sending two lines of tears down her face.

"We start over," Janae suggested. "Let's stop letting the streets ruin us. And stop thinking we need a man to make it in life."

Gogo nodded and wiped her eyes. "We can leave Asheville and get a place together."

"Sounds like a plan." Janae smiled.

Gogo grinned. "Uh, when you said we don't need a man, you wasn't going lesbian on me were you?"

"Girl, please!" Janae laughed. "I'll never be that stressed out. But seriously, we need to get our shit in order and stop fucking these no-good niggas who ain't worth our time."

Janae went mute when the female doctor knocked once and entered the room. The white doctor with brunette hair smiled at Gogo before turning her attention to Janae. She held an iPad that she viewed while standing at the foot of the bed.

"How does your head feel, Janae?" the doctor asked.

"Just a slight ache."

"Feeling nauseous?"

"Not like I did this morning."

"Has this happened before?"

Janae gripped the bed sheets. "Uh, about a week ago. But it wasn't this bad."

The doctor nodded and glanced down at the iPad. "How long have you known?" The doctor looked up from the iPad with an eyebrow raised.

"Known what?" Janae asked defensively.

The doctor tapped the screen and turned it around for Janae to see the test results for herself. "I checked your past medical records, Janae, and I'm sure you know what you're looking at."

Janae's heart knocked her breath away as she stared astounded at the screen. Gogo jumped from the chair to see what the hell was going on with her bestie.

"Oh my God!" Gogo gasped and covered her mouth as Janae lost the battle to hold the tears at bay.

Janae cried for a retest as Gogo held her in her arms. Her protests didn't help the case or her new issue. The two girls from the hood cried together in face of the world that seemed so much against them.

Chapter Thirty-four

Janae lay on the couch, nursing her ever-growing stomach. She was excited about the new life growing inside of her.

She wasn't sure whether the baby was Bryson's or Lloyd's, but she did regret the circumstances of how her new life came to be. For the last few months, she'd been low-key. Got a part-time job at Ingles ringing up groceries and doing light stocking for as long as she could stand it. Janae wasn't sure she was going to like the job at first because she knew how she was when people were rude to her. Janae learned quickly to suck it up and smile.

Being a cashier wasn't too much different from tricking. Both positions required her to wear light makeup and put on her best face. Both required that Janae move around and be flexible with her life and schedule. At times, both jobs required that she get on her knees to get the work done and spend a considerable amount of time in different positions. She reported to a supervisor at her job; she needed a pimp's protection in the streets.

The only difference to some degree was the pay. Her minimum-wage rate of pay was reported to the IRS and state government, and she got what she worked for. Her pimp passed along pennies on the dollar for what she tricked. The income she earned wasn't even hers.

Janae was surprised at how fast she and Gogo had become friends, especially after Lysa's death. Gogo had taken her out to eat, helped her with her prenatal appointments, and helped her deal with Lysa's death.

When she asked about Leshaun, all she heard and saw was that once Leshaun got the money to get the Gamble Property up and running, she focused on other business ventures. Leshaun built a Dame's Paradice club near the heart of downtown. The club was more female-centered and had some of the same themes as the clubs she owned in Charlotte and Birmingham. Leshaun was pleased with the gay club she helped finance in Nashville, Tennessee and the Web series she sponsored, which brought business to the club.

In Asheville, she bought two bed and breakfasts that were thriving. Leshaun focused on expanding her rental properties and hosting events. She even helped a local promoter bring major rap and R&B artists to the Orange Peel and to Dame's Paradice.

Prince left IHOP to manage one of the bed and breakfasts. There was no word on if he and Leshaun had gotten together, but the only time Janae saw him was at the new property or occasionally chilling in the Barnes & Noble, typing fast on an Macbook. Kofi had a new car and drove for Uber. Janae was surprised the first time he picked her up because she didn't remember seeing his name as the driver. Janae and Kofi made small talk. He told her he was back in school at Western Carolina University and pursuing a biology degree. Kofi was the one who told her that Zay had been cremated and that his ashes were in an urn next to Tiana's in her old suite that was remodeled at Price Street Hotel. He also revealed that 9ine moved forward with the adult entertainment business that he and Zay had always talked about.

Janae knew she was having a daughter. She really wanted a boy, but she was happy that her daughter was healthy. She hadn't thought of a name for her yet, but she did know that she didn't want her daughter to turn out like she had. She wanted her daughter to be more than somebody's ho. She wanted her to grow up and become a self-sufficient woman who could take care of her own needs. Janae wanted her daughter to become the woman she wanted to be and worked toward.

The phone rang, and Janae reached on the coffee table and picked it up. She recognized Gogo's name and smiled.

"Hey, girl." Janae slid the TALK button and spoke.

"You feel like some sushi?" Gogo offered.

"Girl, yes." Janae smiled. Gogo always seemed to know when she was hungry and up for some food. "I have this craving for ginger. I drink ginger ale, season my food with allspice and nutmeg. It's like I'm craving sweets, but don't have to have sugar."

"Every pregnancy is different," Gogo replied. "I'm downstairs in a black 2017 Toyota Avalon. I'm renting it while my car is being fixed. I'll be up to get you in a minute."

"Cool, give me a few minutes to get ready."

"Okay, girl."

Janae hung up the phone and was thankful she took a shower earlier in the day. She had laid out a maternity outfit in case she decided to go somewhere. It took her a minute to put on the dress and then fit into the wide tennis shoes that made walking easier. She gave herself a once-over. Her hair was wrapped tight in a bun, her face glowed, and she didn't look or feel a mess.

Janae locked the door and made her way to the car, which was parked in the handicap spot. Gogo got out of the driver's seat and helped her get in the passenger's seat. Then Gogo got back into her seat and put on Pandora so they could listen to today's R&B and hip-hop instead of being stuck with the local pop station they'd both grown to detest.

"So where are we going?" Janae asked.

"It's a little Japanese spot on Patton Avenue. It's behind where Denny's used to be ," Gogo answered.

Janae struggled to remember the restaurant. She always went to the fast food place in the mall when she wanted teriyaki, or she just bought the sushi rolls from the Ingles she worked at. The last time she had Japanese at a restaurant, she and Lysa went to Asaka's on Biltmore Avenue, not too far from the Grand Bohemian Hotel.

Gogo maneuvered her way to Patton Avenue, and Janae enjoyed the ride. They pulled up to the white building that had Japanese script written on it.

"Doesn't look like we are going to be alone," Janae commented as she closed the car door.

"Naw, I doubt that," Gogo answered. "Have you ever seen the hibachi chefs do their knife twirling act while they make your food?"

"No. I didn't even know they did that."

Gogo smiled. Janae was up for the feeding and entertainment. They walked into the restaurant and were greeted by a host who led them to their table. The hibachi chef squeezed some oil on the grill and set some rice on top.

"This is going to be a good show," Gogo told her as she helped her in the chair.

Once Gogo was seated, Janae noticed Prince, Kofi, and 9ine making their way to the table from the back. 9ine sat next to her and smiled. Prince and Kofi sat on opposite ends.

"Looks like the show is about to begin." 9ine grinned at Janae.

Her heart beat fast. She knew Leshaun operated dirty and she wondered where she slipped up that she didn't see this move coming. Gogo was her sister—first mistake. Janae should've tried to kill Gogo before she found out she was pregnant instead of relying on their truce. Zay had gone nuts, and that threw her off guard.

"Ma, you're here." 9ine got up and greeted the woman behind him.

Janae almost didn't recognize her. Leshaun was still a big girl, but a little slimmer. Her hair was in a giant, asymmetrical Afro similar to what Pepa of Salt-N-Pepa had in the eighties. Leshaun's face was full, colored by autumn and earth-colored shades. Big hoop earrings hung from her ears.

"Pregnancy looks good on you," Leshaun complimented her as she leaned in for a hug.

Janae tried to hide her discomfort and hugged her back. If Leshaun was going to kill her, she could've done it by now. So what did she want? And why bring her to a Japanese restaurant to do it?

"So are you having a girl or a boy?" Leshaun asked she made her rounds and then took a seat next to Prince.

"I'm having a girl," Janae answered.

"It's been awhile since I've had one of them." Leshaun put a napkin in her lap, and the chef started the show.

Janae looked around the table to figure out how each of them may try to strike her at any time. The knives flew in and out of the chef's hands and, when they weren't flying, they clashed and slashed. As the chef continued moving the food, 9ine kept telling everyone what he was doing, like he was an expert on Japanese cooking.

"Now that I almost have everything up and running, I'm going to celebrate," Leshaun announced as the chef started serving their meals. Everyone had chicken teriyaki with vegetable sushi rolls, fried bananas, and steamed vegetables. "Outta Tiana's Purse is doing well in its location on Hendersonville Road. The store has a nice mix of urban and professional gear and the programs to dress young women for success continue to thrive. I'm thinking about opening a sister location in Birmingham. We'll see. The Price Hotel is up and running and for the first time in seven months, and is at full capacity."

Everyone clapped, except Janae. "Not only that, but I completed the purchase of the property near Merrimon Avenue by the Ingles, which brings my bed and breakfast total to three. No more B&Bs, Prince."

Prince nodded his head as everyone chuckled.

"We've really come a long way as a team. I want to thank Gogo for being my rock and not letting me falter, even when I wanted to. Prince, you big-dick asshole, we been together twenty long years and our daughter pretends like she doesn't know either one of us at times. 9ine, you've branched into your own world. I'm sorry you're having to do it all without Zay but you know I love and support what you do. Kill 'em in the A and bring the money back home. Kofi, I'm glad you're back in school. I wish Chasity were here, but she's on special assignment for me in the Triangle and should be returning later tonight. And, Janae, I have to hand it to you; I wouldn't have had to rebuild everything if it weren't for you."

Janae looked around again. All eyes were on her, especially the chef's. *This is it. This is the moment where Leshaun has me killed. And my baby, too.*

"Well, I can't give you all the credit." Leshaun lifted up her glass for a toast. Everyone else did the same and Janae looked around. "Stop being paranoid. Lysa had as much a hand in everything as you did. You want to know why you're here and she's not?"

That was an interesting question and one that, if she were breathing her last moments, she'd like an answer to before she met her Maker.

"'Definition of a Bad Girl' is one of my favorite tracks. It's a little over a minute long and should've served as the title cut for Total's debut album. Pam speaks about what it takes to be a strong, independent woman who's not scared to make every sacrifice to take and reclaim what's hers. Janae, I suggest you listen to that song again."

Janae exhaled. "Look, if you're gonna—"

"I'm not done," Leshaun cut her off. "I spent seven months rebuilding what you and another bitch had the audacity to try to destroy. If you wanted to leave, you should've just left. After all, I am what I am, and I play by the rules. I don't get mad when you choose someone else. I'm pissed when you take the extra step to destroy what is mine in the process.

"So I'm gonna cut to the chase. After you give birth to your daughter, I'm going to give you six months to recuperate. Nourish and bond with your baby. Love her like I love my two children. And after six months, you will begin the process of paying me back. And I want all of my money back, with interest. The quarter of a mil was just the beginning. The city of Asheville assessed me with a five thousand dollar fine. It cost me about seven thousand dollars in travel and lodging expenses to live from one hotel to the next. It cost me another four to send Kofi, 9ine, Zay and Chasity across the country to raise the money. I invested another fifteen thousand in supplies and rental fees to secure the lodge and to use my properties in other cities to raise the money. I also had to pay out almost four thousand dollars in refunds and replace another five thousand dollars in property. So when we add it all together, you owe me two hundred and ninety thousand dollars, plus interest."

Janae's breathing became labored. Three hundred racks was a lot of money to come up with, and she wasn't ready to put that much miles on her pussy.

"Oh, and one more thing: I hope you were real cool with Lysa because that money she stole from Lloyd, he wants that back, too." Leshaun let it slip while she put a piece of teriyaki chicken in her mouth. "I told him he can't touch you because you're still my girl. So the fifty thousand y'all screwed him out of, I'm arranging for Chasity to make that payment to him now. And once she comes back, that will be added to your tab too, with interest."

Janae shook her head. Lysa helped her get into this mess, and now she wasn't around to help her fix it. "And, let me guess, you're giving me seven months to pay it back."

"Bingo. And, by then, you'll learn the definition of payback. Eat up. I want your baby to come out big and strong and for her to be a better woman than the both of us."

Leshaun continued eating and said nothing else directly to Janae for the rest of the meal. Her heartbeat was still fast; she wasn't sure how she was going to come up with all that money to pay Leshaun back. Janae knew two things: one, she had about two months to think of how and from whom she was going to get the money; and, two, she knew that seven months after her daughter was born, if she didn't have the exact amount of money she owed Leshaun down to the penny, she'd never see her daughter again.